CW00486853

lucky penny

Thank you for reading,

L.A. Cotton xx

l. a. cotton

Titles by L. A. Cotton

Fate's Love Series

Fate's Love

Love's Spark

Love Collides

Chastity Falls Series

Loyalty and Lies

Salvation and Secrets

Tribulation and Truths

Standalone Novels

Lucky Penny

To keep up to date about future releases you can sign up to L A's newsletter at http://eepurl.com/20pJv

Published by Delesty Books

First Edition

Copyright © L. A. Cotton 2015

All rights reserved.

This book is a work of fiction. Names, characters, places, and events are the product of the author's imagination or used in a fictitious manner. Any resemblance to actual persons or events is purely coincidental.

No part of this book may be reproduced or used in any manner without the written permission of the publisher, except by a reviewer who may quote brief passages for review purposes only.

If you are reading a copy of this book that has not been purchased from a licensed retailer please destroy it. Thank you for your support.

Edited by Jenny Carlsrud Sims of Editing4Indies

Cover designed by Daniela Conde Padrón of DCP Designs

Image and Model: Mandy Hollis at MHPhotography

Interior Design and Formatting: Champagne Formats

ISBN-13: 978-1519266958

ISBN-10: 1519266952

Love me or hate me, both are in my favour
Love me and I'll always be in your heart,
Hate me and I'll always be in your mind

~ *Unknown*

prologue

"Do you think about life after this place, Blake? About what will happen?" Penny gazed over at me as if I was her world, causing my stomach to knot tightly.

I wanted to be—her world. I wanted to give her the moon and the stars and everything between. She deserved it and so much more. She deserved life; one better than the shit we put up living with Derek and Marie.

"All the time. Come here." I looped my arm around her neck, not caring if anyone spotted us, and drew her in tighter as we lay beyond the yard staring up at the night sky. Tiny lights sparkled like diamonds on a smooth black canvas. It was beautiful. A little slice of heaven in our own fucked-up version of hell. "Eighteen more months, Penny, and then we're free and it'll be just you and me."

Penny sighed beside me. It was full of hope. I felt it in the way her hand lightly squeezed mine, and how her body relaxed into the ground as the breath left her lungs. We both wanted more. More than the shit hand we had been dealt. We had dreams and hopes for the future, just like any other sixteen-year-old kid. Except we weren't like most other kids. We had already lost so much… lived so much.

It was what brought us together in the first place, but now… now, things were different between us. Sometime in the last two years, my best friend had become my reason for breathing.

My everything.

"Eighteen months. We can make that, right?" Her voice was unsure, and I hated them for taking away the last shred of fight she'd had when she arrived at the Freeman group home with just one bag and a shitload of nightmares.

I rolled slightly to face Penny, my eyes taking in her delicate features. Chocolate brown eyes set against pale skin with a peppering of freckles that covered her perfectly shaped nose framed by loose dark waves rolling over her slim shoulders.

Trying to push down all of my anger for the things she'd faced in this place, I choked out, "You're my lucky Penny. With you by my side, we can survive anything."

chapter one

"It's not you, Pen. It's me."

I winced at Cal's words, but not for the reasons most girls would. Most people experienced being dumped in their lifetime, usually more than once. As a rite of passage, relationships began and they ended. Friends turned to lovers and fizzled back into the friend zone. Personalities clashed and partners decided the grass was greener. Or sometimes, the spark that was once burning so brightly simply flickered out into the darkness. Sure, they all lived to tell the tale, but that was usually after weeks of drowning their sorrows in a bottle of whatever liquor burned away the hurt or at the bottom of a carton of the sweetest ice cream.

Anything to forget.

Just for a little while.

But I didn't wince because Cal had finally decided to cut me loose. My eyes weren't pooling with tears for the loss of our love. No, it wasn't that his words didn't cut deep.

The truth cut deep.

And the truth was that it wasn't Cal, it was me.

It would *always* be me.

After hugging me awkwardly, Cal held me at arm's length as if he no longer recognized me. He offered me a weak smile and left. I watched him disappear into the distance before I strolled back through Tuttle Park. My arms held me together as I watched the world go by. It was a warm evening, which usually brought out a crowd. People walked their dogs, couples in love walked hand in hand making plans for their futures, and families played tag with their children. And here I was again.

Alone.

Despite the sliver of regret stabbing at my heart, I knew it was for the best. I'd tried—really tried—to make things work. Cal was my third attempt at a normal relationship in the last four years. A year older than me, he had a steady job, a nice apartment in Indian Springs, and he was motivated. If Mom were around, she would have called him the perfect guy.

I knew there was something different about him when I had let him touch me. It had taken four months, a lot of persuasion, and two panic attacks, but we had finally managed to be intimate in ways I hadn't been with anyone else. But in the end, it wasn't enough. Cal had wanted more—something I couldn't give. And although I'd seen the signs long before today, when Cal started to pull away, I let him. I couldn't blame him. What twenty-four-year-old guy wanted a girlfriend who struggled with simple touch, let alone intimacy? And besides, I wasn't planning to stay in Clintonville forever. Really, our relationship was doomed from the beginning.

Just like your life.

By the time The Oriental Garden came into view, daylight was disappearing on the horizon and taking with it the last shreds of my deteriorating mood. I'd lived above the takeout restaurant for almost two years, but it still didn't feel like home. Nowhere ever did. When I'd viewed the supposedly renovated one-bedroom apartment in Clintonville, the owner had failed to mention the hand-me-down kitchen and touched-up damp walls. Add to that the lingering smell of fried egg rolls and the window that overlooked the back alley of the local student bar, dumpsters and all, and I wouldn't call it homey. But it was all my meager wage from Vrai Beauté could afford, and it was better than the last place I'd lived—and the one before that.

I nudged open the stiff door with my knee and stumbled into the apartment, immediately assaulted by the scent of grease and lavender. The walls seemed to absorb it from downstairs. I'd tried everything I could find to mask the grotesque smell. Lavender was the only thing that seemed to make it almost bearable, but I still spent as little time here as possible. If I hung around for too long, I ended up smelling like Chinese takeout on legs.

After collecting the pile of mail on the doormat, I heated some leftover lasagna, turned on the small television in the corner of the room, and made myself comfortable on the threadbare couch. My fork poked and prodded at the congealed pasta and meat, but I couldn't bring myself to eat it. Between seeing Cal and having to face my boss, Tiffany, tomorrow, I had no appetite.

At the thought of work, my eyes drifted to the calendar pinned to the wall by the refrigerator. Sixteen black crosses stared back at me, which meant fourteen more days and then I was out of here for the whole summer.

No more egg rolls.

No more damp, flaky walls.

No more being kept up all night by drunk students.

I was trading my less-than-comfortable surroundings for even fewer home comforts. But I had been looking for this chance. My fresh start. An opportunity to do something with my life. It was only one summer, but one summer could change everything. I knew that better than anyone did.

Only this time, I hoped it would change my life for the better.

"Penny, there are rails to organize," Tiffany, the owner-manager of Vrai Beauté, barked disapprovingly. "You've been very distracted this week."

I moved toward the rack of dresses and started reordering them with trembling hands, scanning the shop to make sure it was empty. Tiffany didn't like chitchat when there were customers. The nerves somersaulted in my stomach again, but I inhaled deeply and recited my mantra. *You can do this.*

"Actually… there's, hmm, there's something I need to discuss with you."

She glanced up from the counter and arched her eyebrow with a look that said 'what could you possibly have to discuss with me.' "Yes?"

I opened my mouth and spluttered my words. Irritated, Tiffany said, "Well, don't just stand there. Out with it, Penny."

"Well, I applied to work at a camp for the summer. Camp Chance out in Hocking Hills. They offered me a position, and I'll be gone for eleven weeks."

When I'd spotted the ad for summer work at Camp Chance, a camp for fostered teenagers situated in Hocking Hills State Park, I had applied with no expectations. With no experience working with kids and only a couple of childhood camping trips on my resume, I didn't expect to make it past the paper application. But in less than two weeks, I would be packing my bags and leaving for the summer.

"Aren't you a little old for camp?" Tiffany replied running her eyes up and down my body as if she was mentally assessing my age. "And eleven weeks? I'm not sure I can hold your job here for that long, Penny, if that's what you're asking."

My shoulders sagged slightly. Of course, she couldn't just congratulate me or show any interest in my news. It was exactly the reason I'd put off telling her until now.

"If you can't hold it, I understand." I gulped down the disappointment swimming in my stomach.

Tiffany pursed her lips into a thin line and looked like she might say something else, but obviously thought better of it as she dropped her eyes and continued checking over price tags.

It was silly really. Tiffany wasn't someone I'd developed

a friendship with—I didn't develop friendships with anyone—and she only spoke to me when the job required it. I think she only hired me because she had felt sorry for me the day I interviewed for the job. I'd missed the bus and had to walk five blocks in the heavy rain. By the time I arrived, water was running off me like a river, but I'd insisted on continuing with the interview. I needed a job, and I didn't like to rely on second chances.

The doorbell chimed, and I glanced up to watch a group of girls enter the store. They were laughing about something, and I immediately busied myself with the rail trying to ignore them. Over the last year, it had gotten easier. My job at Vrai Beauté was my first customer service position, all part of the heal Penny plan. *You need to be around people more, you need to learn to live again,* the therapist had repeatedly told me. He didn't count my previous job at the university's library working in the storeroom or the job before that where I worked in the kitchen of a busy hotel. I guess he had a point. I liked to stay hidden in the background. The spotlight was a place for perfectly primped girls like the ones currently cooing over the lingerie section at the back of the store.

"Excuse me, Miss."

I inhaled deeply and turned around, plastering on my best fake smile. "How can I help you?"

"Do you have this in a four? There's only sixes and eights on the rack." She smiled back, and it seemed genuine. Not like some of the customers who came from all over the Columbus area to get their hands on the latest fashion trends stocked by Vrai Beauté.

I snatched the silky material out the girl's hands and

answered a little too abruptly. "I'll go check for you."

Tiffany shot me a questioning look as I hurried past the counter and into the back. I was restless about going to Camp Chance next month. Excitement laced with terror, and my head was an exhausting place to be. It would mean living in close quarters with the other counselors and getting to know them. People like the ones in the front right now. The last time I'd been around a group of people was five years ago in foster care. The day I walked out of the Freeman group home in Lancaster was the day I became truly alone. With the exception of Bryan, Michael, and most recently, Cal, I'd been alone ever since. I rarely made friends, not ones that stuck anyway. But my therapist was right. It was time to move forward and to let myself heal.

It was time to step out of the shadows and live.

chapter two

On my last shift at Vrai Beauté, Tiffany barely managed to wish me luck, but much to my surprise, her parting words were that she would try to hold my job open. Kylie, one of the part-timers, was willing to pick up my shifts over the summer until she started back at school in the fall. It was better than nothing. I couldn't find it in me to be relieved I still had a job, not with how preoccupied my mind was. An endless stream of questions plagued my thoughts. What would the other counselors be like? Would I survive the five days of intense training? Or would I be packing my bags before I had them unpacked?

The bus out to Hocking Hills was quiet, just me and a handful of campers taking the sixty-mile journey out of town. When we passed through Lancaster, my blood ran cold. Five years later and my fresh start had led me right past the one place I wanted to erase from my mind. I closed my eyes, turned up the volume on my iPod, and let the music force out the unwanted thoughts.

It wasn't until the bus came to a halt that I dared to open my eyes again. The campers exited the vehicle with their laden rucksacks and headed toward the visitor's center.

"Next stop is yours, little lady," a gruff voice sounded from the driver's chair.

I nodded up at the rearview mirror but didn't reply as the engine rumbled to life, and we started moving further within the thick forest. The road cut through the dense green wall as trees swayed gently in the breeze. It was peaceful. Calm. Somewhere I could imagine spending time, despite having never visited this part of Ohio before.

After ten minutes, a crooked hand-painted sign welcomed us to Camp Chance, and the woods expanded into a clearing. A large wooden cabin stood proudly in the center with smaller cabins arranged off to the side. The driver parked in a dirt parking lot and opened the door. "This is you."

"Thanks," I murmured as he offered his hand to help me off the bus.

Clutching my bag tighter, I made no attempt to accept his courtesy... or touch. I silently scolded myself. Shrinks had been telling me for the last four years to face my fears. Baby steps, they'd all said. A graze or two of a pinky, shaking hands, holding hands, hugging, kissing. The cognitive behavioral therapist I spent six months visiting last year told me to focus on the person I was with at that moment, to hold onto the reality that their touch was not *his*. Easy for them to say sitting in the confines of their sterile offices. In practice, it wasn't that easy, and while I didn't intend to let the driver pucker up to me, I knew I should have accepted his offer of help. But my past had conditioned me to fear touch. To abhor being touched.

If the driver was offended, he didn't show it as he retrieved my other bag from the luggage hold and placed it on the sidewalk.

"I'll be seeing you."

"Bye."

He climbed back into the bus and pulled out of the lot, and I was once again alone.

My feet wouldn't move. I don't know how long I stood there glued to the sidewalk. A few people came and went from the central cabin, but no one noticed me. I was relieved. I needed more time to psych myself. The rational part of me knew this wasn't the Freeman group home. There were no Dereks or Maries here. This place helped and nurtured teenagers who lived in foster care. To give them the kind of chance I never had.

Nothing will happen here.

But the little voice of doubt that kept me shackled to my past refused to stay quiet.

"Hey, are you here for the staff training?" A tall, slim girl joined me dropping her rucksack down at her feet. "I'm Marissa."

I turned slightly to face her, stepping back instinctively to put a little more space between us. "Hi, I'm Penny, and yes, I'm here for the summer."

"Me too. Counselor or activity instructor?"

"Counselor."

Marissa smiled at me knowingly. "Nice. First year, I take it?"

I glanced around. Was it that obvious? Of course, it was. I nodded, and she laughed. "Don't look so worried. You're in for one hell of a summer. I hope you brought insect repellent. The bugs out here take no prisoners."

"I brought everything on the list," I replied, nervous energy vibrating through me.

"Shall we head inside? Troy and Tina will be waiting."

I nodded, following Marissa's lead as she moved toward the buildings. She wasted no time going inside, but I paused to give myself a few seconds to calm my erratic pulse.

"There she is. Get over here, Marissa. It's been too long," a male voice called.

I stepped inside to find a tall man with a fuzzy beard and a red bandana tied around his head smiling in our direction. Marissa was a few steps in front of me and jogged into the man's open arms. "Troy, what in hell's name has Tina been feeding you? You look like you gained twenty pounds."

"Not you as well." He laughed drawing Marissa into a bear hug.

"I told him to take it easy after his operation, but did he listen?" a woman called over from a table which was pushed against the wall.

"I listened." The man I'd deduced was Troy released Marissa and stepped back shooting the woman—Tina—a goofy smile. She rolled her eyes with a smirk that caused her cheeks to dimple. "You did not. Wait until the regular kids show up. They'll remind you every day."

"Fine, fine, so I gained a little weight." He rubbed a

hand over his stomach. "But I still got it, right?"

I stood awkwardly watching their exchange. It was obvious that Troy and Tina were a couple—just something about the way they looked at one another—and Marissa seemed to know them as well.

"Oh, hey, you guys, this is Penny. One of the new counselors."

"Penny Wilson, right?" Tina came to join us, smiling directly at me, and I felt my free arm come up around my waist. "Good to have you here. Come in. Don't just stand there. We don't bite."

"She does," Troy joked, moving to wrap an arm around her. "But only when she's really angry."

"Ignore him. The others are around here somewhere. A couple members of the team won't get in until tomorrow night, but you'll have plenty of time to get to know everyone. It's your first camp, right? How are you feeling? Nervous?"

I opened my mouth but nothing came out, and I ended up standing there gawking awkwardly.

"She's good. Right, Penny? I thought we could bunk together?" Marissa said.

"You got it. Marissa will show you around and get you settled. You'll be part of the Chance family in no time. We'll see you at the meet and greet." Troy took Tina by the hand and led her away from us leaving me behind with Marissa.

"Thanks. I totally froze."

"Hey, we've all been there, and besides, they can be a little full-on." Marissa smiled and some of my nerves settled. "I guess I should include myself in that, but I'm good people. You'll see. Now, let's go get us a cabin."

The warmth of the fire licked my face, but I welcomed it as I leaned in closer. It had been a crazy day and every part of my body ached with overuse. Even if it wasn't for my sore muscles demanding proximity to the heat, something about the flames captivated me. The hypnotic flicker of orange, the crackle of the wood snapping under the pressure of the heat, even the charred smell drew me in.

"Okay everyone, bring it in." Troy stood up in the circle and tipped his bottle to the rest of us. "Welcome to another summer at Camp Chance. I hope we didn't push you too hard today?"

Heads shook and a couple of people called out, but Troy ushered them to silence. "I look around the fire and see some familiar faces. In some cases, I see some very familiar faces, but I won't mention any names, Marissa." He coughed under his breath, and Marissa grumbled something from her seat beside me while the rest of the circle broke out in muffled laughter.

"And I also see some new faces. But old or new, it doesn't matter because do you know what else I see? I see people who want to make a difference to the kids who will pass through those gates this summer. Kids who need to remember that being a teenager can be fun. The next few days will be intense, but you'll need it because these ten weeks won't be a walk in the park. If you think that, then now's the time to pack your bags and get the hell out. Some of the kids we will work with this summer will test your patience until you want to throw in the towel. But they need this, they need us…"

I didn't take my eyes off the fire, but I heard every word coming from Troy's mouth, and each syllable punched me in the chest. Risking a glance around the campfire at my colleagues, I didn't know their stories, but I knew my own. I'd been the kid Troy was talking about, except there had been no Camp Chance for me.

"We get two weeks with these kids. Fourteen days to give them an experience they'll never forget. One that will stay with them forever. One that could put them on the right path in life. One summer, a lifetime of possibilities. Let's make it count, people."

Someone clapped and another joined until the whole circle was clapping. I joined in, but I wasn't in the moment. I was too lost in my own thoughts. I knew my past was going to affect my present, but until now, I hadn't realized just how difficult it was going to be to separate the two.

"Hey, everything okay?" Marissa nudged me and smiled.

I nodded and forced my lips into a weak smile, but I saw her skepticism.

The epitome of athletic, Marissa had a toned body, broad shoulders, and lean, muscular arms. But despite her build, Marissa was still very feminine. I envied her. She was comfortable in her own skin, confident, and even though I'd only known her a little over twenty-four hours, I instantly warmed to her. She didn't give you any other alternative.

After showing me our cabin yesterday, which was actually one room with two cots, a small bathroom off to the side, one dresser, a wardrobe, and a couple of chairs, Marissa and I had hung out for a little while. Thankfully, she liked to talk, and I'd sat and listened while she filled me in on everything there was to know about Camp Chance.

A year younger than I was, this was Marissa's fourth summer in Hocking Hills. She was qualified for everything from canoeing and abseiling to knots and orienteering and had just graduated from the University of Akron with a physical education degree. I was already glad she had been the person to find me standing in the dusty parking lot.

"I think we've all heard enough of Troy's voice for the evening, so I'd like to switch things to serious for just a second." Tina stood up next to Troy and a chorus of boos echoed in the warm air.

"Okay, okay, this won't take long. Firstly, you're here to work. This isn't a vacation. The days are long and the pay sucks, but work hard, be the best you can, and you'll be rewarded. Secondly, tonight is the exception. Enjoy the food and lukewarm beers because starting tomorrow there's a zero tolerance rule. Anyone caught with alcohol or drugs in camp will be marched out of here quicker than Troy gained his twenty pounds. Lastly, this isn't prison. Make the most of your downtime between camper groups, but no funny business. And, yes, I mean what you think I mean. No screwing around with each other. Not in your cabins or out by the lake where you think no one can see you."

Someone wolf whistled and Tina's eyes narrowed in their direction. "Trust me. It won't be the first time or the last time. It's only ten weeks, people. Save it for after the summer camp."

"My wife, everyone. The country's solution to birth control." Troy stood up beside Tina and grinned. "Now that we have that out of the way, how about a song?" He lifted a guitar off the ground and slipped the strap over his neck, letting his fingers strum the strings gently.

Troy led the campfire in song, and I lip-synced along to the ones I knew. The self-conscious person inside of me wanted to sink back into the shadows and remain hidden, but that wasn't why I was here. I was here to heal. To move forward. So I wrapped my arms around my waist, holding myself together, and started to sing along quietly with the rest of the group.

I was busy humming to an unfamiliar song when I noticed two figures approaching the campfire. Tina, noticing them as well, leaned over to Troy and whispered something in his ear. He nodded, all the while strumming the strings. Tina rose from her seat, an overturned tree trunk, and went to greet the two shadows. The song ended and the three of them came to join the group. The two guys sat across the fire, opposite Marissa and me. There was something vaguely familiar about the taller guy, but it was dark and I couldn't quite make out his face. It seemed my heart didn't need the light, though, because although my eyes couldn't get a good enough look to recognize him, my heart knew him. I felt it with every fiber of my being.

"You look like you've seen a ghost, Penny." Marissa nudged me again, only this time when I turned to face her she was wearing a look of confusion while I was trying to fight back the panic rising in me.

"I, I'm not sure. The tall one, he looked familiar."

"You mean Blake?"

Blake?

My heart beat in double time.

And then crashed.

And for a moment, I was certain it stopped beating.

Everything stopped.

I couldn't breathe.

I couldn't swallow.

I couldn't get out the words almost choking me.

"Penny?"

My eyes snapped up at the sound of Marissa's voice, and something caught my attention. Through the flames, I saw the two guys talking. The one I thought I recognized was listening to the other guy, but he wasn't looking at his friend. His blue eyes were set firmly on me.

Eyes I'd spent days and nights dreaming of.

Eyes that had kept the nightmares at bay.

Eyes I thought I'd never see again.

"Penny, you're freaking me out a little over here."

Marissa's voice deflected off my impending meltdown. I came to Camp Chance to heal. Not to have every scar ripped open again and laid bare.

But my past and present had just collided.

I never thought I'd see Blake Weston again, but he was here, sitting across the fire from me.

A ghost from my past.

Looking right at me.

chapter three

The second the music stopped and Troy packed away his guitar, I fled into the woods with Marissa calling after me. For the last three songs, I'd managed to avoid looking across the fire again, but memories I'd fought hard to forget over the last seven years assaulted my mind.

Seven years.

"Penny, wait up." Marissa's voice was closing in, but I pushed harder, pain throbbing in my already tired legs with every pound of my feet on the ground.

I hadn't planned to run; it just happened. My fight or flight instinct had kicked in, and flight had won. Lucky for me, because I was in no way ready to face Blake. Not yet. So here I was, running in the darkness through dense woods with absolutely no idea where I was heading.

"Penny, will you just slow down for a second? We can talk. I'm here for you."

Marissa's words brought me to an abrupt halt, and I

dropped my hands onto my thighs and tried to get a handle on my ragged breathing.

I'm here for you.

No one had been there for me in a long time. I dealt with life's curveballs on my own. Alone. Yes, I'd had a therapist. Yes, I'd dated three guys over the past three years, but I had never had someone to really talk to, to confide in. Not the way friends talked to one another. But somehow, here I was sprinting through Hocking Hills like a crazy person while a girl I'd only known a little over twenty-four hours chased after me because she cared.

Leaves rustled behind me, but the hand landing on my shoulder startled me and sent me into a blind panic. I lunged forward, shrugging Marissa off me.

"Hey, my bad." Her voice was laced with regret. I turned slowly expecting to see the confusion on her face, but all I found was concern as she held up her hands in a peace offering. "Geez, you run fast. I almost lost you back there. I covered for you, by the way. I blamed it on Troy's grilling skills."

An unexpected laugh bubbled up and tumbled out of my mouth, but as quickly as it had arrived, it disappeared into the night.

"Ready to talk?"

I shrugged, my eyes darting from side to side. How did I even begin to explain things to Marissa? A girl I barely knew.

"Okay, well, you might be quick, but you have a crappy sense of direction. The cabin is back this way." She motioned to a path behind her. "Come on, let's get back. I have a whole summer's supply of Reese's."

I followed her, my breathing slowly returning to normal, and we walked in silence for a few minutes. Laughter and chatter from camp carried through the air but was quiet enough that I knew I'd ran further than I thought.

It didn't take long for Marissa to break the quiet between us. "So I'm going to go out on a limb and say your little stunt has something to do with seeing Blake tonight?"

"What is he doing here?"

It wasn't supposed to be a question for Marissa. That question had consumed my thoughts ever since my eyes landed on him across the fire. Why here? Why now?

Why does the Universe hate me so damn much?

"He's here every summer, Penny."

"He is?" I slowed down, unable to digest what Marissa was saying.

She nodded. "Next to Troy and Tina, Blake is Camp Chance's longest serving summer counselor. This must be his sixth or seventh summer."

I didn't respond as we started to walk again, but I felt Marissa watching me out of the corner of her eye as she tried to piece together the puzzle. The pieces obviously fell into place quicker than expected because she said, "You went pretty pale when Blake arrived. You two have a bad history?"

My whole body tensed. If only she knew how Blake Weston was a part of the worst time in my life, a time I wanted nothing more than to erase. But it wasn't that simple because he was also a part of some of my most treasured memories. The kind that, no matter how hard you tried, refused to go away. The kind that had hit me like a home movie running through my head the second I'd recognized him. Stolen kisses in the yard when no one was looking, and sneaking out to the lake at Cenci Park. There had been a time when Blake was my world.

But that was then, and this was now.

And now we were nothing but strangers.

When I didn't answer, Marissa said, "Fine. I get it. We all have pieces of our past we would rather keep to ourselves, but your past is Camp Chance's golden boy, Penny. He's not going anywhere. Can you deal with that?"

That was the million-dollar question.

Could I?

When Troy had said the training would be intense, I expected long days and some challenging teambuilding exercises. I didn't expect crash courses in everything from first aid to fire starting, how to deal with aggressive behavior to how to deal with wild animals, and how to tie the perfect knot to how to feed eight campers on basic rations. My hands were sore, my head was pounding, and my shirt was stuck to my body with a fine layer of sweat.

I was exhausted.

On the upside, I'd managed to avoid Blake for the whole day. He had been assigned to the other group, which was fine by me. After spending the whole night tossing and turning, I'd decided that Marissa was right. Blake was here to stay… and so was I.

I needed this.

And besides, maybe having him here was a sign—my one chance at full and complete closure. Maybe my luck had finally turned.

Marissa assured me that once the first round of campers arrived, there would be little time to worry about bumping into Blake. Each counselor had a small group of same-sex campers assigned to them and would live in one of the cabins with their group for thirteen nights. There were six counselors, three male and three female, and six activity instructors. Troy and Tina handled the day-to-day camp management, and a team of 'behind-the-scenes' staff helped everything come together. Meals, cleaning, maintenance—that kind of thing. There was another full day of training followed by a team debrief on Friday, and then a day off before the first group arrived on Sunday.

"Intense, right?" Marissa breezed into the cabin as if she hadn't just spent the last eight hours paired with me. My lack of coordination was apparent when it came to pretty much anything that involved rope, paddles, or maps.

I nodded as I peeled the damp t-shirt off my body and grabbed my wash bag. "I'm going to take a quick shower."

"Great, then we can head to the campfire. We managed to talk Troy into grilling out again."

"Hmm, I'm not sure. Is it mandatory?"

"No, but what are you going to do instead? Hang out here alone?" Marissa's eyes bunched up.

Actually, that was exactly what I planned to do. Blake would no doubt be there, which meant I would not.

I padded into the small bathroom ignoring my roommate's pleas. She didn't understand; I hadn't given her any reason to. All Marissa knew was that Blake and I had some kind of history. If I was going to survive the summer here, I needed my past to stay just that—in the past.

The hot water lasted five minutes, cutting short my plans of a long soak under the trickle of soothing warmth. I wouldn't even have this luxury come Sunday when I moved into my camper's cabin. Campers had to use the communal block for washing. There was one for staff and one for campers.

After drying myself and brushing out my hair, I pulled on my shorts and tank top and rejoined Marissa.

"That didn't take long," she said with a knowing smirk.

"Let me guess. You knew the hot water would last a full two minutes?"

"Something like that. Besides, it means you can come with me now."

"Marissa," I warned.

"What? You can't hide in here all weekend. We can avoid him, I promise, but you're going to have to face him eventually."

Not today.

"Fine."

Marissa wasn't the only one surprised by my reply. Maybe it was my sense of achievement from the day—the fact I'd let Marissa support my body weight twice—that had me feeling determined to not only survive the summer but to also make the most of it.

"Really?" A smile formed on Marissa's face, and I found myself smiling back.

"Yes, really. Now, come on, before I change my mind."

Everyone gathered around the campfire. Troy and a couple of the other guys—Malachi and Liam, I think—grilled burgers and hot dogs on a smaller fire contained within a huge steel drum. Tina seemed more relaxed than she had last night and made sure to go around to all of the new staff to see how we were doing. And, of course, Blake was there. I had felt him before I saw him. One brief look and now, I was forcing myself to look anywhere but in his direction. It was hard; harder than I thought it would be. But apparently, what the head let itself forget, the heart did not, and every time I heard his voice, my heart flipped violently in my chest.

As the night wore on, I became less and less comfortable. Everyone seemed more than at home making new friends and reacquainting with old ones, and I sat on the periphery unsure of how to edge my way in. Marissa tried her best to include me, but people gravitated toward her. She pulled them in without even realizing. Me, not so much, and eventually, I slipped away and wandered down to the lake. It was close enough to still see the campfire, but far away enough that I wouldn't be disturbed.

The water rippled gently, deflecting the moon's glow. It was beautiful. Serene. I sat down at the water's edge, and my hand searched the ground for a flat stone. When I found one suitable, I rolled it in the palm of my hand, over and over, feeling its smooth surface. It was perfect. Drawing my hand up, I tilted it slightly and gripped it with my thumb and forefinger. With a snap of the wrist, I sent the stone flying across the lake. It landed on the water's surface and skimmed across. One. Two. Three. Before disappearing with a small splash.

"Nice," a voice called from somewhere behind me, and

a deep sigh reverberated in my body.

"Do you mind?" Blake dropped down next to me, his shoulder almost touching mine.

The proximity should have bothered me, but I couldn't breathe, let alone move. His voice had pinned me to the very spot in which I sat.

"It's really you. Fuck, Penny, I can't believe this is real."

I heard his words, but my eyes remained on the lake glistening before us.

"Say something, anything."

"It's beautiful out here."

Those words were safe. Detached. If I said any of the things I really wanted to say, I risked falling apart into irreparable pieces.

Neither of us spoke again. The silence hung between us, thick and heavy, and I felt sure it was going suffocate me.

After what felt like an eternity, Blake said, "There's so much I want to say. Things I want to explain, but I… this is, shit, I'm messing all of this up. I didn't expect this."

Out of the corner of my eye, I watched as Blake swept a hand through his hair and ran it across his head.

"I've missed you so damn much. It's really you, Penny. My lucky Penny." The pain in his voice was almost tangible. Something I could reach out and touch.

A single tear formed in the corner of my eye and rolled down my cheek.

And just like that, Blake Weston pieced together the broken parts of me, all while tearing them back down.

For the second time in my life.

chapter four

Blake

Age 12

"Have you seen her yet?" Bennett asked me as we sat on the wall of the Freeman group home, our legs dangling beneath us.

"Another girl?" My face scrunched with disapproval.

That made five in the last year. They came, stayed for a few months, and left. Girls were always first out of here. A couple looking to adopt preferred girls, or at least that was what Marie liked to tell us repeatedly.

"Yeah, Mase saw her already. Marie has her in the house giving the grand tour," he smirked and flicked his head back toward the house.

We both knew what the grand tour meant. A quick look around the house and then a rundown of what Derek and

Marie expected of us while we stayed. House rules, they liked to call them. They expected each of us to do chores and keep our rooms tidy. But rule number one was to be seen and not heard, which was almost impossible given we were teenagers. Well, not me. Not yet. I'd just turned twelve, but in a year, I would be a teenager, and then I would stand up to the Freeman's shit.

"Don't go there, Blake."

"What?" I shrugged kicking my feet on the sidewalk.

"You have that look again. You have to rein it in, dude. You've already been grounded three times this month. Don't go causing trouble. It's not worth it. Besides, I kinda like having you around. You might be the youngest here, but you have a good head on your shoulders."

Pride swelled in me. Bennett was the oldest kid living in the group home. He was strong and protective of the younger kids, like me, and he knew all the ways around the house rules. I got along well with Mase and Peter, the other two boys, but I looked up to Bennett. I wanted to be just like him when I was older.

"Okay, Bennett. Sorry." I ducked my head not wanting him to see my red cheeks.

"Hey, don't apologize, okay? Just keep your head down and remember you won't be in this place forever." Bennett shoulder checked me and hopped down off the wall. "Come on, let's go and meet her. You know what Amy can get like when a new girl arrives."

I followed Bennett up the path to the porch and took a deep breath.

He was right; one day, I would be free.

And I was counting the years.

"Why are your eyes so puffy?" Amy snarled at the new girl, Penny, and folded her arms over her chest like it was a crime to cry.

"Amy, back off," Bennett said. He was slouched back on the worn couch in the den; the one room in the house we were allowed to hang out in besides our bedrooms.

"You're not the boss of me, Bennett Foley. I can ask her a question if I want to."

I looked over at Penny from underneath the bill of my baseball cap. She seemed to shrink further into herself, wrapping her arms around her waist. She looked so broken. I hadn't been happy about another girl showing up, but I didn't like how sad she looked. I squirmed uncomfortably in my seat.

"Bennett's right, Amy. It's obvious she's upset, so let's give her some space," Jessica, the oldest girl, said.

"Fine. Fine, I have homework anyway. Catch you losers later." Amy stormed out of the room.

Bennett and Jessica shared a look, and he said, "She's getting harder to manage. Can't you do something?"

"Me? She's not my responsibility, Bennett." Jessica glared at him.

"No, but she's making too many waves. Derek and Marie will take this room away. They did it before, and they'll do it again. And you know what that means. It means lockdown."

I glanced around at my foster siblings. Mase sat next to Bennett looking as comfortable as I was. Mia was sitting on the stained beanbag in the corner of the room watching the exchange between Bennett and Jessica. Peter hadn't been allowed to come down since he was late doing his chores yesterday, and Penny was silent looking down at her hands clasped in her lap.

If I were older, like Bennett, I would have stuck up for her or asked her if she was okay. Penny was new to the system; it was written all over her soggy face. Arriving at the Freeman group home was scary enough when you had been in the system for a while but arriving here as your first foster home—I couldn't imagine how she felt or what was going through her head.

"Fine, I'll go talk to her." Jessica glanced over at Penny and smiled sadly. "It'll get easier, I promise. If you need to talk, I'm here. So is Mia, right?"

Mia nodded like Jessica was her mom, and Penny lifted her head and managed to nod back. We all watched the two girls leave the den.

"Okay." Bennett smoothed his hands down his jeans and stood. "I'm turning in. Don't stay in here past eight. They don't like it."

Mase followed him but paused at the table. "Coming, Blake?"

I rose and murmured that I was coming. Penny had dropped her head again, but it didn't feel right just to leave her all alone. Not on her first night.

"Actually, I'll be up in a bit, Mase."

He shrugged and went after Bennett. There wasn't a door hanging from the frame in the room, that wasn't allowed, but once I heard Bennett and Mase on the stairs, I knew we were alone.

My heart thumped in my chest, and I gulped back my nerves. I didn't understand why I was being such a girl. She wasn't going to bite; she couldn't even look me in the eye, for Pete's sake.

"Hmm, hi, I'm Blake. Penny, right?" I asked, approaching her chair.

She slowly lifted her head and sniffled. "Yeah. Hi."

"Sorry about earlier with Amy. She has a giant stick up her butt."

A small smile spread over Penny's face, and I stood a little taller, puffing my chest out. I'd made her smile. *Me.* No one else had managed to make her smile.

"That's okay."

"No, no, it isn't. She's always like that. It's because no one likes her." I sat on the arm of the couch closest to Penny.

"Okay, it's not okay. Got it." Her smile was gone, but she didn't look so sad anymore.

"It's your first time, right?" Penny nodded, and her eyes teared again. "My bad, sorry. I didn't mean to make you cry."

Shaking her head from side to side, she choked out, "It's not you. It's, it's been a sucky few days."

An idea sprang into my mind. It was risky, and Bennett would kick my ass when he found out, but it always made me feel better. And if there was a chance it would make Penny feel better, then it would be worth the consequences.

"Hey, want to get out of here?"

Alarm replaced sadness, and Penny's mouth fell open like she was ready to tell me no.

"I sneak out sometimes. It'll be okay, I promise."

Disappointment started to fill my chest. She was going

to say no and then things would be awkward between us. She didn't look like the type of girl who would break the rules, but I just wanted to take her mind off whatever it was that was making her so sad.

I stood ready to bolt from the room when she told me no, but instead, she surprised me by saying, "Okay."

When I had first arrived at the Freeman house almost a year ago, I'd been quick to work out all the escape routes. I had been in a couple of foster homes before this one, and although the foster parents weren't as strict as Derek and Marie, most had rules. Over time, I became a master at climbing, jimmying windows, and crawling out of the smallest of spaces.

Backing onto Cenci Park, the house was the perfect place for an escape. The yard was long and narrow and cloaked by trees along one side that snaked across the bottom. That was the perimeter of the park. If you stayed close, the shadows swallowed you up so someone looking out from the kitchen window couldn't see you. We didn't risk it a lot, but when I'd first arrived, Bennett had brought me out here a couple of times after lights out. He said I was a natural at escaping.

Penny… not so much.

She had almost cried when her sweater snagged on the window lock, and then she let out a squeal when I returned from checking to make sure the coast was clear. She was a sucky accomplice, but we finally reached the trees and followed the path down to the bottom of the yard.

"Are you sure we won't get caught?" she asked for the twentieth time.

"I've done this before. We'll be okay as long as you can keep quiet. You almost gave us away back there." I glanced over my shoulder and watched Penny chew her bottom lip between her teeth.

"Sorry."

"It's okay. Come on, it's not much further." I turned back and continued down the yard, using my arms to shield my face from the branches.

The end of the yard wasn't fenced off; it was a border of thick trees separating it from the park. On the other side was what we called No Man's Land. We figured it was the outer perimeter of the park, but no one ever came out this far, and the main paths were a way away. When we couldn't walk any further, I told Penny to stay put as I used my hands to feel for the hole we had created between the trees.

"Got it. Come on," I whispered, straining to make out Penny's face.

I felt her move toward me, and then she was almost face to face with me. My heart did that weird thing again.

"Where does that lead?" she asked, and I blinked remembering where we were and what we were doing.

"Follow me."

Penny stuck close behind me as we ducked into the trees. Bennett got out to meet his friends this way sometimes, making the path well worn. After a few seconds, the trees opened up around us, and we spilled out into the clearing. I wasted no time and dropped down onto the grass to lie on my back.

"Wha-what are you doing?"

I patted the space next to me, and Penny slowly inched down until she was kneeling next to me.

"You have to lie back or you won't see them."

"See what?"

"Just trust me. You'll want to see them," I said.

She lay back and a few wisps of her hair brushed my face. We were shoulder to shoulder staring up at the sky.

"Wow." Her voice was so quiet.

"Yeah, wow," I replied admiring the stars.

They shone even brighter when it was a clear night, and tonight was perfect.

Neither of us said anything else. Besides, I didn't bring her out here to talk. I just wanted to share this with her. The first time Bennett had brought me out here, he told me this was ours. Somewhere we could come when things at the house were too much. I didn't know what he meant back then, but I quickly learned.

My eyes tracked the stars, trying to identify the constellations Bennett had pointed out to me over our nights spent out here. I could still only identify Cassiopeia. I was halfway to making out Ursa Minor when Penny cleared her throat quietly.

"Thank you."

It was only two simple words, but they changed everything.

chapter five

Being a camp counselor was hard work. The days were never ending, my time was no longer my own, and I hadn't felt clean in two weeks, but it was hands down the most rewarding thing I had ever done.

"First group is done. Congratulations, people." Troy clapped his hands together and grinned at the campfire.

I turned my head and smiled at Marissa. Despite no longer bunking together on a daily basis, we had become close friends. I still hadn't opened up to her much, but I was starting to trust her. She had joined me with my group of girls for breakfast a handful of times and helped me deal with a couple of teen girl dramas. We made a great team, and for the first time since the accident, I finally felt like I had purpose.

The only thing holding me back was my anxiety at the close physical proximity to the girls and the instructors. I was generally okay when I expected it, like a high-five from one of the girls or when I had to help them climb or hold something, but I still couldn't handle the unsuspecting moments.

At the end of the first week, Chelsea, one of the youngest girls in my group, had finally managed to complete the Camp Chance obstacle course. She was so proud of herself that she hugged me without thinking. Instead of sharing in her excitement and personal achievement, panic at her slender arms wrapped around my waist suffocated me. Somehow, through my alarm, I'd managed to pat her on the back. She didn't notice the way I stepped back ever so slightly to put space between us without actually shrugging her off.

"Penny, earth to Penny, are you with us?" Troy was staring right at me, and I blinked rapidly before murmuring something unintelligible while my cheeks exploded with embarrassment and I ducked my head.

"Good job with the girls last week." He winked and turned his attention to someone else.

I could still feel eyes on me, but I knew it wasn't Troy as he was busy singing praises of John, one of the other counselors who'd had a particularly difficult group. Even though I knew who I would find looking in my direction, I couldn't resist the urge to lift my head.

Blake's head was resting on his fists, which were propped on his knees as he leaned into the fire. He sat opposite Marissa and me again, just as he did every time we congregated at the campfire.

"He's watching you again," Marissa whispered under her breath.

It had become our ritual. We would sit around the fire, I'd look up to find Blake watching me, and Marissa would point out the obvious.

Since the night by the lake, I had tried my hardest to avoid him. Whenever our paths crossed, I smiled and whispered a polite hello, but I couldn't give him more than that yet. It was too soon. Too raw. Besides, I didn't know if he even wanted more after the way I'd fled from him when he had laid his feelings out on the line.

Lucky Penny.

That nickname had once made me feel like I could survive anything. It *had* helped me survive so much. But now it was a distant memory—the kind that felt more like a dream than reality.

Marissa nudged me in the side, snapping me from my memories, and when my eyes refocused, Blake was no longer looking in my direction.

My heart sank.

"The next buses arrive at five in the afternoon tomorrow, so the next twenty-two hours are yours to do as you please."

"Except each other," one of the guys called out causing the whole camp to burst into fits of laughter. I smiled, but the joke was lost on me.

"Okay, smart aleck, you know where to find us if you need us. Enjoy your downtime. The lake is warm this time of year if you catch my drift." Troy waved his hand in the air behind him as he and Tina headed back toward the central cabin. Laughter followed them.

A couple of the guys stood up and yelled, "Last one in cooks."

They set off in the direction of the lake peeling off their clothes as they went. Without stopping, they both leaped off the dock and bombed into the water. A huge wave rose up and splashed around them.

Marissa chuckled and stood up next to me. "You game?" She yanked her tank over her head and stood there in front of everyone in just her shorts and bra.

"Hmm, I don't think so." I pulled my arms tighter suddenly feeling self-conscious.

She shrugged, unbuttoning her shorts and shimmying them down her toned legs. "Suit yourself. Keep hold of my clothes for me. Last year, some jackass hid them, and I had to walk back to the cabin half naked."

Marissa took off, catching up with Sheridan and Liam, who had already stripped down to their undergarments. I scooped up her clothes and walked down closer to the water, taking a seat on one of the overturned trunks. As I watched everyone swimming in the lake, a feeling of sadness washed over me. Here I was, one of the oldest counselors and yet, the most sheltered. I had never experienced this, right here. Never thrown caution to the wind and just let go. I was a prisoner of my past, and for all my progress over the last few months, I was still captive to my fears.

"This seat taken?"

My eyes fluttered shut and my breath caught in my throat as the person I'd been trying hard to avoid sat down beside me.

"You're not going in?"

I shook my head, my fingers finding the edge of the carved-out bark. I dug them in feeling the rough edge bite into my skin, but I welcomed the sensation, needing it to ground me. My breathing became shallow as I concentrated on relaxation techniques to try to keep in control.

Blake's presence brought out intense feelings in me, and I wasn't used to feeling such confusion. On the one hand, I wanted to run far away again like the night I'd first found him across the fire, but part of me—the part that remembered—wanted to bask in him. To reach out and touch him to make sure this wasn't a dream. To confirm that the guy I'd given my heart to such a long time ago was really here.

"I'm sorry about the other night," he said staring out at the lake.

My eyes took in every detail of his face, a face I'd once known almost as well as my own. His brown hair was longer, falling over his eyes a little when it was damp, and he had a thick layer of stubble covering his jaw. Seven years had been good to him. He had filled out in all the right places. But despite his sameness, something about him was different. I couldn't quite put my finger on it. My heart had recognized him right off the bat, but after catching glimpses of him around the camp over the last couple of weeks, my head realized the guy I had once loved was changed.

But then, weren't we all.

Lost in the lines of his side profile, I didn't sense him turning to face me until two blue pools stared back at me.

"Okay, can we start over? As crazy as it is seeing you here, for as much as I'm trying to get my head around what it means, we have to find a way to be around one another."

I inhaled another deep calming breath. Blake was right. We had to find a way to make this work.

"You're right."

His reaction to my words caught me off guard; I could feel the relief rolling off him as if he couldn't believe I had actually replied…and agreed.

Blake cleared his throat, and I was sure I caught a nervous quiver, which made little sense. Things might have been awkward between us, yes, but what did he have to feel nervous about?

"Okay, I'd like that. To get to know you again, I mean. It's been a long time, Pen."

Seven years.

"Weston, get your ass over here," a voice called out from the lake and Blake sighed. "I guess I should go join them. Are you sure I can't persuade you?"

I shook my head feeling that earlier discomfort creep in. Blake opened his mouth as if to say something but didn't. Instead, he smiled before leaving me. I watched him walk toward the lake. He hooked his hands under his shirt and pulled it clean over his head. My mouth instantly dried. The last time I'd seen Blake, he was sixteen. But as I watched the boy I'd once known slide his cargo shorts off his legs, causing tanned, taut muscles to flex across his shoulders, and start sprinting toward the dock in nothing but his boxer briefs, it was obvious he had been replaced with a man.

And I didn't know how to feel about that.

"So tell me again. Exactly what did he say?"

Marissa and I stood with the rest of the counselors waiting for the new group to arrive. We could hear the approaching buses, but they hadn't yet broken through the trees.

"He said he wants to get to know me again. What does

that even mean?"

Marissa smirked. "I think you know what it means, Penny."

Heat burned through me, and I knew my cheeks had a crimson stain to them. If I had learned anything about Marissa over the last two weeks, it was that she was comfortable with her body, and that included talking about sex.

"Marissa, can you stop? Please. It isn't like that." I leaned back against the wooden fencing that sectioned off the parking lot.

"I'm just saying. I've seen how he looks at you across the fire. Like he's remembering."

I groaned. Although she hadn't pushed for details about the history Blake and I shared, Marissa had started to draw her own conclusions.

The buses came into view, and I stood upright, wiping my hands down my shorts, butterflies fluttering in my stomach. The first group had, for the most part, been easy. I knew I had gotten off lightly.

"Ready?" Marissa asked.

"As I'll ever be."

The buses rolled to a stop and dust sprayed around them as the driver hit the brakes.

"Fingers crossed we get it easy again," Sara, one of the other counselors, said with a smile.

It went from calm to crazy as the doors opened and twenty-four over-excited teenage girls rushed off the bus.

"Okay, okay, girls this way," Tina yelled over the chatter. "Counselors, you're up."

I rounded the crush to join Tina, Sara, and Sheridan. Tina started giving out instructions, and my eyes wandered over to the other side of the parking lot where the male counselors were meeting the boys.

Blake looked at eased as he goofed around with a small group of boys and something stirred in me.

"... Brianna, Lacey, Tonya, Jenny, Lucy, Erica, and Crystal, you're going to be with Counselor Penny for the next two weeks."

I raised my hand and waved, trying not to shrink into myself as I remembered one of the first things Tina had told us during our first training session. *'These kids will smell your fear and use it against you. Even if you feel like you don't have it under control, your body language says you do. Got it?'* Hearing her words replay in my head, I straightened and rolled back my shoulders looking right at the eight girls gathered in front of me. I smiled. "Hi, I'm Penny. I'll be your camp counselor during your stay."

A taller girl with cut-off shorts and a baggy t-shirt arched her eyebrow and huffed. "Awesome."

"Erica, come on, give her a chance." A smaller girl glared at Erica and then glanced back at me, smiling weakly.

"Okay, grab your bags and I'll show you to our cabin."

Once the girls had their bags, we started the short trek to the camper cabins, or cabin row as we called it, set further into the woods than the staff quarters. I alternated between walking forward and backward so I could talk to the girls. Erica and another girl—Brianna, I think—obviously didn't want to be here. Their bags hung off their shoulders as if they were carrying the weight of the world on them. I only hoped their worries were the regular girl variety and not the kind I experienced growing up.

We hadn't even reached the cabin when Erica dropped her bag to the ground and folded her arms over her chest. "I'm not sleeping in there," she spat out.

"Bagsy top bunk," a girl with long red hair yelled, running for the cabin door.

"Go ahead," I said to the girls hanging behind, waiting for me to give them permission to enter.

"Erica, are you going to join us?" I didn't approach her. She wore her hostility like a coat of armor, but I could see the cracks. Her hands trembled slightly as they hung at her sides.

"I'm not going in there."

"Okay. When you're ready to join us, we'll be inside."

I could try to talk her into it, but something about the hard girl in front of me told me it would do no good. She was defensive and unwilling for a reason.

Turning my back on her, I walked up the cabin's steps. The sounds of chaos spilled out of the tiny cracks between the wood. Before heading inside to try to instill calm, I glanced over my shoulder at Erica. "You might not think it, but I've been in your shoes before. It's okay to let your guard down once in a while." I smiled softly. "I look forward to getting to know you, Erica."

It was the truth.

Something about Erica called to me. Gut reaction, intuition—I didn't know what to call it, but I saw some of me in her. I'd been that girl before—lost, scared, and alone—and someone had helped me. He had showed me that living in foster care didn't have to be all bad.

Now, maybe, I could be that person for Erica.

chapter six

"That's it, Lucy. You can do it. Just a little farther. Reach, REACH," I yelled, willing her to stretch a tiny bit farther to grab the ledge. My words seemed to give Lucy the strength she needed, and with one last push, she extended her arm, stretching as far as possible until her fingers touched the ridge of the wall and she managed to get a firm grip on it.

"Go, Lucy! Pull yourself up."

Her small hands held on for life as she tried to find a foothold in the wall to hoist herself up.

"Come on, Brannon, Lucy is almost over. We can't have the girls beating us. We're men, Brannon. Men."

I shot Blake a questioning look, and he grinned across the obstacle course at me. This was the second time this week our cabins had been paired together to participate in activities. Although the cabins completed most of the activities individually, some—like raft building, the obstacle course, and games day—built teamwork by pitching one cabin against another in competitions.

Blake continued to shout words of encouragement to Brannon while pride settled in my stomach as Lucy kicked herself over the wall and tumbled down the other side into the mud pit. Her shrieks caused the other girls behind me to laugh. I turned to face them and said, "Is that how we support our teammates? Get over here and cheer our girl on."

They joined me, yelling words of support to Lucy. Erica, although she had participated in the activity, stood positioned away from us slightly and didn't join us to cheer on Lucy.

"Erica, we all cheered for you," I said, hoping she would find it in herself to show Lucy some support.

She shrugged refusing to meet my eyes. "So. I didn't ask you to."

Unwilling to engage in her attempt at an argument, I ignored her.

Five days in, and I was still no closer to breaking the ice between Erica and me and the other girls. Brianna—Erica's only friend—had even warmed up a little, participating fully in all the cabin and camp activities, although she still seemed wary of me.

Lucy reached the end of the course, and we all rushed over to her to celebrate her achievement. As the smallest and youngest girl in our cabin, the obstacle course had worried Lucy. The huge grin on her face showed just how important it was for her to be able to complete the course.

"Boys, what do we say?" Blake led his group of disappointed faces over to us.

Reluctant mumbles of 'well done,' 'good job,' and 'congratulations' came from their group. Blake stepped forward and bent slightly to address Lucy. "Good job, little one."

He held his hand out for a high-five, and Lucy beamed as she swatted her hand down on his. "Now, who wants s'mores?"

A chorus of cheers deafened us, and Blake caught my eye in the crush. Something passed between us. I don't know if it was the excitement of the activity or seeing Lucy beat Brannon on the obstacle course, but we were sharing a moment. The excitement I had been swept up in transformed into confusion. The same confusion I felt whenever our eyes collided. He was trying to tell me something. Or, at least, that was what it felt like, but I wasn't ready to find out what. I was still adjusting to him being here. In my life.

My present.

Fifteen minutes later, Blake had the fire burning and sixteen happy campers were feasting on charred s'mores. I helped myself to a bottle of water out of the cooler and sat on the empty trunk, letting the kids have some time to themselves.

"I think there may have been a little bit of cheating going on earlier. It's the only explanation. Team Weston never loses."

I smiled. It was impossible not to when Blake was being playful—something I'd realized was a big part of the new Blake. I watched him interact with the kids, with the other counselors, even Troy and Tina. He was charismatic, a total charmer, but he was also warm like the sun, and people gravitated to his light.

"It had to happen at some point. Besides, my girls rocked it."

Blake tipped his water bottle at me. "That they did. So how are the girls?"

I glanced over at them laughing and joking with the boys. "They're okay. Erica isn't responding yet."

He followed my gaze to where Erica sat on the edge of the huddle with Brianna. They were toasting marshmallows on their skewers but didn't have the same expressions as everyone else.

"It doesn't happen right away, not for them all. Give her time."

"I keep forgetting you're a pro at this."

Blake shuffled beside me, sliding off the trunk and sitting against it on the ground with his knees bent. "Pro? Nah, I just get them. Hell, we were them, Penny. After-"

"Agh, I'm on fire. Someone help me, AGH." Trevor, one of the boys, was leaping around on the spot waving his rapidly burning skewer while the rest of the kids all laughed hysterically.

Blake got to his feet. "Trevor, drop the skewer. It's on fire. Not you, buddy. Just let it go."

Trevor stopped and glanced at Blake and back at the skewer, which was completely charred on one end. He threw it out in front on him and started stomping on it over and over.

"Trevor, I think you killed it." Blake laughed and Trevor stopped, ducking his head with realization.

"I- I thought I was on fire. My bad." He skulked back to his seat and shrugged off a couple of his friends.

Blake didn't come back to sit with me. Instead, he joined the boys. It had felt like he was going to say something before the fire incident. Something significant. But now he was avoiding me. Dusting myself off, I joined the girls. Even if it was something significant, what did we know about each other anymore? I didn't even know where he lived, what he did with his life. We really were strangers to one another.

And maybe it was for the best.

"I'm not doing it. No way. You can't make me." Erica stood in her usual pose; arms folded over her chest, an icy glare aimed in my direction.

Ten days, and I was still no closer to cracking her. It was like whatever I did or said sparked a reaction from her. It was the same with most of the adults in the camp. It was frustrating, but more than that, it concerned me. Most of the other kids relished the opportunity to be free for two weeks; to play and experience and grow. Some of the kids who came through the Camp Chance program were fortunate enough to have supportive and wholesome foster families. Those kids stood out—they were confident and wore a smile in their adventures. But others, like Erica and Brianna, were wary and unsure, and the foster kid in me knew it stemmed from their experiences back home.

Home.

If Erica was anything like I was when I was her age, home was not a word used to describe my foster home. It was hell on earth—a time in my life made bearable by one person. That was the reason why I couldn't let Erica walk away from Camp Chance without doing something… anything, to give her hope of a better life. It was also the reason I needed Blake's help, but that would have to wait until the group campfire tonight because, right now, I had to get eight girls across the lake on canoes.

Marissa was our instructor for the afternoon, and she had an endless amount of patience with the girls as they struggled to stay upright in their kayaks. Lucy, being small, was surprisingly buoyant and had managed to navigate across half the lake with little support. Marissa was working closely with Crystal and Brianna, and the rest of the girls were goofing around, flicking water at one another with their paddles.

"We have to get across the lake, Erica. That's what today's activity is all about. Perseverance and determination. We could-"

"I'm. Not. Doing. It," she hissed.

I sighed glancing away from her to watch the rest of the girls out on the lake. The water was glistening in the afternoon sun making the water look inviting, but not enough that I was particularly looking forward to canoeing across it.

Being the calm and compassionate counselor was getting me nowhere, so I wrung my hands in front of me, bent down to pick up the paddle for the canoe pulled up onto the embankment and thrust it at Erica. "Let's go."

"Wha-what?" She blinked staring at me as if I had totally lost it.

"I said let's go. In the canoe. You and me. Now." I pushed the paddle at her a little farther forcing her to take it from me and then spun on my heel to push the canoe to the water's edge. "Let's go, Miss I'm-not-doing-it."

Inside my chest, my heart was pounding so hard I felt

a little nauseous. This was out of character for me. All the kids had me pegged as the quiet one. A lot of them liked that about me, but with Erica, it didn't work. I couldn't reach her that way. Blake had told me to give her time, to let her come to me, but time was running out.

"Move it, Erica. We haven't got all day," I shouted glancing in the direction of where I'd left her standing. Only she wasn't standing there anymore. She was moving toward the canoe with a look of pure hatred on her face.

"If you capsize us and I drown, I'll sue." She climbed in the back end of the vessel and huffed loudly.

I couldn't help the slight grin on my face as I sat down and started to shimmy the canoe forward using the paddle to push off the ground. The vessel whooshed into the water and started to float away from the shore. My smirk grew into a full smile, feeling pretty pleased with myself on both fronts—getting us out onto the lake without sinking and coaxing Erica to join me.

My smugness didn't last long.

Marissa was busy showing off to the girls up ahead of us by creating ripples with her paddles to make their kayaks rock. Laughter echoed around the lake each time she did it, as they rocked from side to side. But by the time the ripples reached us, they had merged into waves rolling toward shore.

"We need to paddle into them, I think," I called back at Erica, trying to remember what Marissa had taught me during our staff lesson out on the lake.

Erica muttered something I couldn't make out, and we both started to rotate the paddles in the water to force the vessel forward into the gentle waves. Marissa spotted us and said something that caused the rest of the girls to look in our direction. The next thing I knew, six girls started copying Marissa's action with their paddles, sending ripples rushing out toward us.

"Marissa, seriously?" I yelled, still paddling forward, my pulse quickening.

The canoe seemed to ride the waves with ease, even if the slight rocking churned my stomach.

"How long is this going to take? I hate it out here," Erica muttered sounding almost bored.

"Keep at it. I can't do it alone."

Concentrating on the movement of the paddles, I didn't notice Marissa instruct the girls to turn their kayaks in full circles. The force of their vessels cutting through the water created stronger waves that started lapping at the front of the canoe. "She's crazy," I murmured under my breath. My panic was rising; I was beginning to feel as if capsizing might be a valid concern now.

We continued forward, despite having to grip onto the sides a couple of times, and by the time we reached Marissa and the girls, they were all in fits of hysterics.

"That was not funny, Marissa. I thought we were going to capsize," I said breathlessly. Really, I wanted to shout a string of expletives at her, but that would have to wait for later.

"You were fine. We didn't make big enough waves to flip you."

Sensing Erica watching me from the back of the canoe, I glanced behind me and smiled. "You good?"

She nodded. It was the most positive thing I had managed to drag out of her all week. I returned her nod and turned back to Marissa, but not before I caught a slight smile on Erica's face. It was barely there, but I saw it. Relief flooded me. Finally, I was getting through to her, and my mind immediately went to the one person who would understand the hugeness of my small win—the only person who would really understand how important this was for me.

Blake.

chapter seven

The sound of Troy's guitar floated on the summer's breeze. Tonight was group camp, the last one before the final goodbye camp in three days' time.

"I can't believe it's almost time to leave," Lucy sighed dramatically, and Crystal pushed her from behind with a snicker. "What? I don't mind it with the Peterson's, but Camp Chance is so freakin' cool. I don't ever want to leave."

I chuckled amazed by how far the small girl next to me had come in just ten days. Troy had been right; Camp Chance really did change lives.

"We all have to leave eventually, Lucy." I ruffled her hair, and she ducked away from my hand smoothing it back down.

Some of the girls took group camp very seriously. It was one of the few times they had to interact with the boys. Gone were their daytime scruffs, replaced with cut-off shorts and pretty tank tops and tees. Even Erica had made an effort tonight, and although she hadn't spoken to me again since her slip earlier, something about her felt less detached.

We entered the clearing, and my eyes did a quick count. We were the last cabin to arrive, it seemed, and everyone else sat quietly around the fire.

"You made it." Marissa came to the edge of the circle to greet us. "Hi, girls. Come on, Troy's about to start."

We hurried behind Marissa to our section of the circle and the girls squashed in beside Sheridan's group. When the girls finally settled, I looked up and my eyes found Blake.

"Okay, now that everyone's present and accounted for, how about a song? Everyone remember flea fly?" Troy strummed a note on the strings and a sea of heads nodded.

"Flea," he said.

"Flea," the circle responded.

I tried to turn my head to Troy, but Blake's intense gaze refused to let me.

"Flea fly."

Flea fly. My lips moved but nothing came out, and a slow grin spread over Blake's face. He knew exactly what he was doing, and yet, I still couldn't drag my eyes away from him.

What in the hell was happening?

"Flea fly flow."

I heard the words, heard the circle repeat them, but they sounded distant as if someone was turning down the volume button.

"Feasta…"

Hi. Blake mouthed at me, his mouth hooking up in a smile.

Just look away. This is dangerous territory. What are you

doing?

Hi. I mouthed back with a coy smile ignoring the little voice in my head. The familiar flutter of butterflies started in my stomach. It was a feeling I was becoming used to whenever Blake was near.

"Cooma lotta, cooma lotta, cooma lotta feasta."

Hi. He mouthed again, and I dropped my eyes. It was too much all at once, and I needed to break our connection. I had felt things change between us the other day, but I hadn't expected to feel so exposed around him. Just as I did when we were kids, Blake always saw me. Not the front I tried to put on or the brave mask I wore so often, he saw *me.* The real me. Broken, tired, alone. The girl holding on by a thread. I wasn't exactly that girl anymore. I was stronger. Hardened.

I was a survivor.

But it didn't matter because, looking at me across the fire, it had felt as if Blake could see straight into my soul.

"Oh, no, no, no, na feasta," Troy's voice rang out loud startling me.

I didn't risk glancing back up at Blake. Instead, I joined in with the rest of the song. I tried to think about anything but the boy who once saved me and how it might have been more than just coincidence that we found our way back to each other seven years later at a camp for kids living what we had lived.

"There she is." Troy approached me as everyone around us mingled. "How are you enjoying camp so far? I've been hearing good things about you." He smiled, and I felt myself shrinking into my hoodie not used to such compliments.

"Of course, you have. She's a natural." Blake slung an arm around Troy's neck and smiled directly at me. "Right, Penny?"

I nodded, unsure if there was a hidden meaning in his words.

"We change lives, but I never thought we would bring together two lost souls either. It's a beautiful day, people. Live. Love. And be happy." Troy clapped Blake on the back and lifted his head at me before leaving us.

The girls had long abandoned me to sit with their friends—new and old—and Marissa was busy talking to Liam. She denied there was anything between them, but I'd caught her checking him out on more than one occasion.

"Come on." Blake motioned to the lake in the distance. Without thinking, I rose and followed him.

"Won't anyone notice we're gone?" I asked remembering Tina's warning about counselors taking their relationships too far.

"We're just talking. It's fine. You can trust me, Penny."

I was transported back eleven years to a time when a broken girl had given her trust to a boy with grass-stained jeans and unlaced chucks.

So much had happened since then.

"So Troy is an interesting guy," I said trying to evade the memories flooding my mind.

"He's great. He really gets the kids and the work. He's just a little free spirited. I think he and Tina were hippies back in the day."

"He called us lost souls? What did he mean?"

Blake swept a hand through his tousled hair and blew out a long breath. "I've known Tina and Troy for a long time, and they know some of our story."

Something flashed in Blake's eyes, causing me to tense, and my mind immediately went to a place I didn't want to remember.

Ever.

"Hey, nothing like that," Blake said reassuring me. "They just know we were in a group home together and haven't seen each other in a real long time. Too long. I have a confession to make…" I tugged the zipper of my hoodie, suddenly feeling a chill despite the adrenaline coursing through me. "I knew you were coming."

My feet stopped dead. "What?" I asked sure I must have heard him wrong. "What do you mean you knew I was coming?"

"I stay in touch with Tina and Troy throughout the year. When Troy had his operation back in the spring, Tina asked me to step in and help her vet the applications. I saw your name and read your application. I instantly knew it was you."

He knew. He had acted as surprised to see me that first night as I was to see him.

As if he could hear my thoughts, Blake went on. "I saw you across the fire, and it was like I'd been sucker-punched. I guess I wasn't as prepared to see you as I thought."

Well, that explained some of his shock, but it still didn't make me feel great that he knew all this time. Blake started to walk again, but when I didn't follow, he doubled back.

"Shit, Penny, I know there's a lot we still haven't talked about but just give me a chance. Please."

We hadn't talked at all. We had been polite and skirted around one another, and then tonight, there had been the moment across the fire, but we had yet to say *any* of the things we needed to say.

For a long time after Blake left the Freemans, I imagined what I would say if I ever saw him again. I wanted answers. Where did he go? How could he leave me behind? Derek and Marie refused to tell me anything; they said it was confidential. As if that wasn't bad enough, Amy took great pleasure in taunting me. She said I was too clingy and Blake had requested the move to get away from me. I knew that wasn't true; Blake loved me, he'd told me only the night before I came home from my summer job at the local store to find him gone. But Amy did have a point because he was gone, and I was still there wondering what in the hell had happened.

That question haunted me for a very long time. But now he was here, standing next to me, asking—no, pleading—for a chance to explain.

"Penny..." His voice cracked, and he swallowed hard. Although it sparked off something in me, all I could do was nod. There was never a choice to make, not where Blake Weston was concerned. My head might have learned to hate him. To blame him. But my heart never forgot him. Never forgot the love it once felt for him.

Still felt for him.

The moon's reflection illuminated Blake's face as I stared at him with my jaw hanging open. "I still can't believe they found you. After all that time."

"Yeah. Apparently, I was one of the lucky ones. Uncle Anthony hadn't spoken to my mom for years, so he didn't even know I existed until he moved back to Columbus and hired a PI to search for her. His search led him to Lancaster which led him to me."

I closed my mouth trying to make sense of everything, but one thing still didn't add up. "So he found you and petitioned the courts?"

Blake nodded.

"Okay, but why the sudden disappearance? And why didn't you know about any of this beforehand? Surely, someone should have told you that you had family who wanted you?"

"Uncle Ant knows a lot of the right people, and he pulled some strings to make it happen quickly. I wanted to say goodbye. I fought with them so hard, Penny, but they said it was for the best. I was confused and angry, and my head felt like it was going to explode..." Blake dropped his head. "And as selfish as it was, a little part of me was relieved I was finally getting free from them. From that hell. I thought I'd get out, get my shit together, and come back for you."

I understood that part. I did. But Blake's honesty stirred something in me. For as much as I wanted to get the hell away from Derek and Marie, I couldn't imagine ever leaving without him.

Ever.

"You left me all alone in there." Tears streamed down my face. "Do you know what it was like to come home that day and find you gone? To have Derek and Marie revel in the opportunity to hurt me even more than they already had? They wouldn't tell me a word. No one would. Nothing. You just disappeared into thin air."

The force of my sobs wracked my body, and I had to grip the rickety bench to keep myself upright. I was foolish to let Blake's earlier playfulness distract me. Our past had been staring me in the face ever since I laid eyes on him because *he* was my past. A reminder of everything I'd gone through. Everything I'd survived.

"Wait, what?" Blake's head whipped up, and now, he was the one looking at me with utter shock.

I stared at him in disbelief. Surely, he didn't expect me to bare myself like that again?

"They didn't tell you?"

"Who?" I asked confused.

"Derek and Marie? They didn't give you my letter?"

Letter?

Realization dawned on Blake's face, and he cursed something under his breath. "Of course, they didn't. Fuck."

Wiping the tears away from my eyes, I said, "Can you please tell me what is going on?"

He looked at me with such sadness that, even though I had thought it impossible, another piece of my heart broke. They say the eyes are a window to the soul, and sitting there in front of a lake just as we did in another time, Blake was baring his to me.

So entranced in the pained looked on his face, I missed his fingers inching closer to mine until they were brushing. My eyes darted to where our hands rested between us. Slowly and carefully, Blake entwined his fingers in mine as if he thought I might shatter under his touch.

My heart began to pound in my chest. Blake was touching me, and I was freaking out. But not because his touch repulsed me… or scared me… or hurt me.

I was terrified because it didn't.

chapter eight

Blake

Age 13

"I can't believe he's gone." I kicked my feet into the dirt and dropped my head.

"You knew it was going to happen, Blake. Bennett finally turned eighteen."

I sighed. "I know, I know. It's just he was the best."

Penny nudged me with her shoulder and curled one of her small hands around mine. "I know. He looked out for all of us. But you're right. It won't be the same without him."

I looked down at our joined hands. She was always grabbing my hand and linking our fingers. I wondered if it made her feel all funny inside the way it did me. If it did, her face didn't give her away, and I was too chicken shit to ask her why she was always doing it.

One day, not long after she moved into the Freeman group home, it had just happened. We had risked sneaking out to No Man's Land one night, just the two of us, and we almost were caught. Penny was so scared that she grabbed a hold of my hand and held on for dear life.

It kind of became Penny's thing after that. Now, it was more like *our* thing.

Amy had to take a cheap shot whenever she spotted Penny's hand in mine, but Penny just shrugged it off. According to her, there was nothing wrong with holding hands with your best friend.

Best friend.

When Penny first called me that last year, I had just stared at her blankly. She thought of *me* as her best friend? The messy-haired kid with the quick temper and hand-me-down chucks. My last best friend had been a one-eyed stuffed bear called Frederick when I was seven. Sure, I had Bennett and one or two other friends during my time in foster care, but no one had ever called me their best friend.

No one.

But Penny was a girl, and boys and girls weren't usually best friends, were they?

"Hey, where'd you go on me?" Penny stared at me wide-eyed, her long hair spilling in front of her face. When I blinked out of my trance, she grinned at me.

"Just zoned out. Come on, let's head inside."

"Already? Can't we stay out here a little longer?"

I shook my head. "You know the rules, Pen. Chores before dinner and we're already late."

"Fine, fine, lead the way."

"Blake, Penny, where have you been?"

Marie was waiting for us as we entered the house. Arms folded over her chest, her face was beet red and her eyes were narrowed. When neither of us replied, it turned another shade darker, like the blood vessels might burst at any second. "Well?"

"Sorry, Marie. It was my fault. I wanted to stay in the yard. It's such a nice day, and well, I wasn't ready to come inside."

Shit, Penny, I silently cursed. Penny knew better than to take the blame, especially with Marie. She was meaner than a witch on a good day. When she got mad, it was better to stay in your room than risk crossing her path.

"Penny, do you not remember the rules of this house? *My* house?"

Penny tensed beside me. "I remember. It won't happen again."

The throbbing vein in Marie's thick neck pulsated. The thing looked like it needed its own food supply.

"Blake, go and help the others clean the kitchen, please."

I risked a sideways glance at Penny. If she was scared, she wasn't showing it, but I still didn't want to leave her.

"I can stay. I was late, too."

"Blake," Marie's voice said in that way grown-ups did was something was final.

When I had first arrived at the house, Marie terrified me. She was short and stocky with eyes that burned right through you. Over the last two years, my fear had lessened, but it didn't mean I just went around breaking the rules. If you did, Marie liked to dish out punishment to everyone. It was her way of exercising her power because she had it all… and we had none.

"What's going on back here, Marie?" Derek stomped into the kitchen.

Unlike his wife who was short and round, Derek Freeman was as tall as he was wide. His stomach hung over his baggy dress pants and his thick arms stuck out of his creased white shirt. Bennett thought he must only own two shirts. One for Sundays and one for the rest of the week because, by Friday, it was usually a dirty shade of gray and covered in stains. The smell was enough to make you puke whenever he was near.

"Penny here was just telling me how she wanted to stay outside instead of coming inside to do her chores."

Derek pushed Marie aside and stood right in front of Penny, bending down slightly to come level with her face. "That right, Penny?"

"Yes," she said her whole body rigid.

"Yes, what?"

My fists started to clench. I hated the way he thought he could speak to the girls. Talking to us—the boys—like that was one thing, but intimidating the girls was just plain wrong. My daddy might have been a bad seed, but he always taught me that a man should never make a woman feel scared.

Derek was nothing like my daddy; he got off on making the girls scared.

Penny breathed in harshly and then said, "Yes, sir."

"There, that wasn't so hard, was it?" Derek stepped

closer to Penny, only a sliver of space between them. His smell wafted to me, and I gagged trying not to make a sound. I could only imagine how bad it was for Penny who was literally breathing him in.

"Now, what are we going to do with a pretty little thing like you?"

His words punched me in the gut. I'd seen the way he acted around Jessica, but she was older. She looked more like a woman. Penny was just a girl. A kid—like me. It wasn't right for him to be talking to her in that slimy tone of his and leering at her.

"There's a toilet in our room that needs cleaning up real nice." Marie laughed. The sound was like nails grating on a blackboard. It went right through me causing my hairs to bristle.

Derek didn't reply. He just stood there staring at Penny, beads of sweat forming on his almost bald head while his chest moved up and down from his short breaths.

"Well, don't just stand there, girl. Get in the bathroom and make a start."

Marie's orders seemed to snap Derek out of his fixation, and he muttered something under his breath before leaving the room. Marie followed him but not before reminding Penny that she was to clean the whole bathroom, bowl and all.

"That was the most disgusting thing I've ever done in my life. They're both pigs."

After Penny had cleaned the Freeman's bathroom while

the rest of us ate dinner and made the most of our free time in the den, I'd slipped her a note as we passed in the hallway asking if she wanted to sneak out. I instructed her to meet me at our usual spot half an hour after lights out.

"Jessica had to do it once. She puked."

Penny pushed up to her elbows and craned her neck around to look at me. "Really? She never told me that."

I shrugged. "Is it something you'd want everyone to know? She was grounded for two weeks after that."

"I hate them."

We all did, but only a few of us were brave enough to say it out loud. Jessica, Penny, and me. The others agreed but never said the words. Bennett wasn't afraid to say it, even to their faces. He'd told them as much the day he left. It was awesome; the look on Derek and Marie's face as Bennett walked out of their house and down the path flipping them the bird and shouting 'so long, fuckers' at the top of his lungs. I got caught laughing behind their backs. They grounded me for a week and gave me extra chores.

But it was so worth it.

"So do I."

"Derek gives me the willies."

"The willies? It's two-thousand-and-four, Penny. No one says willies anymore."

She punched my arm playfully and replied through her laughter, "Okay, Blake, the word master, what *do* people say these days?"

I shifted up to my butt and gripped my ankles with my hands. "Creeps, heebie-jeebies, shivers. I don't know, but they don't say willies, that's for sure."

"Whatever, Weston. If I want to say willies, then I'll say

willies. Willies, willies, willies," Penny called out into the darkness, breaking into fits of laughter.

Before I knew it, I was laughing along with her. The events of earlier long forgotten. Once our laughter started to die down, Penny's face hardened. "I miss them."

"Your parents?"

Penny didn't talk about her parents much. I knew there had been some kind of accident that killed them, but that was all.

"Yeah. I miss them so damn much." Her voice cracked, and a tear slipped down her cheek. I reached out to brush it away, and Penny turned her cheek slightly to rest it in the palm of my hand. She smiled sadly. "How have you survived for so long?"

"What? In foster care?" I snatched my hand back, not feeling comfortable with the way touching her made me feel, and shrugged. "Just have, I guess. My first family wasn't so bad. They had a son my age, Daniel. He was cool. But then Maddie got pregnant again and they decided they couldn't look after a new baby and me, so I was moved."

"And what happened then?" Penny looked at me as if I held all the answers.

I picked up a blade of grass and twirled it in my fingers. "The second home wasn't as nice. The kids were mean, and no one wanted to get to know the new kid on the block. I grew up a lot."

I had to. I didn't say the words; I didn't want to scare Penny.

"I don't get it. Why do people foster if they don't like kids? It's obvious that Marie and Derek hate all of us."

"The money, I guess. People do strange things for a few

bucks."

Penny flopped back down on the grass and stared up at the stars. "Well, it sucks. This isn't how I imagined my life turning out."

I lay back next to her. "Tell me what you imagined."

"I wanted to travel. To see the Eiffel Tower in Paris and Big Ben in London. And I wanted to go to college to study to be a grade school teacher. At college, I'd meet a guy, someone sweet and really good looking. We would date all through junior and senior year and then get engaged. Move to the suburbs and live happily ever after..." Penny's voice trailed off, and I looked over to see if she was crying again, but she wasn't. She'd closed her eyes and slightly scrunched her face, but she seemed peaceful.

My fingers spread out almost grazing hers. Didn't she realize she could still do all of those things? Foster care wasn't the end; that was what Bennett always used to tell me.

"You can still do all of those things, Penny."

Her eyes fluttered open, and she turned her head to face me. "Everything changed when they died, Blake. Everything. I have no one. No family, no friends, I had to move to this hell. How am I supposed to do any of the things I wanted?"

"You fight." The words came out without even thinking.

"How? Tell me how?" Her glassy eyes pleaded with me.

"One day, we'll be free of this place. You have to hold onto that."

Penny was silent for a moment, but I could tell she was thinking about telling me something. It was the way her nose scrunched up.

"You can tell me, Penny. Whatever it is, I'll listen."

"Leah and Sophie cornered me again in free period."

"You promised to tell me if it happened again. What the hell, Penny?" I pushed up off the ground and rose to a standing position, anger pulsating through me.

Penny jumped to her feet and came to face me. "I know, I- I just didn't want to cause any trouble."

"I don't care about getting into trouble, you know that, but I do care about them talking shit to you."

Leah and Sophie were the high school's mean girls. They had singled Penny out the second she arrived. It only got worse when Penny had to start wearing the hand-me-downs of the older girls and the clothes from the Goodwill store Marie had us all wear because she'd grown out of her own clothes. Jessica had tried to get them to back off, but they disliked all of us Freeman home kids, so it didn't do much.

"Blake." Penny reached out and entwined her hand in mine forcing me to look at her. "I can handle a couple of mean girls. I've survived worse."

Without thinking, I tugged Penny to me and wrapped my arms around her. She buried her face in my chest, slipped her arms around my waist, and hugged me right back.

She was my best friend. I don't know why I ever doubted it. But as we stood there, in No Man's Land, holding on to one another, a thought crossed my mind.

What if she was more than just my best friend?

chapter nine

Everything was a mess.

My feelings were all over the place. I was confused and weary, but most of all, I was hurting.

Hurting over things that had happened years ago. Things that were out of my control.

Things that could have been so different.

After revealing the truth to me, Blake went on to explain that he'd lived with Uncle Anthony and his wife, Miranda, until the summer before he was nineteen, at which point he enrolled in Ohio State to study sociology. After leaving me, he had gotten into some trouble. Blake was angry. He lashed out at everyone and anyone he could, and his first summer at Camp Chance was supposed to be his way of giving back to the community. But it ended up being more than just a chance to right his wrongs. Blake fell in love with it and had been coming back year after year.

Ever since our talk two days ago, something had been bugging me, eating away at me like a slow spreading poison. Even though Blake had filled in some of the blanks, I just felt like he hadn't given me any details, not really, and there was still so much I didn't know about him. It was my constant reminder about how much time had passed between us. We weren't the same people anymore.

"Penny, it's time."

I pouted at Marissa. Saying goodbye to this group was going to be hard. I had developed a soft spot for many of these girls, especially Lucy, and even Erica, despite her ongoing resistance to the program—and me.

"Come on. The girls want to say goodbye."

I rose from the bed already choked with emotion. Goodbyes were something I avoided. Just another residual behavior from my past.

Outside, eight sullen faces greeted us. "This sucks." Lucy stepped forward. Her head hung low, and I heard the emotion in her voice. In an attempt to make her feel better, I ruffled her hair and bent down to her level. "You should be so proud of all you have achieved, Lucy. No one can take these two weeks away from you. They're stored in here." I tapped my head. "And here." I moved my hand to my chest right above where the heart was.

"Now, does everyone have everything?" Marissa cut the mood, and I glanced up at her hoping she would know how to make this easier.

Heads nodded, and we set off toward the parking lot.

The buses were already waiting and bodies filled the lot. Kids hugged their friends and exchanged contact details. It filled my heart with hope knowing that most of the kids passing through the program were leaving with a few more allies in their corner and a whole heap of memories no one could ever take from them.

"Okay, guys, five minutes to say your final goodbyes and then it's time." Marissa wrapped her arm around me, and I bristled.

I couldn't help it.

She knew I didn't feel comfortable when someone touched me, but she had been pushing my boundaries lately. Although she still hadn't come right out and asked why I opposed touch, it was as if she was trying to use shock therapy to cure me.

"Hmm, Penny, can I talk to you in, hmm, in private?" Erica stood awkwardly looking down at her feet.

I ducked out of Marissa's hold, instantly feeling myself relax. "Of course, you can."

Marissa gave us some space, and I motioned to the bench off to the side. Once seated, I turned to Erica and waited.

"I just wanted to say sorry for giving you a hard time. I know you've only been trying to help me, and I've been a total bitch, and now, it's time to go back, and I don't want to leave."

Erica's eyes filled with tears, and I swallowed hard. Anguish etched into her face. Inside of her. This was a teenage girl who was confused and scared and alone, and I related to that more than she would ever know.

Clearing my throat, I said, "It has been my pleasure getting to know you, Erica. You are smart and determined, even if it is determined to do the opposite of everyone else."

At that, Erica laughed.

"Living in foster care isn't easy. I know that better than anyone does, but it doesn't have to define you. Figure out what you want in life and go for it. Remember, a lifetime of possibilities."

Erica nodded, even managing a small smile. "Thank you." She rose from the bench. But before she walked away, she turned back and said, "My foster family… they're not bad people. They just don't get me. I just thought you should know that."

I swiped the tears from my eyes as I watched her leave. When I looked back over the sea of people, I found Blake watching me with sadness in his eyes.

It was as if he knew. Knew what had just passed between Erica and me.

Somehow, he always knew.

"Two down, three more to go. Good job, guys. Keep up the hard work. Enjoy your downtime." Troy applauded the circle and left us to go in search of Tina, who hadn't made it to the debrief this time.

I pulled my hoodie tighter around my body. Although the sun kept the days warm, evenings were starting to cool down already, and I noticed no one seemed as eager to skinny dip in the lake tonight.

"How are you feeling?" Marissa asked me as she edged closer to the fire to toast a marshmallow.

"Okay, I guess. I was sad to see them leave."

"Yeah, it doesn't get any easier. Some groups are harder to let go of, but tomorrow is a new day and a new set of teenage attitude."

Sheridan was sitting next to us, and she muttered

something that sounded a lot like an amen to that, but neither Marissa nor I asked her to repeat it.

"Okay, since Troy isn't here to kick us off with a song, I don't mind stepping in." Blake stood up, retrieved Troy's guitar, and slipped the strap over his neck. His fingers plucked at the strings a couple of times as if he was getting reacquainted with the feel of them, and then he sat back down on the overturned log.

Everyone watched him like it was a completely normal occurrence, even the new counselors. But to me, it was just another thing to add to the growing list of things I didn't know about Blake Weston.

"I wrote this song a while back."

Blake could play. His fingers worked the strings with ease, blending together to create a soft melody, but it wasn't his guitar skills that had me in awe. It was his voice. Deep and gravelly, his sound filled the space around us until I was lost in his words.

I've never been one to say how I feel
Talk comes cheap and I wanted it to be real
A touch of our hands as we lay under the sky
With you by my side I felt like I could fly

She's my lucky penny, my lucky penny
She's my lucky penny, my lucky penny
Lucky, lucky, lucky, my lucky penny

You walked into my life and turned things around
Showed me how it felt to be found
We had everything and nothing all at the same time

My best friend, my heart, my partner in crime

She's my lucky penny, my lucky penny
She's my lucky penny, my lucky penny
Lucky, lucky, lucky, my lucky penny

I didn't realize I was crying until Marissa pressed a tissue into the palm of my hand. I blinked down at the white paper and sniffled. To my relief, everyone was as entranced by Blake as I had been and no one except Marissa noticed my emotional state.

Excusing myself, I made my way back to our cabin, the ghosts of my past weighing heavy on my shoulders. I felt Blake's eyes follow me as I disappeared into the trees, but I didn't look back.

I couldn't.

Marissa didn't follow me. It was most likely she had pieced together our story after Blake's song. How could she not? It was as if he had weaved our entire relationship into his lyrics. I could feel his sixteen-year-old self singing every line to my sixteen-year-old self. Although, I was pretty certain the sixteen-year-old Blake I'd known then had no clue how to play the guitar.

After washing the tearstains from my face, I brushed my teeth. It was still early, but I couldn't face going back out there, so I changed into my shorts and tank top and climbed into bed. Sleep would be impossible, but at least here, I was safe.

Most people felt lonely in solitude, but I welcomed the silence. I embraced it even. Something about the quiet, the knowledge no one else was around, comforted me. I knew it made me different. I didn't need a shrink to tell me that, but it didn't change the fact that I found sanctuary in being alone.

I lay there not really allowing myself to think. Thinking was dangerous; it led to remembering, and my memories were stained with pain and hurt and the kinds of things that made most people's nightmares look like a walk in the park. Instead, I tracked the uneven cabin ceiling. My eyes followed the planes of the wood from one end to the other and back again until they grew heavy.

A knock on the door startled me sending my already restless heart into overdrive and I rubbed at my eyes.

"Hello?" I called out hoping to hear Marissa's voice, but I knew it wasn't her. She wouldn't have knocked; she would have barged right in and demanded answers.

"Penny, it's me."

I squeezed my eyes shut, but my mind betrayed me as an image of Blake's face filled my head.

Another knock.

"Penny."

Forcing myself to sit up, I swung my legs over the edge of the bed. He wasn't going away. Blake—our connection—was something I was going to have to deal with sooner or later, and from Blake's admissions over the last few days, it seemed that he was making the decision for me.

My legs were like lead as I walked to the door. It swung open and Blake stood there looking at me with such reverence in his eyes I almost crumpled. Maybe I did crumple because, before my head had time to process what was happening, I was in Blake's arms, and he was holding on to me like he needed me to breathe.

"I've missed you so much. I've tried to stay away, to give you space, but I can't. I can't spend another day feeling like you might slip through my fingers again."

One of Blake's hands buried itself in my hair and cradled my head holding me to him. My face pressed up against the collar of his hoodie, and I breathed him in. He smelled familiar, like damp grass and fresh air, of a time when things were less complicated, and my heart ached for us. At that moment, we weren't two strangers reunited by chance; we were sixteen-year-old Blake and Penny.

And we needed each other to survive.

chapter ten

I was twelve when I watched my parents die in the collision that should have killed me as well. With no family to take me in, the state had no choice but to put me in foster care. At the time, I was too numb to care. My world had been ripped apart, and if that wasn't enough, it chewed me up and spat me out. I wanted to die. Wished over and over that the accident had taken me as well. But instead, I ended up on the front porch of a run-down house in Lancaster, Ohio. 'The Freemans are good people,' my social worker had said to me on the car ride over. I didn't care if they were the fairy godmother and Santa Claus—no one would ever replace my parents.

Being all alone in the world is a scary place when you're a child. But I wasn't alone for long. Blake was the only other kid in the group home who tried to get to know me. The others were okay, except a mean girl called Amy, but they didn't want to be friends.

Blake was different.

He stuck up for me, made me laugh, and enjoyed my company. He wanted me around.

He was my best friend at a time in my life when I thought I'd never feel whole again, and in the end, Blake had done the impossible. He had started to piece together some of the brokenness in me. Although he could never replace my parents, he did make living each day a little bit less painful.

And then one day, he was gone—taking with him a part of me that had never been replaced.

The day I aged out of the Freeman group home, the social worker had asked me what the first thing I was going to do now that I was an adult. I looked at her, choking down the tears building behind my eyes, and said 'never look back.'

And that was exactly what I did.

I didn't dwell on what had happened to me at the hands of Derek and Marie. I didn't allow myself to cry any more sleepless nights over Blake. I lived each day as it came and learned how to navigate the world on my own.

I became a survivor.

Even if I wasn't really living and only existing, I didn't let myself get close to anyone or put my trust in others. I built walls around me so high that it was virtually impossible to climb over them, and when I did finally let someone in, my anxieties prevented me from taking the next step.

Or, at least, that was what I had thought until I saw him again. But now, as I sat across the room from Blake, I couldn't help but wonder if my attempts at relationships had all failed because he was the benchmark. Because the sixteen-year-old guy I had fallen in love with, who understood me like no other, still owned my heart.

"What are you thinking?" Blake broke the heavy silence between us.

After I let him into the cabin, I'd returned to the bed and he had taken the rickety chair in the corner of the room. We had been sitting like that for the last twenty minutes.

I pulled at the frayed hem of my shorts. "Nothing. Everything."

"Just like my song, huh?"

"Yeah, I guess. I didn't know you played the guitar?"

"I didn't. It's a recent thing. Troy is a great teacher. Listen, I'm sorry if the song was too much. I wrote that a long time ago when things were, well, when things were confusing. I didn't plan to sing it tonight, but I saw you and it just came out."

I dropped my eyes and took a deep breath. Blake seemed to have no problem talking about us, when all I wanted to do was talk about anything but us.

When I didn't look back up, Blake whispered, "I never forgot about you, Penny."

This was getting us nowhere. Being around Blake made me feel like I was drowning, and if I couldn't breathe, how was I supposed to articulate all of the feelings rushing through me?

"I'm not sure I'm ready to do this." I lifted my head slowly to meet his eyes and replied honestly.

"Do what? I'm not asking anything of you. I just can't keep pretending like it's nothing that we're both here."

What does that even mean? I wanted to yell at him, but my voice failed me. Instead, I said, "And I can't keep reliving the past. It was a long time ago. I've made my peace with what happened."

It was a lie. I hadn't made my peace; I just didn't want to keep dredging it back up. Blake's eyes narrowed, and I knew my words weren't convincing.

"I should have come back for you." He dragged a hand over his jaw as if the words were difficult to say. "I'm sorry."

I wrapped my arms around my waist and bowed my head again. Blake was making me anxious. Forcing me to acknowledge things I didn't want to.

"We have to stop going around in circles. What's done is done, and it's in the past. Nothing we say or do now can change that. We're not the same people we were back then. Look at you, you're a guitar playing, camp counselor with a sociology degree, and for all I know, you have a wife and two kids back in Columbus."

Blake laughed, but the strain in his voice did little to appease the nerves swimming in my stomach. When I met his eyes again, he smiled sadly and said, "And who are you, Penny Wilson?

"That's exactly what this summer is supposed to be about. Finding myself. Kind of sad, isn't it?"

"I don't think it's sad at all. Sometimes, we find ourselves in the strangest of places."

And just like that, the suffocating tension started to ebb away.

Blake and I spent the next hour talking about safe topics. Troy and Tina, his college days, my job at Vrai Beauté. I left out details of my less than homely living situation and Blake skirted over his relationship with Uncle Anthony and Aunt Miranda. I got the sense there was far more to that story than he was willing to share, which was okay. There were things I didn't want to reveal yet either.

The time passed and so did some of my earlier apprehensions. Talking to Blake was actually effortless, and we soon fell back into the ease of childhood conversation. We gossiped about our fellow counselors and shared stories about the funnier side of camp, like my near miss with the canoe last week.

It wasn't until Marissa arrived to inform us that everyone else had turned in for the night that the earlier tension creeped back in.

Blake stood and flashed me a smile. "Walk me out?"

I nodded, ignoring Marissa's questioning look and her gaze burning a hole in the side of my head.

The door clicked shut behind us, and I paused on the balcony, not wanting to drag out goodbye any longer than necessary. We would be seeing each other tomorrow.

"What, you're not going to escort me back to my cabin?" Blake said with a hint of amusement in his voice causing me to half smile.

"Go on, get out of here. I'll see you tomorrow."

"I can't leave without doing this." Blake retraced his steps back up to where I was standing.

My heart was pounding so hard in my chest I felt lightheaded. Surely, after everything, he wasn't going to try to kiss me?

Blake's hand brushed along my jaw into my hairline, and he leaned into me. I stood frozen unable to move. Was this really going to happen? More importantly, did I want it to?

His mouth inched closer and then swept across my

cheek pressing a kiss to my skin. The feel of his lips caused my stomach to pool with warmth, and I knew without a doubt that I was blushing from my neck up.

"Good night, Penny."

Good night, Blake, I mouthed, still rooted to the spot. I held my palm to my warm cheek and watched him make his way across the row of cabins and out of sight.

"Spill." Marissa pounced on me the second I entered the cabin.

"What?"

"Oh, come on, you can't pull that with me. I walked in on something earlier, and I want details. You've been holding out on me."

My mouth opened in an attempt to explain, but nothing came out. I paced the room a couple of times before inhaling a deep breath and climbing under the comforter.

"Blake was my everything."

"You don't say. Those lyrics, wow. He was talking about you, right? You're the penny in his song. His lucky penny?" Marissa sat cross-legged on her bed and rolled her neck.

"I'm lucky Penny."

"Wow. This is… holy shit balls. I knew there was history between the two of you, but I had no idea it was epic."

"Epic? Really, Marissa? What are we, twelve?"

"Oh, give this girl a break. I'm just excited. Camp Chance is reuniting first loves and creating second chances. One summer, a lifetime of possibilities." She mimicked the camp's slogan, and I flopped back onto the bed covering my eyes with my arm.

"Oh, no, you don't, Penny Wilson. I want deets. Liam is evading all my best moves, so I need to live vicariously through you."

I groaned into my forearm. Was she for real? She was making my life sound like something out of a romance novel, when it was anything but.

"If you want a fairy tale, then you're talking to the wrong girl," I said quietly, half hoping she wouldn't hear me and would let it go for the night.

"Come on, it can't be that bad." I felt movement at my side and peeked out from under my arm. Marissa had edged toward the side of my bed and was looking down at me with a pouty face.

"You can talk to me. I promise I'm a good listener. I know you have secrets, but sometimes, it helps to share."

Reluctantly, I shifted up on my butt and pressed back against the wall to give Marissa room to sit down on the edge of the bed.

"I was put into foster care when I was twelve…" A wave of sadness crashed over me sucking the air from my lungs. Marissa's eyes widened, and I saw the concern there. But she had asked, and I wanted to trust her with this. To trust someone for once in my life. Someone other than Blake, or one of the numerous therapists I'd visited over the years.

"My parents died in an accident. I walked away with barely a scratch, but there was no one to care for me. No family, no friends, no one. I was placed in a group home. Can you imagine what that's like?" I stared at the door looking right past Marissa, unable to meet her eyes.

"The Freemans were mean. The worst. To this day, I

still wonder how they ended up with a foster license because it was pretty obvious from the second I stepped into their house that they hated kids. Especially broken kids like me."

"Wha-what happened?"

My eyes fluttered shut, and I whispered, "Blake happened..."

For the next twenty minutes, I unraveled our story to Marissa. Stolen moments out in No Man's Land, the way he stood up for me at school and in the group home. How he tried to make my crappy life seem that little bit better. And then, I told Marissa how the messy boy with the goofy smile had given me hope in bleak despair. How he became my everything.

When I finished, Marissa looked on the verge of tears, and the only word to leave her mouth was 'epic.'

"Really, Marissa? I think tragic is more fitting."

"You would say that because you lived it, but from someone looking in, it's the real deal. I can't imagine how it must have felt to see him again, after everything."

I mashed my lips together, swallowing down the lump in my throat, and shrugged.

"Don't do that. Don't play this down. Your bond exceeded first love, Penny. From what you've told me, you guys saved each other in that sorry excuse for a foster home."

"He left me, Marissa. Every time I see him, that's the first thing I remember. Getting home that day to find him gone. He was my world, and he just left."

Marissa shuffled forward until she was right in front of me. Instinctively, I pressed further back into the wall, but she reached out and caught my hand in hers.

"Don't you think that you both being here, at this moment in time, could be a sign? A do-over?"

Of course, I'd considered it. I'd done nothing but consider it for the last four weeks, but I knew better than to believe in second chances. Life was hard and cruel and full of disappointment, and opening myself up to the possibility of second chances was too risky. My head wholly agreed with that. It knew the rational thing to do was to see the summer out and then go back to reality. My reality. The one where I worked a minimum wage job and lived in an apartment hardly fit for an animal.

But my heart wanted to believe there was a reason for this. A purpose behind fate's decision to cross our paths at this precise moment in time.

"Everyone deserves a second chance, Penny."

chapter eleven

The weeks passed in a blur of sticky summer days filled with laughter, tears, and teenage tantrums. I tried hard to heed Marissa's words of advice and give Blake what he wanted—a chance to get to know me again. We spent what little downtime we had talking and discovering the people we had become in our years apart, but both of us were still holding back. I knew Blake felt it as much as I did, but all I had asked of him was to take things slow, and he kept true to his word.

It was already the end of the eighth week, and Blake and I were at our usual spot by the lake. The sun beat down on us, but the breeze balanced its afternoon heat, and I lifted my face to enjoy the cool rush of air over my damp skin.

"You're a natural with the girls now."

I glanced over at Blake and smiled, pride swelling deep in my chest. "I feel more confident. I'll be sad when it comes to an end."

Something flashed in his blue eyes, but I didn't push

him. Neither of us looked ahead to the end of the summer. We had only just found one another again and the thought of saying goodbye made my stomach drop. It was still hard to believe we had lived in the same city for the last four years and had never crossed paths before this summer. But Blake's regular job as a legal investigator with his uncle's law firm required him to travel a lot, so I knew I probably wouldn't see him all that often if at all.

There was every chance we would leave camp and become a distant memory to one other, and my summer spent at Camp Chance would just be another place I turned to when things in my life became too much to bear. A place to escape to, a sanctuary… a dream.

Comfortable silence lingered in the space between us until Blake shuffled next to me. "So I know I promised to take things slow, but it's killing me not to know." He sat upright and twisted around to face me, his eyes glistening in the sunlight. "Is there someone waiting for you back home?"

Blake's question caught me off guard. We hadn't talked about our personal lives much, but I was more hung up on his reference to home.

Home died the day my parents left me alone on this earth. Nowhere would ever be home again. We had talked about it enough when we were younger, and I always thought Blake understood that, but I guess it was just another thing separating us. He had moved on, and I hadn't.

I couldn't.

"No." My fingers plucked a daisy from the grass and swirled it around. "There's no one."

"Oh."

I couldn't place the emotion in Blake's reply. I wanted to believe it was relief, but it could have been disappointment.

"Is there someone waiting for you?" I asked deflecting the limelight from me to him.

Blake swept a hand through his hair. It had grown after a summer without luxuries, but it looked good on him along with his scruff. "It's complicated."

"Oh." My stomach dropped the way I imagined it felt when you rode the roller coasters at Cedar Point. Of course, there was someone. Blake was everything a girl could want in a guy—funny and easygoing with his just-walked-out-of-*GQ* magazine look. It didn't come as a surprise, but my response did. My head immediately went to a time when Blake had been mine. A time when I couldn't imagine living without him.

My heart echoed the words. *Mine.*

"Don't you want to know more?"

Staring at the daisy, I shrugged and refused to make eye contact with him. "It's none of my business."

"Things are fucked up," he said ignoring me. "I'm supposed to be here working things out."

"And how's that going?" I lifted my head slowly to meet his intense gaze.

Blake's lips drew into a thin line, and he released a slow breath. "It's complicated."

Exhausted by his cryptic responses—and unsure if I was ready to hear the truth—I changed the subject. "Do you speak to anyone else from back then?"

"I found Bennett after I left. Well, more like he found me. We still keep in touch."

I nodded. If I had bet on one relationship withstanding

the test of time, it would have been theirs. Blake looked up to him like a brother, and Bennett always held a soft spot for his younger foster sibling.

"How is he?"

"Good. Life turned out real good for him. He won't believe this when I tell him."

Ignoring another cryptic statement, I simply replied, "That's good."

We sat enjoying the peace of our surrounds. The water lapped at the shore at one end of the lake, and the trees surrounding the area swayed gently in the breeze. The sound soothed me. Everything about this place was healing, and I could see why Troy and Tina picked it to do the work they did.

After a few minutes, Blake shifted again. "Penny, what happened after I left?"

I let out a small groan. "Geez, Blake. Talk about turning all serious on me." I tried to follow with a smile, but I was too tense. I knew if I looked in the mirror, I'd be grimacing.

Frustrated with myself… Blake… our whole predicament, I glanced back at the fire needing a few seconds to center myself. The others were goofing around, making the most of our downtime before the last group arrived tomorrow. Marissa cozied up in front of the fire next to Liam who, despite her best efforts, still looked more interested in the fire than in her. She sat so her body angled toward us, making me smile. Marissa had become a really good friend. I was going to miss her.

"I'm sorry." Blake sighed. "I just feel like we're losing time, and there's still so much I want to know. There's not enough time."

You don't want to know, I whispered silently to myself.

"I don't want to walk away from here in two weeks and regret things. *More* things."

He was making up lost time or, at least, trying to. I got that. I did. But opening up didn't come easy for me. I was used to bottling things up until I was like a pop bottle ready to explode, and even then, I could only give so much. Only things that felt safe to reveal.

"After you left, things were okay for a while. Derek and Marie even managed to be nice to us occasionally. I hate to say it, Blake, but it was almost like they were glad to see you go."

Blake tried to look offended but ending up laughing. "Doesn't surprise me. Derek hated me."

Those three words changed the energy around us. The silence no longer felt comfortable but strained.

It was like no matter what we talked about, however hard we tried to avoid it, everything always led back to the one thing too painful to talk about.

This was our legacy.

"Not as much as he hated Chris. Those two really went at it."

"Someone finally stood up to him?" Blake sounded surprised, but I also heard a tinge of regret in his voice.

My eyes dropped from his face and swept down his frame. Blake had clenched his fists at his sides, and his whole body had tensed. He played a good game of seeming as if he was in control, but I saw the truth. Blake was standing on the precipice about to fall over at any second.

Some things never change.

"You could say that." Wanting to bring Blake back to

me, I added, "Remember when Bennett aged out? I'll never forget the look on Marie's face as he strolled up the path yelling at the top of his lungs 'so long, fuckers.'"

Blake's jaw relaxed a little, and he tilted his head at me. "Yeah, I remember. It wasn't all bad in there. I earned your first kiss, if I remember correctly?"

The playfulness I had become accustomed to watching whenever Blake interacted with the boys and other counselors was back, and just like that, some of the tension evaporated. And made my cheeks flush. I didn't doubt it would return. It was always with us—just under the surface.

But for now, we could bury our heads until the next time.

I helped Marissa drag the last of the canoes up the embankment to the storage shed. The girls had gone on ahead to clean up.

"Did you know Blake has someone back in Columbus?" The words almost lodged in my throat, but since our conversation two days ago, it was all I'd thought about. Who was she? What did she look like? Did he love her?

Marissa's smile faltered as she said, "He does? Is it serious?"

"I don't know. He said it's complicated."

We hoisted the last canoe onto its hanger. Marissa dusted herself off and turned to me. "I bet. The love of his life turned up."

"Marissa, can you be serious for once, please?"

She held her hands up laughing. "Sorry. I just can't

resist." We started the short walk to the shower block, the girl's laughter traveling in the air. "Besides, it true."

"It sounded serious," I said quietly.

"No way. I've seen the way he looks at you, the way he watches you across the fire. He never takes his eyes off you. Besides, as far as I'm aware, he hasn't mentioned a girlfriend to anyone here. It's probably just a clingy hook-up who needs a reality check."

It hadn't sounded that way, and the fact Blake didn't give me any details suggested there was more to it. But you didn't willingly argue with Marissa.

As if she could hear my thoughts, Marissa halted and turned to me. "Anyway, would it matter if there was? It's not like you've been jumping for joy at being reunited with him."

"Marissa!"

"Oh, come on, Penny. I know you two have a rough history, but it's just that, history. In the past. You can't let your past dictate your future. Mold you, sure, but define you? Nuh-uh! The Penny I've watched grow over the last couple of months is stronger than that."

Was I?

Most days, I didn't feel it.

I'd made progress, sure, but the truth was that I was still tethered to the ghosts of my past in ways I hadn't even realized until I saw Blake again.

So much pain tainted our story, I didn't know if we could rewrite ourselves a new ending… or beginning.

"You're overthinking this." Marissa took my hand in hers. "I've watched the two of you together. Everything you felt for Blake all of those years ago is still there. It's written all over your face every time you look at him. And I don't doubt for a second that it's the same for him."

Warmth spread into my cheeks, and I dropped my eyes. Why couldn't I just be normal instead of damaged and confused and terrified to step out of the shadows?

Why couldn't I let myself live in the moment for once.

"I know you're scared," Marissa went on. "And that's okay. But tell me one thing, Penny. Can you live with yourself if you leave here without giving him a chance? A real chance?"

I looked over at the lake where Blake's group was attempting to cross the water on homemade rafts. His polo shirt clung to his chest as he helped a boy onto the floatation device.

"Well, can you?"

Could I?

Blake had healed me once, and then he had broken me in a way from which I never truly recovered. But somewhere over the last two months, he had started to put me back together. Piece by piece. My head had warned me, tried to keep me away, but my heart recognized him. They called to each other, sought each other out.

Blake already owned my heart.

He always had.

But could I give him my damaged soul as well?

chapter twelve

Blake

Age 14

"What in the hell have you done to your hair?" Amy scowled at me as she entered the den and snickered into her hand.

Bitch.

I ran a careful hand over my head and shrugged. "Nothing."

"Oh, you soooo have, you styled it. Is it for your girlfriend?" Her voice grated on me like nails on a blackboard, and when Amy folded her pudgy arms over her chest and huffed looking far too pleased with herself, I wished for a moment I was Bennett. He always knew exactly the right thing to say in these situations. But I was never going to be as cool as Bennett was. Instead, I said the next best thing,

"Piss off, Amy."

"Blake and Penny sitting in the tree. K-I-S-S-I-N-G. First comes love, then comes-"

"Cut it out, Amy. Go bother someone who cares." Mason swatted at her, and she shrieked, spinning on her heels and storming out of the room.

"So what is up with your hair, dude?"

"Nothing." I ducked my head.

Did it really look that stupid? All I'd done was sneak a little bit of product from Peter's secret stash underneath his bed. I just wanted to make tonight special.

"She'll notice," my foster brother said with a grin.

"Who'll notice?"

He helped himself to a handful of my chips and slouched down next to me. "Penny, dickwad. Who else?"

"I don't know what you're talking about, Mase."

His eyes sparkled with amusement. "Sure, you don't. Just be careful. If Derek and Marie catch on to the two of you always sneaking out, the shit will hit the fan. For all of us."

I mumbled something under my breath trying my hardest to act cool. He was right though, I knew that. But I didn't care. Not today.

Penny was my best friend, and she deserved a birthday to remember.

Dinner was the longest thirty minutes of my life. One thing Derek and Marie insisted on was that we all ate together. Every evening, we had to sit around and pretend to play happy foster family. Except tonight, Penny's seat was empty. She had joined the debate team at school and they had an away meet. Although I was pleased for Penny since it was the first thing she had showed interest in since arriving here, I now officially hated Tuesdays.

"What time is Penny due back, Marie?" Amy said in her sickly sweet voice, the one she saved just for the foster momster, as Ben, the new kid, called her.

I shot Amy a warning glare and laughed into my glass when she yelped. Mason winked at me, and I knew he had probably stomped on her foot under the table.

"She'll be back before lights out. Now, eat your vegetables."

Since Bennett aged out, I had moved into his seat at the table, which meant I sat farthest away from Derek and Marie. Looking at them across the table was gross enough without sitting within spraying distance like poor Ben. He looked ready to puke as Derek sprayed another mouthful of Marie's disgusting pot roast at him.

"Blake, is your homework all done?"

"Yes, sir," I said biting down on my tongue. He wasn't asking because he was interested, so I braced myself for his next words.

"Good. You're on cleanup duties."

"What? It's not my night. It's Amy's."

"Amy helped me with something earlier. Don't argue with me, boy, or you'll be washing pots all week."

Mason caught my eye and shook his head discreetly. *It's not worth it.* I understood his silent message, but I didn't want to hear it. Not tonight of all nights.

"Fine, but the new kid helps."

Ben's eyes widened and he opened his mouth to protest, but quickly closed it when I shot him a look.

"I'll help."

"Fine. Just get it done and take out the trash while you're at it."

"Is it always like this?"

Ben handed me the last of the pots, and I dipped it into the water and rinsed off the suds.

"We get Sundays off."

Actually, Derek and Marie left us to fend for ourselves while they gorged themselves at the Golden Corral, but he didn't need to know that yet. Besides, it was the one day of the week we could be kids.

"My last placement was this real nice family. They took me to ballgames on the weekend. I liked them. I don't like Marie. She smells. They both do, but it's her eyes. They scare me."

"They're just skin and bone, kid. Keep your head down and stay out of trouble. Who knows, maybe you'll be out of here quicker than you think."

Ben was a sweet kid. Only eleven with a face full of freckles and blond curly hair. He looked like the type of kid a family might want, and although adoption was rare for kids our age, it could happen.

For kids like Ben, not for me.

I'd given up on that dream a long time ago.

Just as we cleaned away the last of the cutlery, the front door opened and footsteps sounded in the hallway.

"That you, Penny?" Derek's gruff voice called out from the living room.

"Yes, sir."

Just hearing her voice improved my mood, and I hurried to wipe the counters.

"Straight upstairs, young lady. It's almost time for lights out."

I hovered near the door. Penny would have to walk right past us. I had my hand buried deep in the pocket of my jeans gripping the folded paper. Her footsteps grew louder, and I turned to Ben and said, "Go take out the trash. I'll wait here."

I felt bad for getting rid of him, but I wanted to see Penny alone. The kitchen door clicked shut behind Ben just as Penny reached me.

Hi, she mouthed, her lips hooked up in a smile.

Hi. Happy birthday, I mouthed back, sliding out the handmade card and handing it to her.

My heart pounded so hard against my ribcage I thought I might pass out. I knew most girls would think a scrappy hand decorated card was lame, but I hoped Penny would like it. Derek and the foster momster hadn't even bothered to buy her a card.

Her eyes ran over my handiwork, but her face gave nothing away.

Later? Usual place? I looked down sheepishly, but she nudged me refusing to let me look away. I nodded as if there was anywhere else I'd rather be. As she walked off, her hand brushed mine leaving a million jolts of electricity buzzing through me.

“I thought you weren’t going to make it.” I stood up brushing off my jeans as Penny appeared in the clearing.

Our place.

She rushed over to me and launched herself into my arms. I caught her midair, and she pressed her lips firmly to mine.

Penny was kissing me.

Me.

It wasn’t my first kiss; I’d fooled around with girls at school before behind the bleachers playing dares, but this was different. My hands held her close not wanting to let her go.

Ever.

But as quickly as her lips connected with mine, she was pulling away leaving a hollow pit in my stomach.

“Sorry,” she said breathlessly, dropping her eyes away from me.

I brought a hand from behind her back and tipped her chin up forcing her to look at me. “Never be sorry. Happy birthday, my lucky Penny.” I leaned in to kiss her again.

It was just a quick peck, but it was everything.

Before things got awkward, I grabbed Penny’s hand and yanked her over to the blanket I’d laid out. For the last couple of weeks, I had been stealing everything I needed to make tonight perfect. A blanket from a box in Derek’s garage and cartons of juice and cookies from the cafeteria at school. I’d even managed to swipe a candle and a lighter from one of Marie’s drawers. She must have confiscated it from them one of the other kids because birthdays didn't happen in the Freeman house. It wasn't much, but Penny's wide grin told me it was more than enough.

"I can't believe you did all of this."

"You're only fourteen once." I offered her a choice of juice. "Birthday girl chooses."

We sat like that, in No Man's Land in the middle of the night, until there was nothing left but wrappers and empty cartons.

Over the last year, our adventures had gotten later and later. With no Bennett to cover for us, it was too risky that someone would see us sneaking out, so we had started waiting for everyone to fall to sleep.

"I feel sick," Penny groaned causing me to snicker.

"You shouldn't have eaten that last cookie." We were lying back on the blanket holding hands looking up at the stars. "I'm sorry I couldn't afford a proper gift."

Penny gasped and rolled onto her side, pushing up on her elbow. "Blake, don't even… this, the card, tonight, it's more than I ever dreamed of. Thank you for making this the best birthday ever."

It was after two when we started to make our way back to the house. Darkness cloaked our two-story prison, and my eyes strained hard to make out the small bathroom window on the ground floor. My senses immediately went on high alert—something wasn't right. I always made sure to leave the light on to guide our way back.

"Shit," I grumbled to myself squeezing Penny's hand.

"What's wrong?"

"The light's out. Either it blew or someone switched it off."

"Crap, what should we do?"

"There's a chance whoever it was has gone back to bed." I pulled Penny close and whispered into her hair. "Come on, as quietly as you can."

I felt her smile against my neck. Stealth wasn't her strong point, and although she could jimmy open the window with ease and climb out the gap undetected, she'd had more than a couple of close calls over the last year.

As we crept closer to the house, my gut was yelling something wasn't right. I'd come to trust my instincts since living in foster care. Forced into this life from a young age, all I had was myself to rely on. I had to grow up and get wise, and right now, the adrenaline pumping through my veins was telling me something was very wrong. But we had no choice but to go back inside. If we stayed out all night, someone would discover us gone anyway.

We ducked out of the cover of the tree line and crossed the yard to the side of the house. The window was on this wall somewhere, and I was pretty certain I could retrace our escape route in the black hole surrounding us. My clammy hand traced the wall looking for the frame. Just as my fingers hooked onto the sill, the kitchen light came on and the door creaked open. I froze, my heart in my mouth.

"So it is true?" a faceless voice said gruffly. "You two have been sneaking out right under our noses. Tut tut, you should know better. Especially you, boy." Derek's voice was eerily calm causing shivers to jolt up my spine.

Penny gasped and pressed herself into my side letting

go of my hand. I wanted to reach back and take her hand in mine—it belonged there, but I knew it would only make our situation worse. So I squared my shoulders and took a step toward the half open door. Derek sneered at me. He looked like he'd just won the lotto, an evil smirk on his scruffy half-awake face.

"Inside." He stepped back to let us past.

Penny moved with me, still pressed into my back as we entered the kitchen.

"Go to your rooms. We'll talk about this tomorrow."

We didn't argue.

We didn't say anything.

We walked the short distance upstairs to our rooms in silence. Derek didn't follow, but I couldn't shake the feeling something was still off.

Penny's room was the second door along the hallway. I stopped and turned to her. "Barricade yourself in. Find something, anything to wedge the door shut, okay?"

I don't know why I said the words, but I couldn't shake Derek's reaction to discovering us returning from No Man's Land. Together. There had been something in his voice. He didn't sound so much angry as he did pleased to have found us sneaking back in.

Penny opened her mouth to argue. I could tell by the way her nose scrunched up that she wanted to tell me I was being stupid, but something changed her mind because she nodded and went inside. When her door closed in my face, I went to my room, the last room on the right. I shared with Mason. Jessica, Amy, and Mia shared, and Peter shared with the new kid. Penny had the smallest room. It was more like a closet, only just big enough for a single cot and dresser.

Mase was snoring like usual. Once he was asleep, nothing could wake him. He slept through storms, breakfast, and he even slept through the one time Derek caught Bennett sneaking out. I tiptoed around his bed to my own and stripped down to my boxer shorts. Once in bed, I pulled up the comforter and stared at the ceiling thinking of Penny.

I woke startled. A layer of sweat coated my whole body like I had a fever, but I felt fine. I must have been dreaming. But then I heard it. Muffled voices. A whimper.

Throwing back the comforter, I swung my legs over the edge of the bed and sat as still as possible to listen for any sounds. Mason was asleep on his back, mouth hanging open, and his chest rising and falling with each throaty breath. Trying to hear anything over his snoring and my pounding heart was almost impossible, so I crept to the door and pressed one ear against the wood.

I heard it again.

Before I knew what I was doing, my hand was wrapped around the door handle and I'd yanked it open. Rushing into the hallway, the cool air hit me slowing me down for a second. What in the hell was I doing? All I knew was that something felt very wrong. The muffled noise was coming from the end of the hallway. It was hard to make out any clear voices or even tell if it was human; it could have quite easily been an injured animal, but my gut knew.

I knew.

Back pressed flat against the wall, I inched my way down the hallway closer to Penny's door. There was a sliver of moonlight coming in through the window at the opposite end of the hallway. My heart beat frantically in my chest while I tried to come up with some kind of plan.

But it was too late.

Penny's door opened slowly, and Derek stepped out in the hallway, one hand adjusting his zipper. I almost stopped breathing trying to make myself invisible. Puke rose up in my throat as I watched Derek smooth down his pants, and I had to clamp my mouth shut.

What was I witnessing?

There was a gentle murmuring sound coming from inside Penny's room. Derek glanced back, pulled the door shut, and headed back downstairs to where his and Marie's room was situated. Everything closed in around me until it felt like all the air had been sucked out of the hallway.

Penny.

I sprang into action moving as fast as I could without making a sound. I didn't risk knocking and slipped silently into Penny's dark room. A figure was curled up on the cot sobbing quietly. The kind of sobs that tell you how much a person is hurting. Dirty, messy, ugly cries. And yet, somehow, my brave, strong friend was managing to contain them.

Penny must have sensed me because she rolled over slightly and looked right at me.

"B- Bl- Blake?" she sniffled, and my chest cracked.

My whole world was crumbling around me, but I managed to ground out, "What the fuck has he done to you?"

chapter thirteen

"What do you think they're doing in there?" Blake leaped up on the wooden railing surrounding the cabin's balcony and smiled down at me.

"Preening themselves, I guess. It's hard work being a thirteen-year-old girl these days." I looked back at the cabin from my position on the top step. The girls had been getting ready for almost an hour.

"I can't ever remember you taking that long to get ready."

I turned back to Blake and met his eyes with a playful smirk. "That's because I never had anyone to impress."

He arched his eyebrow, and a smirk of his own broke over his face causing my stomach to flip. "Oh, is that so? No one to impress, huh?"

Blake held my gaze, and I knew we were lost in our memories. A time when I'd traded my usual jeans and hand-me-down chucks for a summer dress Jessica let me borrow. I'd even curled my hair and swept it to one side with a piece of ribbon I stole from Mrs. Ryson, the home economics teacher at school. Blake had almost tripped over his own feet when he saw me. It was one of the first times I realized he was more to me than just my best friend.

"Oh, hey, girls." Blake shook his head as if he was shaking out the memories. "All set for the campfire? The boys are itching to see you."

I swatted my hand through the railing. It collided with Blake's firm stomach and heat spread through me. Blake must have felt it too because his already taut muscles tensed under my touch.

Breaking our connection, I said, "Don't tease them. Ignore him, girls." I rose from my makeshift seat and turned to the girls gathered in the doorway; their eyes firmly set on the exchange between the two of us.

"Right, I guess that's my cue to go gather my horde. See you soon." Blake flashed us a grin before hopping off the balcony. We watched him jog back in the direction of his cabin. When he disappeared, Shauna and Mindy, two of the older girls, bustled past me rolling their eyes, making their way down the step.

"He's so fine," a voice said from the huddle to my side, and I turned to find Audrina with a doe-eyed dreamy look on her face. "Don't you think, Penny?" she added earning snickers from the rest of the girls.

"Let's go," I said a little too hastily, ducking my head to avoid them seeing my flushed cheeks. "We don't want to be late." I ushered them down the steps and did a quick head count before we set off in the direction of the campfire.

I was going to kill Marissa.

When we had arrived at the fire, we somehow ended up seated next to Blake and his boys instead of our usual spot next to Sheridan's group. My safety blanket had been ripped away from me, and I knew Marissa was somehow responsible. Although, from the smug look on Blake's face, I didn't doubt he was also involved.

"Fancy seeing you here," he whispered. His breath brushed my ear, and my whole body shuddered. I blamed the chill in the air.

"Blake," I warned, trying to nudge him back into his own space. He was being inappropriate. Not that anyone was interested in what we were doing in the outer row of the circle when Troy commanded everyone's attention with his over enthusiastic campfire songs.

"Okay, let's do a round of *The More We Get Together*. Everyone remember this from the first night?" Troy asked the circle, and everyone nodded. "Well, this time I'm going to add some extra verses. Got it?"

We nodded again. Being my fifth group, I knew the routine by now.

"The more we get together…" Troy started us off, and we all joined in.

Together, together.
The more we get together, the happier we'll be.

'Cause your friends are my friends and my friends are

your friends.

The more we get together, the happier we'll be.

"Great, now it's Marissa's in her canoe… and go."

I sang along with each verse. Troy always picked on two or three counselors to get a reaction from the kids. Unfortunately for me, my verse didn't highlight my strength. After a run-in with a huge spider during the first week, I got lumbered with 'Penny's afraid of spiders.' The kids loved it—me, not so much.

"Okay, last one," Troy bellowed his hands making easy work of the acoustic guitar. "Liam's eating all the s'mores."

Troy strummed his guitar, and I inhaled, ready to sing. Liam's name was on the tip of my tongue, but Blake leaned in close to me again and started singing. It was almost a hum, so quiet and low I had to strain to hear him over the noise.

Blake's not ready to say goodbye, say goodbye, say goodbye.

Blake's not ready to say goodbye, unhappy he'll be.

'Cause you're still his lucky Penny, do you know that, do you know that

Blake's not ready to say goodbye, unhappy he'll be.

I didn't dare look at him. I wanted to cry, to let the tears building behind my eyes fall. I wanted to smile at him, to share this moment with him. But most of all, I wanted to lean into him and show him that I felt the same. That after all this time, my heart still remembered him.

It never forgot.

Very slowly, I inched my head around. Blake was leaning into me enough that our mouths were close. Close enough I could feel his breath on my face. He pulled away slightly giving me his eyes—eyes that held so many memories—and then they dropped to my mouth.

I swallowed hard.

"Good job, everyone." Troy's voice was a like a bucket of cold water, and I used the harsh awakening to shuffle as far away from Blake as possible. It wasn't far enough; given we were packed like sardines on the benches. I was aware of everything. Of his hand gripping the edge of the bench, his fingers grazing mine. The gentle rise and fall of his chest. The way he kept glancing at me and then looking away if I turned my head in his direction.

It was a game of cat and mouse, and I was most definitely the mouse. Only, I wasn't sure what would happen when he eventually caught me in his trap.

"Night, guys. Get some rest because you all have a busy day tomorrow. Remember—one summer, a lifetime of possibilities." Troy and Tina waved us off as we set off back to our cabins.

I was relieved to leave the campfire. The last hour had been excruciating, and although Blake didn't say another word to me, something was building between us. The pull between us was just too strong, and for as much as I had tried to deny it, I couldn't any longer.

Marissa had been right all along.

"Come on, girls. We have an early start." I herded the girls toward the path back to the cabins. "We'll get our wash bags then go brush our teeth and hit the sack for the night, okay?"

A couple of the girls groaned, but it was only the fourth day, and most of them were still finding their feet. Once they felt a little more at home, I had no doubt I would be dealing with more attitude than a few groans.

"Finn makes me brush my teeth twice before bed. Once for the clean and once for good measure," a small dark-haired girl called Phoebe said.

"Twice? That's stupid," one of the older girls replied. "You should tell him he's an idiot."

"Audrina," I said sternly.

"What? It's the truth. No one brushes their teeth twice. Isn't it bad for them or something? Finn sounds like a dick."

So much for finding their feet. I spun around and stopped, effectively blocking Audrina's passage. "Audrina, we don't talk like that here. There are rules."

She studied me for a second and then narrowed her eyes to almost a scowl. "I thought Camp Chance was supposed to be fun."

"It is fun, a lot of fun, if you stick to the rules. No cursing and no making anyone feel bad."

"I wasn't making her feel bad. I was just saying Finn sounds like a di- I mean, a douche."

"He's not," Phoebe stated confidently. "He's nice actually. He helps me with my homework and takes me to the library on Saturdays."

Audrina redirected her attention from me to Phoebe. "The library?" she hissed. "He sounds like a boring douche."

"Audrina, enough!"

I didn't raise my voice a lot. In fact, in eight weeks, I could count on one hand how many times I lost my patience, but occasionally, something touched a nerve, and it was almost impossible to ignore. Right now, I didn't like that Audrina was trying to tarnish Phoebe's relationship with Finn. One thing these girls didn't need was someone tearing down the positive relationships they had with their foster parents.

Silenced, Audrina folded her arms over her chest and walked ahead in a huff. I lingered in the back with Phoebe wanting to check that she was okay, but she beat me to it.

"I don't care what she says. Finn is the greatest. One day, I hope he and Maggie adopt me, and I can live with them forever," she said her voice filled with hope.

My heart swelled and then slowly withered. I had never had the luxury of hope when I'd entered foster care. I'd lost everything. Had nothing else left to lose. But maybe that was the better place to be. Phoebe still had hope. She could still experience so much pain and hurt all because of her young naïve hope. Part of me still envied her. Envied that blissful state of unaware. Envied how fond she sounded of her foster family.

I didn't have the heart to be the voice of reason—to tell her not to get her hopes up. Instead, I simply smiled and nodded my head. Enough disappointment and upset filled the lives of so many of these kids. I couldn't face being just another person to add to that. My response seemed to appease Phoebe, and she skipped back to her friend.

Almost forty minutes later, after being persuaded into cocoa and scary stories, it was time for lights out. I arrived at camp thinking it would be strange to share a room with eight hormonal teenage girls, but I'd soon gotten used to the bedtime gossip and chatter. Hot days spent active around Camp Chance meant that most of the campers were ready to sleep when lights out rolled around.

"Night guys," I called into the darkness, only a sliver of moonlight reflecting through the glass window at the front of the cabin.

A chorus of good nights echoed off the wooden beams, and I stared at the bunk above me. It was empty. Counselors took the fifth set of bunk beds, positioned slightly away from the rest of the bunk beds next to the front window, giving both our campers and ourselves a little more space. It also meant counselors slept closest to the door to catch any late-night escapees. The first time I caught two girls trying to sneak out, I'd smiled to myself. That was me, ten years ago, sneaking out to meet Blake. Of course, they had been trying to meet up with some boys from one of the other cabins. I'd had to reprimand them, but I'd done it with half a smile. I could relate. More than they knew.

Within minutes, silence descended over the cabin. Nothing but the sound of heavy breathing and the occasional shuffle of sleeping bags. Sleep didn't come easily to me. It never did. Not here, and not back in my apartment above The Oriental Garden. Sleep brought darkness, and the darkness brought nightmares. Although since being here, they happened less often. I didn't know if it was the exhaustion or something else entirely.

I had been lying there for at least thirty minutes when a gentle tapping against the cabin startled me. My whole body went rigid listening for the sound again. *Tap, tap, tap.* I slowly unzipped my bag and swung my legs over the edge of the bed careful not to make a sound. The last thing I needed was eight tired and overexcited girls letting their imaginations run wild with them. Especially if my suspicions were right.

Tiptoeing around the bed, I hooked a finger around the simple curtain and pulled it back. The moon illuminated cabin row; a single lamp hanging from the porch lit up each cabin, but I couldn't see anything—or anyone. *Tap, tap, tap.* I jumped back, my heart leaping into my mouth. My hand gripped the handle and turned it carefully. The door clicked open, and I pulled it back enough to slip through and close it behind me.

"Hello," I called out into the eerie surroundings.

Nothing.

I listened for a few more seconds, convinced I must have been hearing things, until movement caught my eye. Blake was standing in the shadows between my cabin and the next. His hood was pulled up, but I knew it was him.

My heart knew.

Our eyes locked, and I questioned him silently.

Come on, for old time's sake, he mouthed.

What was he thinking? We could be discovered at any moment. It was totally crazy, not to mention against the rules, and yet, I found myself tiptoeing down the steps.

Hi, he mouthed as I reached him.

Hi, I replied my heart beating so hard I felt a little light-headed. This was not a good idea.

So why did it feel so right?

Blake's hand reached out for mine, and he interlaced our fingers. I didn't stop him; I didn't even think about yanking my hand away. It felt right to feel his hand encase mine. It felt familiar and warm and safe. Like my body had avoided touch for so long because it was waiting for something. Someone.

It had been waiting for Blake.

The sane, rational part of me knew I was more messed up than any doctor or shrink had ever determined, but at that moment, with Blake's fingers entwined with my own, I couldn't find it in me to care. His touch didn't repulse me or scare me. It soothed me. And as he led me into the woods, my heart wasn't rapidly beating out of fear—it was racing for things to come.

chapter fourteen

"Blake, slow down. Where are we going?" I asked stumbling behind him as he led us deeper into the woods.

"Shh, just a little farther," he whispered his voice full of mirth.

Nervous energy tingled in my stomach setting my whole body alive. I had spent so many nights sneaking out of the Freeman group home with Blake in the cover of darkness secretly escaping to the one place we could be free. The *only* place we could truly be ourselves. This felt the same and yet, somehow different. Something had changed.

"Here, see." Blake pulled me through two trees standing so close together they reminded me of the secret passage cut through the trees lining the end of the Freeman's yard. We stepped into a circular clearing. The moonlight shone down giving everything an ethereal quality. It was breathtaking.

"Look up," Blake said watching for my reaction. I tilted

my face toward the sky and gasped. A ceiling of stars hung right above us, and I felt sure if I reached out, I could touch them. "I knew you'd like it."

Like it? It was everything.

Blake tugged me down next to him and with his hand still wrapped firmly around mine leaned back on the grass. I followed his lead until we were lying side my side our hands clasped between us.

"I couldn't let you leave without seeing this. Do you remember?"

Of course, I remembered.

Over the years, the stars had been my reminder that Blake was real, that he had existed at a time in my life I thought I wouldn't survive. Blake loved the stars. Bennett had tried to teach him the constellations, but by the time Bennett had aged out, Blake could only pick out Cassiopeia. That didn't stop us from naming the stars. We would spend hours pointing out funny patterns and giving them crazy names and stories. Blake even named a constellation after me—Lucky Penny. It just looked like a misshapen circle of stars to my eyes, but he said if you looked closely, you could see my smile.

"I remember," I whispered, too choked up to say anything else.

"Do you see it?" Blake extended his free arm and pointed up at a cluster of stars. All I could see was random patterns, and I strained to see what he saw.

"Lucky Penny. One of the brightest constellations there is."

"Blake..." The next words lodged in my throat. What was I supposed to say here? I didn't do this—I didn't bare myself to people. Let alone to the one person who had known me so well once upon a time.

"Don't, Penny. Not tonight, just enjoy this. Just this." His thumb rubbed circles along my hand.

Finding comfort in his words—no matter how cryptic—I allowed myself to let go. At that moment, I wasn't broken Penny trying to find the right words to say to the guy who had once been my world. I was just a girl lying next to a boy watching the stars.

Blake sighed quietly as if he was about to say something more, but when his body relaxed again, I knew the moment had passed. Maybe some things were just too hard to say—better left unsaid. Life had taught me never to take for granted the good moments because they always ended. And no sooner than we had lay down in the grass, Blake let go of my hand and rose to his feet.

"We should probably get back."

"Okay," I said unable to meet his eyes.

The buzz I had felt earlier following Blake into the night ebbed away and was replaced with something much more unsettling. Was this his way of saying goodbye? We still had a little over a week left; there was still time, and we were both returning to Columbus. It was goodbye but not forever. I hoped.

The short walk back to cabin row was awkward, and I fell into old habits, hugging myself tight. Blake seemed just as tense, his hands jammed in his cargo pockets and his hood still pulled up over his head. The path started to widen like the pit gnawing in my stomach. The lost me wanted to flee back to the cabin, close the door, and hide away from the emotional turmoil warring in me, but the stronger me—the me I had become thanks to Camp Chance—didn't want to leave things like this.

"Blake..." I paused and turned to face him. "I don't want to-"

Blake closed the distance between us and stood almost toe to toe with me. His eyes locked on mine and he stared down at me; full of unspoken promise, his gaze sent my heart into overdrive. "I shouldn't have waited so long to do this." His hand brushed along my jaw and into my hair drawing me close to him. He leaned down and covered my mouth with his own.

And I let him.

My body didn't just fall against him; it melted. His touch. The feel of his lips moving against mine. How did I ever let myself forget this? Force myself to forget? His smell. The way he tasted as his tongue licked the seams of my lips before parting my mouth.

Since my first kiss, at the age of fourteen, I had kissed only three other guys: Bryan, Michael, and Cal. Bryan made me cry because he didn't understand my anxieties, Michael was patient and kind as we explored my boundaries, and Cal made me feel nice. But none of them came close to making me feel the rainbow of emotions I was experiencing wrapped in Blake's arms.

I didn't ever want it to end.

Blake deepened the kiss, and my arms wound themselves around his back slipping underneath his hoodie. Warmth radiated from him. My hands traced the planes of his back, just needing to feel his skin; *I* needed to feel it, to know this was really happening. Blake obviously didn't feel the same, and he brought his hand down to mine removing it. "There's no rush," he whispered into my mouth with a half-smile.

Rush?

I pulled back suddenly staring at him confused. "Rush?"

Blake frowned and opened his mouth to say something, but it all clicked into place in my head. "Oh God, oh no, you think, oh God." I stepped back and started pacing back and forth in a short line.

"Whoa, Penny, let's slow down a little. I'm confused. What are you talking about?"

I stopped pacing and dragged my teeth across my bottom lip feeling very exposed and stupid. Oh, so stupid. "What are *you* talking about?"

He was still smiling, but now Blake looked more concerned. "You first."

"I, I…" The words were right there, right on the edge of my tongue, but if I said them, they would change everything.

"Is it about him? About what happened in that hell? Because you said you didn't want to talk about it, that it was in the past." The fear in Blake's eyes rendered me speechless.

I'd been lying to myself when I thought I could survive the summer without letting *him* ruin things. But he had been there all along like a dark, angry storm ready to strike at any moment.

"Penny…" Blake's voice cracked, and he swallowed hard. It was too much; my eyes fluttered shut, and I inhaled deeply.

Just breathe.

He can't hurt you anymore.

Just breathe.

A sense of peace washed over me. I came to Camp Chance with the hope of healing. Blake being here was a sign—my chance at closure. With a deep breath, I opened my eyes and said calmly, "Almost a year after you left, Derek tried to rape me."

The color drained from Blake's face until his pallor looked gray under the moon's light. "I, fuck, I… Christ, what happened? I thought he'd stopped with, you know."

I knew.

The first time Derek came into my room and touched himself, I was fourteen. He'd caught Blake and me sneaking back into the house. It was my birthday. Blake knew something was up, had warned me to barricade myself in, but I thought he was overacting. Sure, Derek had an unusual fixation on me, but he was the same with all the girls. Always leering a little too long. Especially Jessica, but she had boobs and long legs and hair that made her look a lot older than her teenage years. I was just a girl. A tomboy, at that.

My eyes flew to the door as it creaked open. Blake, it had to be Blake sneaking in. But then Derek's huge form came into view, the light from the hallway illuminating him. He looked like the devil. He stood with his eyes fixed on me as I pulled the comforter up around my chest, panic surging through me, my heart slamming against my chest. Why didn't I listen to Blake? He knew; he knew something was off about Derek earlier. He never came in my room, ever, and I knew something was very wrong. When he stepped fully into the room and closed the door behind him, I started to cry, tears trickling down my cheeks. Derek placed a single finger on his lips reducing me to silence.

I. Couldn't. Move.

He joined me on the bed. It groaned and rattled, protesting under his bulky frame. I was terrified, but through my tear-stained eyes, I noticed Derek was nervous, mumbling and trembling. It didn't ease the storm. His eyes... they were hardened. Dead. He didn't speak as he lay down beside me. I held my breath waiting...

He didn't move.

I didn't move.

Neither of us made a sound.

And then I felt his hand move, a zipper being pulled down. Rough, callous hands reached out for me.

"Tried to? You mean he didn't? Please tell me that fucker didn't actually do it?" The desperation in Blake's voice ripped me from the nightmare and I shook my head trying to rid myself of a time I'd tried so hard to forget. "No, he didn't. He couldn't. It wasn't for lack of trying, but no, he didn't."

Blake thrust a hand into his hair and cursed something under his breath. The hostility rolled off him like a stormy sea. I knew it would do this. Blake's temper had always been a loose cannon.

"Why didn't you tell anyone? I was gone. There was nothing he could threaten you with like before."

"No one cared about what happened to us in there. You know that. Besides, I refused to let him break me. To give him that kind of power over me."

That's what I told myself. Whenever Derek used to sneak into my room and lie down beside me and start touching himself, I tuned him out. I focused on my happy place—at home with my parents or in No Man's Land with Blake. I went to another place, one happier and brighter and full of laughter. I never allowed myself to be there with him. I was an empty vessel, and he couldn't hurt me.

Only Derek Freeman had hurt me in ways I wouldn't come to realize until I left the group home.

"I should have been there." It came out a whisper on the breeze.

But you weren't.

"What happened after he..." Blake gulped, pain etched into his strong features. "After he tried to hurt you?"

"He got up, zipped up his pants, and walked out of my room. He never bothered me again. I checked out after that. I only had a few months left before I aged out, so I kept to myself. Jessica was long gone, Amy and Mason too."

"I should have put that fucker in the ground when I had the chance." The venom in Blake's words didn't surprise me. He had always hated our foster dad.

When Blake discovered Derek leaving my room that first night, I'd wrapped myself around him and begged for him not to go after him. It wasn't until Blake finally calmed down that I was able to pass on Derek's message: Tell anyone and he would ensure we never saw each other again. He used our friendship against us, holding us prisoner to his will, and it seemed the sick man loved getting off while lying next to young girls stroking their innocent skin.

Emotionally spent, I said the only words I could muster. "He'll get his." I had to believe that. One day, Derek Freeman would pay for his crimes.

"We should probably get back," I said hoping to snap Blake out of his own thoughts. He shook his head and blinked. "You're right."

As we walked back the rest of the short distance to cabin row, the distance between us seemed wider than ever. Just as I had predicted, my revelations changed everything, and as much as I tried to tell myself that Derek didn't still hold power over me, this was proof he did.

My cabin came into view and an empty feeling washed over me. It was ironic really that what started as possibly one of the single best moments of my life would end this way. Blake called me his lucky Penny, but I was all lucked out. Had been for most of my life.

"This is me," I said turning slightly to Blake. He looked pensive and avoided meeting my eyes. The pit in my stomach expanded. "Good night, Blake." I started toward the cabin stairs. My legs felt heavy as I took the first step. The truth was supposed to set you free, but it all had done tonight was ruin things.

When I reached the last step, I turned back. Blake was standing where I left him. Rigid and unmoving, he watched me intently. I couldn't place the emotion on his face, and a sinking feeling spread through me.

"Thank you for taking me tonight," I said softly before quietly opening the door and stepping inside, leaving my past behind.

chapter *fifteen*

Blake didn't try to kiss me again.

In our last few days at Camp Chance, we didn't share any more heated looks over the fire or stolen glances across the lake. Blake went out of his way to avoid me. I still watched him; my eyes refused to look away, but he never returned my stares.

He had pulled away, and the only thing that had changed was my revelation about Derek.

After Blake kissed me and I told him about Derek, I thought I had finally found closure. But once again, I was lost in my past. I moved through the days spent out at the lake or in the woods with the girls, but I had checked out. I was stuck in my memories.

"And what do you hope to gain from working at Camp Chance, Penny?"

My eyes focused on the bookcase behind Dr. Merth. "To prove to myself that this thing, my anxiety, doesn't control me, I guess."

"Does this have anything to do with Cal?"

"Cal?" I met Dr. Merth's questioning eyes with my own. "Why would it be about Cal? We ended. It's done."

The smartly dressed man regarded me. He looked more like a young hip college professor than a psychologist. "Exactly, Penny. You were making progress with Cal. You dated, for what, nine months? You trusted him enough to let him touch you?"

I winced and my eyes fluttered shut as I remembered. How I'd cried the first time Cal had tried to touch me. How scared I'd been to let him see me, kiss me, feel me. I had let him touch me, and we'd been intimate, but it wasn't easy.

"Penny," Dr. Merth's voice pulled me back into the room. "I'm not here to judge. I'm here to help you explore your feelings and to make sense of what is happening." He smiled and I relaxed into the leather chair a little. "I think, that maybe, you're looking for something or someone to fix you. But it doesn't work like that. You have to deal with your experiences first. Make peace with what happened and try to find a way to make sense of it. What you feel, how you respond to touch, your fears… they are completely normal for someone in your situation. You experienced a great loss and then someone you should have been able to trust took you advantage of you. There is no quick fix for that, Penny. Baby steps, remember."

I nodded, the lump in my throat preventing me from garnering a reply.

"Now, I'll ask again. What are you hoping to gain from working at Camp Chance?"

I came to Camp Chance to prove something to myself—to fix myself—only I got more than I bargained for, and now, I was more lost than ever. Marissa tried to console me. At first, she said I should try to talk to Blake, to give him a chance to explain his sudden coldness. But I didn't need to see that look in his eyes again. The void I'd seen as he watched me walk into the cabin that night.

Maybe this is just how it's supposed to be.

In the end, our second chance was just a naïve fantasy.

An illusion.

"All packed?" Marissa barreled into our cabin in her usual fashion. I nodded. We had said goodbye to the last group yesterday. Our last campfire debrief was this evening, and our buses left tomorrow.

"Aren't you going to start packing?" I asked her glancing at the empty bag sitting on her bed.

"Nah, I'll do it first thing. I want to make the most of our last few hours. We're going down to the lake. Troy and Tina always end the summer with this silly counselor versus instructor competition. You're coming, right?" She eyed me warily.

"Of course, I'm coming," I shot back a little too defensively.

Marissa smiled weakly. I wasn't fooling her with my attempt to hold myself together.

"Awesome. Bring a change of clothes. Things usually end up wet."

Great.

I followed her out of the cabin and shut the door behind me. Tomorrow, life would return to normal. I would return to my shitty apartment and underpaid job, and soon enough, Camp Chance would become a distant memory.

Just like Blake.

You shouldn't have told him, a little voice whispered.

But I knew the truth. If Blake still cared for me the way I was starting to believe he did, what I told him wouldn't have mattered.

"Okay, welcome to our fourteenth annual counselors versus instructors showdown. The rules are simple. First team to build their raft and make it across the lake wins the coveted title of Camp Chance champions."

I rolled my eyes at Marissa; she sat on the opposite bench with the other instructors with a smug grin painted on her face, wiggling her eyebrows in a way that said 'I'm pro at this.'

"Starting positions, please," Troy bellowed. He was enjoying this far too much, and it made me wonder just how old he was exactly. He rarely acted older than a teenager did himself.

Reluctantly, I joined Sheridan, Sara, Blake, Malachi, and John. The guys were already discussing how best to fix together the materials—four drum barrels, various ropes, and a series of wooden poles—to make a floatation device.

"First one across wins. GO!" Troy yelled sounding the air horn.

"Okay, let's get the thing laid out first then we can work on tying the barrels together before we add the poles," Blake directed the rest of us, well, Sheridan, Sara, Malachi, and John. I was too busy focusing on not watching him.

It was the closest we had been in ten days when he'd held me close and kissed me as if I was his air.

"Grab that rope, Penny," someone said pulling me from

my thoughts.

"Hmm, yeah, sure, here you go." Sara flashed me a concerned look, and I smiled weakly.

In less than twenty minutes, our group had fashioned a raft and were wading into the water to see if it was buoyant.

"Remember, teams. Everyone has to travel across on your rafts," Troy shouted from his stool with a huge grin on his face.

I cursed under my breath as I watched my teammates climb onto the wooden base one by one. When Marissa had said bring a change of clothes, I don't know what I thought, but it wasn't that I might end up falling off the raft into the lake.

"Come on, Penny." Blake extended his hand to me, but not ready to acknowledge him, I rounded the other side of the raft and waded into the water. My body shuddered at the cold temperature, but I ignored it and hoisted myself up. The whole thing wobbled, water lapping up the sides.

"It's not that bad, Penny," Sheridan joked shuffling up to give me space.

"You won't be saying that when we end up in there." I glanced down at the dark blue water.

"Nah, they have this down to an art. Right, guys?"

They laughed, but I didn't. I was too busy focusing all my energies on staying as still as possible while Blake and Malachi used paddles to sail us across the lake. I knew the other team was right on our tail.

About halfway across the lake, one of the guys' expertly tied knots started to loosen under our weight. Malachi was certain it would hold, but I watched it slip looser and looser until the last pole started to drop away from the others.

"I'll grab it," John maneuvered onto his knees and shuffled to the edge of the raft.

"No, leave-" Blake yelled, but it was too late.

John leaned over the side a little too far and toppled headfirst into the lake. The raft tilted with him. I grabbed a hold of Sheridan who grabbed Sara. When it landed back in the water with a thud, it sent all of us crashing into one another. Nearest to the edge, I lost my balance and rolled backward.

The cold water hit me like a force field, and I gasped as the water closed around me. Icy liquid filled my mouth, and I choked and spluttered trying to kick my way to the surface. I'd survived a wild summer here, managed to keep forty teenage girls alive, and yet, here I was, about to drown on my last day.

Hands grabbed me around my waist and just for a second, I felt paralyzed.

And then something in me broke.

Panic surged through me, and I started kicking and lashing out. My arms and hands contacted with something solid. Water splashed around me.

"Penny, Penny, calm down, it's me. It's me."

I blinked rapidly trying to clear my eyes. Blake stared back at me with such reverence, I stilled. "Hi." Blake had his arms wrapped firmly around my waist. He was supporting us both in the water, keeping us afloat.

The panic subsided; I regained control of my limbs and demanded my feet kick.

"Are you okay?"

I nodded.

"Come on." He released one arm around me to pull us

closer to the raft. Sara held out the paddle for him to grab, and she and Malachi pulled us in.

Blake pushed me to the edge of the raft and a soggy Peter and Sheridan helped me up. I was completely soaked and very embarrassed. I heard Blake pull himself out of the water behind me, but I didn't dare turn around.

"I told you you'd end up wet," a voice from across the lake shouted. We all turned to find the other raft passing us and a very smug looking Marissa with her hands cupped around her mouth.

Everyone around me burst into laughter, and I felt Blake's eyes burning into my back. I turned slightly. Our eyes locked and the emotion behind his blue depths winded me. Sucked the air right out my lungs. What was he trying to tell me?

"WINNERS." The air horn sounded again and cheering broke through our moment. The other team had reached the other side of the lake. They had won.

We had lost.

Only I had a sinking feeling I'd lost more than just a silly competition.

After watching the other team crowned as Camp Chance champions, I returned to the cabin to dry out.

And to escape Blake.

His efforts to avoid me all week had been telling me one thing, but when he looked at me after saving me from drowning in the lake, his eyes told me something completely different. Marissa was right; I needed to talk to him.

Before we left tomorrow, I needed to clear the air. Even if I didn't like the outcome.

I showered and changed into a dry pair of shorts, a tank, and my blue camp hoodie. My bag was packed and resting against the wall. I glanced around the room; I sure was going to miss this place. The last ten weeks had tested me, exhausted me, but most of all, strengthened me. I still had a way to go until I would completely heal—if that was even possible—but I was stronger. Even Blake's presence, despite throwing me for a loop in the beginning, had given me a chance to face some of the ghosts of my past. When I returned to Columbus, I was finally going to exorcise my demons.

"Oh, hey, you are here." Marissa slipped into the cabin and smiled. "What have you been doing all this time?"

"Getting dry," I said sarcastically.

"Are you okay? Sheridan said you panicked. I didn't realize."

"I'm fine." I sat down on the edge of the bed.

"I was thinking it might not be a bad idea to pack now…" Marissa blushed, something I didn't think I'd ever seen her do. "You know, in case, well, in case anything happens tonight."

"You mean in case Liam finally gives in to your advances?" I arched my eyebrow. Marissa refused to accept his blow offs.

"Exactly. Give me a hand with my stuff?"

I glanced around her side of the room. There were clothes strewn everywhere. "Sure, I guess."

"Awesome, and then we can head over to the fire. Troy is grilling tonight."

Forty-minutes later, Marissa's bag had joined mine by the door, and we headed to the campfire.

"I'm going to talk to him tonight," I said with a lot more confidence than I felt.

"You should. You can't leave things the way they are because you'll regret it. Maybe he just got cold feet? You know how guys are like when they're overwhelmed."

I didn't, but I didn't tell Marissa that. Just as I didn't tell her the real reason Blake had spent the whole week giving me the cold shoulder.

The crackle of the fire grew louder as we cut through the trees to the campfire. Everyone had gathered around to enjoy a celebratory beer, and Troy was at the half-drum barbecuing burgers and steaks.

"Girls, get over here," he called over noticing us arrive.

I followed Marissa, but a hand cut in front of me and Tina stepped into my vision. "Hey, Penny. Can I borrow you for a second?"

Confused, I said, "Sure."

Tina led me to the main cabin. She asked how I had found the summer and commended me on how well I'd bonded with the girls. She was stalling, making small talk, and a feeling of dread started to unfold in my stomach.

"Come in," she said opening the door to her and Troy's small office at the back of the cabin. I followed her inside and took at seat. She sat behind her big wooden desk piled with papers and looked at me with a grim expression. "Please understand. I wouldn't usually get involved with my employee's business like this, but Blake is a good friend. I've known him a long time…"

Blake? What did Blake have to do with this? Oh God,

did she know about us sneaking off the other night? Had someone reported us? Dread turned to nausea and my hands trembled in my lap.

Tina opened a drawer in her desk and retrieved an envelope. "Here. Blake left this for you." She handed it to me across the desk.

Left it for me? I didn't understand.

"Why couldn't he just give it to me himself?"

A sad smile tugged at Tina's lips. "He's gone, Penny. He got a call and had to leave."

Gone?

"He can't be gone. I was just with him. On the lake. He pulled me out of the water."

It hit me like a wrecking ball.

Blake was gone.

For the second time in my life.

chapter sixteen

Blake

Age 16

I traced patterns on the bare skin of Penny's stomach where her top rode up. It was one of my favorite places on her body. Her stomach. The soft skin just underneath her ears. Her lips. Okay, so I liked most of her body. Penny wasn't a kid anymore. Her hips were wider and she had curves… in all the right places. I tried to keep my feelings under wraps, but sometimes it was damn near impossible. Like now, with her lying in the grass in No Man's Land with that ridiculously tight tank top that hardly covered her midriff.

"What are you doing down there?" Penny pushed up onto her elbows, her hair tumbling over her shoulders, and peered down her body at me. I was half-draped over her legs my chin resting on her thigh as my fingers continued to brush her exposed skin.

"Just enjoying the view."

"Well, can't you enjoy it from up here? I miss you." She pouted, and I crawled up the side of her body catching her bottom lip between my teeth and sucking gently. She shrieked and then giggled.

I pulled back and stared down at her; I couldn't imagine life without this girl. Her eyes shone brightly, the way they did whenever she looked at me. Her cute pout melted away, and her lips hooked up into a smile as she curled her hands around my neck and drew me down to her.

Our lips brushed. Penny's tongue licked along the crease of my mouth, and my dick strained against my jeans. *Shut it off, Weston*, I silently cursed. We were only at second base. There had been a semi-naked dry humping incident once, but Penny freaked and we had to stop. I almost came in my jeans. Lately, I seemed to spend more and more time in a cold shower, but I vowed not to push Penny into anything she wasn't ready for. And after what that bastard did to her, I knew she wasn't ready.

We weren't ready.

Even if our bodies were saying otherwise.

I deepened the kiss and rolled my weight onto her a little more. We didn't get to spend much time out here anymore, but it was still our place—the only place we could be ourselves. When Penny's hands started trailing down my back, I ended the kiss. I was the one who had to shut down our play. Penny thought she was ready, she'd told me more than once, but it was too soon. Penny wore a mask, acted brave in the face of what Derek had put her through, but I knew shit like that had to leave some kind of mark. I tucked her into the crook of my arm, and we did what we used to do during our late night visits to Lake Cenci; we lay under the stars naming our own constellations.

After a while, Penny said, "Do you think about life after this place, Blake? About what will happen?" Penny gazed over at me as if I was her world, causing my stomach to knot tightly.

I wanted to be—her world. I wanted to give her the moon and the stars and everything between. She deserved it and so much more. She deserved life; one better than the shit we put up with living with Derek and Marie.

"All the time. Come here." I looped my arm around her neck, not caring if anyone spotted us, and drew her in tighter as we lay beyond the yard staring up at the night sky. Tiny lights sparkled like diamonds on a smooth black canvas. It was beautiful. A little slice of heaven in our own fucked-up version of hell. "Eighteen more months, Penny, and then we're free and it'll be just you and me."

Penny sighed beside me. It was full of hope. I felt it in the way her hand lightly squeezed mine, and how her body relaxed into the ground as the breath left her lungs. We both wanted more. More than the shit hand we had been dealt. We had dreams and hopes for the future, just like any other sixteen-year-old kid. Except we weren't like most other kids. We had already lost so much… lived so much.

It was what brought us together in the first place, but now… now, things were different between us. Sometime in the last two years, my best friend had become my reason for breathing.

My everything.

"Eighteen months. We can make that, right?" Her voice was unsure, and I hated them for taking away the last shred of fight she'd had when she arrived at the Freeman group home with just one bag and a shitload of nightmares.

I rolled slightly to face Penny, my eyes taking in her delicate features. Chocolate brown eyes set against pale skin with a peppering of freckles that covered her perfectly shaped nose framed by loose dark waves rolling over her slim shoulders.

Trying to push down all of my anger for the things she'd faced in this place, I choked out, "You're my lucky Penny. With you by my side, we can survive anything."

I followed Mason into the house. We were too busy laughing and joking about last period that I didn't notice Derek standing at the bottom of the staircase.

"Yo, Derek," Mason said in an indifferent tone as he walked straight past him into the kitchen.

My good mood disappeared, and I locked eyes with Derek refusing to back down. He straightened and said, "Keep walking, boy," as his evil smirk spread wider.

My fists clenched at my sides, and I had to bite down on my tongue to stop myself from saying something I would regret. It was always the same. Derek would catch me off guard, and I'd struggle to rein in my temper. But the dick had me right where he wanted me. If I went after him, he would kick me out, and he knew I would never risk leaving Penny behind. Deep down, I think that's why he went after her in the first place because he knew I liked her. In some sick and twisted way, he was jealous of our bond.

The first time I had caught Derek jerking off in Penny's room, I thought he had hurt her... or worse. Penny explained everything to me, but it didn't make me feel any better. The sick fuck had laid down with her on the bed, unzipped his pants, and jacked off while Penny lay paralyzed next to him. He didn't talk to her or make her touch him; he just got himself off while stroking her skin and then left.

Penny begged me not to do anything; I was one second away from rushing out of the room and pounding my fists into his face. But then Penny dropped a bombshell. Derek had threatened her with splitting us up. If either of us said a word to anyone, he would make sure we never saw each other again.

For that first few months, I was so full of anger and darkness that I pulled away from everyone. Even Penny, to some extent. Every time I crossed paths with Derek, I saw red and it took everything in me not to confront him. It was even worse on the nights he crept into Penny's room. I would lay down the hall listening for the creak of the door and the sound of her muffled cries, plotting ways to end him. But after a while, the cries stopped. When I asked Penny what had changed, she simply said, 'I won't let him break me.' That was the day I knew I had to be strong for us as well.

Derek never returned to her room after that.

It wasn't until Jessica aged out and Penny moved into the bigger room with Amy and Mia that I slept easier, knowing she was in a room with two other girls. Of course, part of me wondered if Derek had done the same thing to any of the others. He had made comments about Amy before, and she was always so mean and yet eager to please Derek that it crossed my mind more than once. But what was I supposed to do? Derek and Marie had been fostering for years; in the eyes of the state, they had a clean record and ran a good home. No social worker would listen to the likes of me; the hot-tempered kid from the drug dealer father and drug addict mother.

With Penny off-limits, Derek came down on me harder. Assigned me extra chores, grounded me for even looking at him wrong, and he even cornered me a couple of times and left me with bruised ribs. But I took everything he had to give and then some. When he bolted down the window in the downstairs bathroom and stayed up extra late to make sure we couldn't sneak out, we found new ways to spend time together. Stolen kisses during our lunch break or a brush of our hands while sitting in the den. Plus, we always had Sundays out by the lake while Marie dragged Derek to the Golden Corral. Last night had been a one off; Marie had dragged Derek to some convention in town. The second they were out of the driveway, Penny and I had escaped to No Man's Land. It was there I'd looked Penny in the eyes and told her we could survive another eighteen months in here. I only hoped I was right because Penny was the only good thing in my life. She was all I needed.

My lucky Penny.

I couldn't lose her.

The next few weeks passed uneventfully. It was officially the summer, which meant our birthdays were finally in sight.

Penny turned seventeen first on September 1st. I followed on September 20th. In just three more months, we would only have twelve months left. Fifty-two weeks before we walked away from Derek and Marie and their stupid fucking rules. Three-hundred and sixty-five days until we were free.

Things were good—as good as they could be in our situation. I caught Derek leering at Penny occasionally, and he still went out of his way to make my life hell, but Marie was having some health concerns that diverted a lot of his attention.

"So what do you want for your birthday?" I whispered to Penny as we walked back from the store with the others. She batted me away. I didn't give a fuck if the others saw us like this—up close and personal—because they all knew about us anyway. But Penny was a private person, and she didn't like to flaunt our relationship in front of them.

"Blake," she warned. "I don't need anything. You know that. Besides, we have the whole summer yet."

I did, but she was turning seventeen. I wanted to make it special for her. I was saving the money I got for helping Mr. Banks out with his lawn across the road. I was surprised Derek and Marie allowed it, but when the old man came and asked them personally if Mason and I could give him a hand, they couldn't really say no. Keeping up appearances was too damn important to them.

"Yeah, I know, but if you could have anything, what would you want?"

Her eyes flashed with desire and her cheeks flushed. *Well, damn, that backfired.*

"Penny..." I smirked, trying to ignore the way she was

looking at me. Like she wanted to jump my bones right there on the sidewalk. She dropped her eyes away from me.

"Hey." I grabbed her hand in my mine and tugged gently forcing her to look at me. "Soon, okay. Soon."

Her eyes widened, and a slow smile broke over her face. I had been the one to make us wait, but maybe she was strong enough for this. Maybe it was time. It had been almost a year since she moved into the girls' room, and I wanted her. God, I wanted her so much. But I didn't want her to regret it or freak out. I didn't want to ruin what we had. If we were really going to do it, I wanted her one-hundred percent with me. I *needed* all of her with me.

The Freeman house came into view, and Penny shrugged her hand out of mine. I jammed my hands in my pockets and jogged away from her to catch up with Mason and Ben.

"Who's that belong to?" Ben said nodding up at the house. The scrawny blond-haired freckled kid was no more. He'd grown up and almost stood as tall as Mase and I did.

"No idea. What's a car like that doing parked out front of their house?" Mase replied.

I didn't join in their conversation. I was too busy wondering what in the hell a black Town Car was doing parked outside the Freeman's house. Its paintwork glistened in the sun; so much so that if you looked right at it, you would probably go blind.

As we neared the path up to the house, the front door opened and a man in a tailored suit appeared. He turned back to say something to Derek and Marie, extending his hand to shake Derek's hand. A shiver ran through me. What kind of business did they have with a man like this?

The man nodded and turned on his perfectly polished shoes and walked out of the side gate. A younger man in a black suit climbed out of the driver's side and went around to open the door for him. The guy had a fucking chauffeur.

"Whoa, did you see that? The dude has a driver. Who the fuck has a driver?"

Ben shrugged and answered, "Someone with money, I guess. What do you think, Blake?"

Not taking my eyes off the car as it rolled away, I said, "I have no fucking clue."

I didn't, but my gut told me it wasn't good.

The feeling didn't leave me for the rest of the day.

chapter seventeen

I kicked open the door to my apartment. Grease and egg rolls assaulted me. The lavender air fresheners had obviously masked the smell more than I realized. My feet shuffled through a summer's worth of mail, and I dropped my bag on the floor by the counter.

Welcome home.

I took in the space before me. Somehow, it looked worse since returning from Camp Chance. What did that say about the place if a wooden cabin in the middle of nowhere was the nicer option?

The door knocked behind me, and Mr. Chen appeared. "Hello, Miss Penny. You return from good summer?"

Nodding, I smiled and motioned for him to come in. He shook his head. "Ahh, no. Just come to say hello. Welcome back." He disappeared back down the stairwell, and I closed the door.

For as much as I hated this place, part of me was relieved when Mr. Chen agreed to let me pay half rent for the weeks I was gone. He even said I could pay upon my return, but I had a small amount of money saved. The thought of having to try to find another place to live was not something I wanted to deal with anytime soon.

Before I went in search of lavender air fresheners, I retrieved my cell phone from the drawer and turned it on. There had been no need for me to take it to camp with me because only a handful of people had my number. The screen flashed to life and it bleeped.

I miss your face already.

I smiled at Marissa's text and typed out a reply, and then set about making my apartment habitable again. It didn't take long to replace all of the dried-up air fresheners, and when I was satisfied the smell of fried food was almost unnoticeable, I carried my bag into my small bedroom and unzipped it. My eyes fell straight to the small white envelope.

Penny,
I'm sorry I didn't get to say goodbye.
I need to take care of some things.
Seeing you again was so much more than I expected.
It was everything.
Wait for me.

Please,
Blake x

There was a cell phone number with Blake's letter. Tina confirmed it was his number but said I should him give some time before trying to contact him. She wouldn't tell me anything else, but I didn't need her to. Blake had told me there was someone else in his life, and now, it all made sense. I suspected he had pulled away because of his own guilt; only, I had wrongly assumed it was guilt over what Derek tried to do to me. Now, I realized it was guilt over the person in his life. A girlfriend, a fiancée… wife. Either way, it didn't matter. I couldn't sit around waiting and hoping Blake would take care of things.

I wouldn't.

The doorbell chimed as I entered Vrai Beauté, and Tiffany looked up from her position at the counter. "Ahh, Penny."

Well, that didn't sound good.

"Hi, Tiffany. How are you?" I said politely ignoring the alarm bells ringing in my head. She rounded the counter mumbling something to Kylie and ushered me to the side so we weren't blocking the entrance.

"Penny, I didn't expect to see you so soon."

She didn't?

"I got back yesterday."

"And how was it? Enlightening?"

I bristled at the hint of sarcasm in her voice. Usually, I would have dropped it, but something in me refused to stay quiet. Proud of what I achieved over the summer, I wasn't going to let her belittle me. Rolling back my shoulders, I replied, "It was very enlightening actually. I had an amazing experience."

Tiffany's face creased. "Well, isn't that just lovely. What can I do for you, Penny?" She sounded almost bored.

"I'm here to check my shifts."

"You really should have called ahead, Penny. Just dropping in like this…" she trailed off. I looked over her shoulder at Kylie, but she dropped her head.

"What's going on, Tiffany?"

Tiffany blew out a dramatic breath. "I'm afraid I'm going to have to let you go, Penny. Kylie did such an excellent job filling in for you, and really, she's a better fit for the shop. I'm sorry."

Tears pooled behind my eyes and my whole body shook with frustration, but I calmly said, "Well, in that case, I'll be out of your hair." I turned on my heels not giving her or Kylie a backward glance. I walked out of Vrai Beauté with my head held high.

My composure crumbled the second I reached the end of the block. As soon as I turned the corner, the tears rushed out with such force that my body wracked violently. People on the sidewalk slowed as they passed me, but no one stopped to ask if I was okay. Giving myself a few seconds to get it out of my system, I turned my back to the road and tucked myself into the wall. My fingers scrambled to find a tissue in my purse, and I dabbed my eyes unsure if my tears were from losing my job or anger at myself for actually believing Tiffany would hold it. She had never liked me, only tolerated me, and I knew I didn't fit in with her shop's standards. I wasn't pretty enough, well put together enough… just not enough.

Stupid, stupid Penny.

When the ugly tears stopped falling, I smoothed down my coat and walked the rest of the distance home. Usually, I would have taken the bus, but Mom always used to say 'the fresh air is good for the soul,' and right now, I would take anything I could get.

As I walked listlessly along the sidewalk, my thoughts turned to my predicament. What in the hell was I supposed to do with no job? The money I'd earned from Camp Chance would cover two months of rent. If I couldn't find something before then, being fired from Vrai Beauté would be the least of my problems.

A sign for an internet café caught my eye from across the street.

Nothing like the present.

I crossed the road, went into the café, and paid the guy for an hour. Within thirty minutes, I had a list of names and numbers to call. The most promising was an agency looking for spare hands for local events. They needed servers and kitchen staff, that kind of thing. I had some kitchen experience, but the ad sounded desperate, and desperate was something I knew all about.

"Penny Wilson." I gave the security man my name. "I'm here for the banquet. I'm one of Mary's girls." I cringed; it made it sound like I was here to give out lap dances not serve canapés to rich folk who liked the finer things in life.

The security man checked his list and then thumbed me inside. "You need to follow this corridor to the end, and the kitchen is back there."

I nodded and scurried past him, smoothing down my knee-length black pencil skirt. 'All I need from you is a pair of hands, a smart dress, and black pumps on your feet. You think you can handle that?' Mary had asked me during my five minute 'interview.' I was beginning to wonder what I'd gotten myself into when she texted me the address of my first job at the Hyatt Regency in Upper Arlington. But she was offering more money an hour than I'd earned at any of my previous jobs. It was too much to turn down even if the thought of serving drinks and canapés to a bunch of wealthy businessmen and their wives made my stomach churn.

The kitchen was manic. Chefs in white jackets yelled out orders to a sea of black and white lingering around the service area. The hotel was hosting some charity event. It was a drinks reception followed by a five-course, sit-down meal. I was down to serve drinks. Drinks, I thought, I could handle. Food service, not so much—or not yet, at least.

"You." A tall girl, probably not much older than me, pointed at me and frowned. "Dump the bag and jacket and grab one of those trays of salmon mousse and follow me."

I glanced around hoping she was talking to someone else, but everyone around me was busy.

Well, okay then.

"Move it," she snarled. "We have hungry rich folk to feed."

Ignoring her jibe, I slipped out of my jacket and wrapped my purse inside. It only had my cell phone and some change for the bus ride home.

"Lockers are back there," the girl said, the annoyance in her voice growing.

I hurried to a locker to shut away my belongings and returned to the kitchen. The girl thrust a tray of mousse-topped crackers at me and motioned for me to follow her. I was so stunned that I didn't even think to inform her I was supposed to be doing drinks. But the tray was small, and I figured how hard could it be?

We exited a swinging door and entered a huge room with floor-to-ceiling glass windows overlooking a courtyard. The gold and deep red accents gave the whole place a regal feel, but the interior design didn't ooze money, the people did.

Ladies were in an array of beautiful dresses and skirt suits, and the men they clung to were sculpted in perfectly tailored suits. It wasn't quite black tie, but for lunchtime on a Friday afternoon, it didn't get much more formal.

Suddenly feeling inferior in my plain black skirt, crisp white shirt, and last-minute chignon, I lowered my eyes to avoid making eye contact.

"You take the left side, and I'll do this side. Once you're empty, go and grab a fresh tray. Got it?" the girl said in a hushed voice. I nodded. "And watch out for the piranhas, they bite." She glided away from me and moved to the other side of the room.

Piranhas?

Stealing a quick deep breath, I readjusted my hand supporting the tray and approached a small group of people. They were laughing at something one of the men was saying. I waited for him to finish before stepping closer.

I cleared my throat and said meekly, "Canapés?"

Shit, was that the right thing to say? I didn't even know what I was serving. I doubted 'would you like a salmon mousse on some kind of cracker' would cut it with these people.

Five faces turned in my direction, and my mouth dried. Sure they could see right through my lack of on the job training or experience, I was surprised when an older woman dressed in a navy skirt and jacket combo with silver-gray hair smiled at me and said, "Why, that would be splendid, dear."

Her friends nodded in agreement, as they helped themselves to the salmon mousse crackers. I smiled back politely and moved to the next cluster of people relieved at how easy they had made it.

For the next fifteen minutes, I worked my side of the room offering people various canapés. There was the salmon mousse thing, some kind of wasabi prawn, and a mackerel pate concoction that made me want to hurl. On the whole, people were polite.

Until I reached the piranhas.

I knew instantly it was the people the other waitress had referred to. Gathered in the far corner of the room, there were four girls around my age. Each had perfectly styled hair to match their perfectly manicured nails and seamless, figure-hugging dresses. Their leader, a slim blonde covered in a long sleeved black lace overlaid dress smirked as I approached them.

"Oh, ladies, look, canapés," her sickly sweet voice dripped with bitterness.

I offered them the tray of prawns and smiled. "Wasabi prawn?"

They each helped themselves. The blonde inspected her prawn up close, and then curled her lip in disgust. "There's a hair on it. What's your name?"

"My- my name?" I stuttered.

"Yes, your name? What's wrong with you? Do you have a speech impediment?" Her friends snickered, and my cheeks exploded with embarrassment. "Well? What is it?"

"Penny, my name is Penny."

"Well, Penny..." She stepped forward peering down at me. Her heels gave her a good two inches over my five-foot-six. "Take this back to the kitchen and tell the chef I'd prefer a little less hair with my prawn." She dropped the canapés onto the tray and rubbed her hands together in disgust. I turned on my heels and fled from the room as quickly as I could without attracting attention, tears stinging the back of my eyes.

Once behind the sanctuary of the kitchen door, I dropped the tray on the counter and leaned back against the tiled wall. The waitress from earlier noticed me and came over. "Let me guess, the piranhas?"

I nodded.

"Don't let them get to you. If you show weakness, Brittany and her little friends will chew you up and spit you out."

"Thanks for the heads-up." I glared at her a little pissed she threw me to the wolves on my first shift.

"Hey, I'm not here to babysit you. If you can't deal, Mary has another ten girls ready to take your place."

I dropped my head to my chest feeling defeated. I needed this job.

"Look, go back out there and show them they can't break you. I'm Tara, by the way."

"Penny," I whispered.

"Don't let them break you. It's your first shift." With that, Tara replaced her empty tray with a full one and returned to the room.

Don't let them break you.

She was right. Brittany was no one to me. Just another self-entitled bitch thinking she was better than everyone and everything. She didn't know anything about my life or me.

I grabbed a fresh tray of canapés and smoothed down my blouse and skirt with my free hand.

I could this.

I could so do this.

chapter eighteen

After my shift at the Hyatt, Mary called me on my birthday to say her eyes had given me the thumbs up. Turns out her 'eyes' were Tara. She had been testing me. And thanks to her little pep talk, I passed and Mary started booking me for regular functions. Sometimes, it was providing catering assistance to high-profile clients at business meetings in downtown Columbus, and other times, I worked more formal functions like the one at Hyatt Regency. But they all had one thing in common: The clients were wealthy. Worlds apart from the life I lived. At least it gave me an excuse to actually celebrate turning twenty-four. Usually birthdays went unnoticed in my life.

During my fourth week of working for her, Mary called me in to cover a charity event at the Arlington Country Club. It was my first black tie dinner gala, and the organizers of the event, West Lake and Associates, provided us with a uniform. The prestigious law firm was hosting the event to raise money for a new state-of-the-art medical center, and according to Mary, everyone who was anyone in Columbus was going to be there.

I rechecked my appearance for the third time. The black pleated skirt framed my legs making them appear longer and the white cap sleeve blouse hugged my chest a little too tightly. To my relief, the black waistcoat fit perfectly making me feel less exposed. Female staff had been instructed to wear their hair in a sleek braid down their backs. Our instructions had been so specific, right down to the shoes we had to wear—black three-inch pumps—that I wondered who these people were.

The ride to the Country Club took almost half an hour by the time I'd caught the connection. Marissa kept me company with her play-by-play text messages. She was on a date with a guy she had been seeing since we returned from Camp Chance. Although from the length of her messages, I gathered it wasn't going all that well.

Have you contacted him yet?

I rolled my eyes at Marissa's text. That was her style. Lull you into a false sense of security and then wham, hit you with the million-dollar question. The answer was always the same. No, I had not contacted Blake. I didn't know if I ever would.

After typing out a quick reply saying that I had arrived, I switched off my cell phone and tucked it into my purse. The bus stopped just outside of the vast grounds, so I'd left in plenty of time to find the main building. When I climbed off the bus, I headed in the direction of the country club. It was a members-only establishment on the outskirts of the city surrounded by luscious green golf courses. The clubhouse was located in the middle of the grounds at the end of a long, winding driveway. Forty minutes early, I took a steady walk to my destination.

Mary was on point tonight. She usually left things to Tara or a girl named Felicia, but West Lake was one of Mary's biggest clients and she couldn't afford to have any slip-ups. I felt the usual flutter of nerves in my stomach but quickly shook them off. This was a good gig. Sure, I had to mingle with high society, but aside from the occasional piranhas like Brittany, the majority of people we served didn't pay us any attention. We were invisible; there to serve and not be seen or heard. It suited me.

"You're early." Tara met me at the kitchen entrance and stepped aside to let me through. "Mary's inside getting herself worked up. It's not like we haven't done this kind of thing before."

I had a strange relationship with Tara. Ever since that first shift when she had warned me about Brittany and her friends, she'd kind of taken me under her wing without really befriending me.

Mary was pacing when I entered the kitchen. She looked up and her eyes sparkled. "Ahh, at last someone who knows what they're doing. Penny, can you go over the order of service again please with Milly and Natasha."

Me? I looked at her with wide eyes.

"You might be new, but you're one of my best girls. Now, don't just stand there. Get over here and whip these two into shape."

Milly and Natasha grimaced, and I half-smiled at them trying to reassure them. Mary was overwhelming. Like a mother who found it hard to let go but wanted her children to fly on their own all at the same time.

I spent the next ten minutes talking Milly and Natasha through the order of service. The gala was a five-course, sit-down meal followed by a silent table auction. West Lake had hired some B-list television personality to emcee the whole event. Touch of Class, Mary's company, was to provide drinks and food service for the evening.

Mary's words lingered in the back of my mind and a sense of pride took root in my chest. Despite my rocky start at the Hyatt, I liked working for Touch of Class. I'd come a long way since my days of hiding behind the scenes and pot washing in a hotel kitchen, and I was eager to work my first black tie event. The dresses, the glitz and glamour, I was intrigued—and maybe even a little excited—to experience a world so very different from my own.

And then Tara delivered four little words that left me with a sour taste in my mouth and a sinking feeling in my stomach.

"The piranhas are here."

I heard them before I saw them. The high octave of their laughter got louder as I worked my section of the room, offering guests flutes of champagne. I smiled and only spoke when spoken to. My back must have been to them because while I could hear their cackles and conversation, I couldn't spot them in the crowded room.

"... he won't be able to resist tonight." I wasn't purposely eavesdropping; they were that damn loud. Another voice said, "Do you think he's getting cold feet? It all happened pretty quickly?"

"Not really, Jenna. We both knew this was coming. Our fathers had this all planned out, and, besides, we're perfect for each other."

I swept around the group I'd just finished serving, and my eyes spotted them against the wall. Brittany Arnold and her minions. I had run into them at more than one event—the piranhas. According to Tara, her family was from old money, born and bred in Upper Arlington. Trent Arnold, Brittany's father, was CEO of Arnold Holdings.

"Oh look, it's Penelope." Brittany's voice dripped with contempt, but I let it roll off me.

Mostly.

My eyes caught the huge rock on her ring finger, and I shuddered inwardly. Who could possibly love someone like her? I had yet to witness one redeeming quality in her. Sure, she was beautiful and never looked less than runway worthy, but beneath all that makeup and money was a cold-hearted bitch.

Feeling riled, I bit out, "It's Penny, actually." I immediately regretted it, and in an attempt to recover my slip, I plastered on a fake smile and said, "Champagne?"

If there was one thing I'd learned quickly during my time working for Touch of Class, it was that you didn't correct these people.

The girls each helped themselves to a glass while Brittany's eyes burned into me as I tried to look anywhere but at her.

"My mistake, Penny. I just love what you've done with your hair. It's very, what do you call it? Trailer-chic."

My heart thudded in my chest. *How dare you,* I wanted to say. But I'd lose more than just my cool if I did. So I simply smiled and turned to leave. Brittany had other plans. She stepped to the side effectively blocking my passage. I tried to veer around her, but she stuck out her foot just as I moved. I felt myself fall. The silver tray clattered to the floor, glass shattering everywhere. All heads turned to me as I landed in a heap, my cheeks a deep crimson. I heard the gasps and low whispers, but only one voice perforated my embarrassment. "You really should watch where you watch step, Penelope."

Tara rushed over to me, handing her tray to one of the other servers. "Are you okay?" Her eyes flitted over my head to where Brittany and her friends stood.

I gave her a terse nod, embarrassment still weighing heavy in my chest. "Yeah, I'm fine. Help me get this mess cleaned up?"

"Ladies and gentleman, dinner will now be served. Please move into the Arlington Suite," a voice said, and I breathed a sigh of relief. The guests started to move away from us, queueing to enter the suite where they would spend the evening dining and donating. Brittany muttered something about how pathetic we were before joining the queue.

"What a freaking bitch," Tara said in a low voice when everyone was out of earshot.

I pushed myself up to my feet and blew out a long breath. "She tripped me."

"Oh, I know exactly what she did. She tried the same thing with me on my first shift. Come on, let's get this cleaned up. I'll sneak up a glass of West Lake's finest when we're done. Before the real fun starts."

True to her word, Tara swiped us two leftover champagne flutes and made me drink it before giving me a breath mint. "Sometimes, all you need is alcohol," she joked. "Feel ready to face them again?"

I shrugged. What choice did I have?

"Don't let them beat you, remember? Hold your head high and plaster the biggest, fakest smile on that pretty face of yours. If it weren't for us, half of the people out there would starve. They need us."

Her speech made me smile weakly, and although it was the biggest pile of utter crap I'd ever heard, it did make me feel a little better. Besides, I'd met worse than Brittany Arnold.

Survived worse.

"I'll swap sections with you. I'll take the piranhas tonight."

"No, I got it. It's fine. You're right."

Tara hopped down off the counter in the back of the kitchen and smoothed down her uniform. "Okay, let's do this."

We lined up with the rest of the servers at the service counter. The chefs were busy putting the final touches on the first course while bellowing orders at us. How to present the dish to the guests, to make sure the shrimp tail faces away. I rolled my eyes when Tara glanced back at me and grinned. When it was my turn, I loaded two small plates on my left arm, picked up another with my right, and followed Annabel, one of the regulars, out the door and into the dining room. Golds and royal blue, the colors of West Lake and Associates, embellished the whole room. I'd never met Mr. West, but some of the girls had worked his functions before. By all accounts, he was a formidable man and demanded nothing but the best.

I veered off to the left and entered my section, tables six through ten. Brittany sat at table six, my first stop. I inhaled deeply and approached her table. She looked up and smirked, but I ignored her and placed the plate down in front of the person seated opposite her. An older woman with gray-blond hair swept up in a sleek chignon sat to her right, and there were two empty seats to her right. *Odd*, I thought to myself, but I served the appetizers starting with the person seated next to one of the empty seats. It was petty, but it meant I would serve Brittany last. My small sense of payback.

I returned to the kitchen and collected three more plates. When I arrived back at table six, I had to clear my throat to be heard over the gaggle. "Will the other guests be joining us?"

"My fiancé and father will be here shortly. Please leave their appetizers." Brittany's bark was worse than her bite, and I tipped my head.

As I walked back to the kitchen, I glanced back at table six.

And stopped dead.

Two men were approaching the table. One, an older man with graying hair, was obviously her father. He had Brittany's eyes. Her evil smirk. He sat in the empty seat furthest from his daughter. The other man leaned over Brittany's shoulder, smiled at everyone, and pressed a brief kiss to her cheek. Her whole face lit up. He sat down. I wanted to sink to the floor. Wanted the ground to open up and swallow me whole. He wrapped an arm around her shoulders. I wanted to throw things at her face. To hurt her for far more than just choosing to make my life as a server hell.

She had the one thing I wanted but could never have.

She had Blake.

chapter nineteen

"Penny, Penny." Someone shook me forcefully, but my eyes were transfixed on table six.

On Blake and her.

Brittany Arnold was Blake's fiancée.

His person was the piranha.

"Penny, what the hell has gotten into you?" Tara barked with such bite that I jumped. "Huh, what?" I blinked at her and then turned my attention back to Blake.

And her.

Her.

"Sorry, I'm fine. Fine." My voice sounded anything but fine.

"Whatever you say," Tara said. "Can you still do your job?"

"Yes, yes, I can do my job. I'm fine," I reiterated as I tried to convince us both.

Tara mumbled something under her breath and rolled her eyes. I didn't take it personally; it was just her way. Besides, I was too concerned with how close Blake and Brittany looked.

Mary breezed into the kitchen beaming. "Fabulous job, darlings. Tara, you handle cleanup, and Sophie, you take point on the second course." Her eyes landed on me, and her smile faltered. "Penny, is everything okay? You look a little pale, darling. You're not getting sick are you? Mr. Weston would be most concerned if you're spreading germs to half of the city."

Weston?

As in Blake Weston?

My lips drew into a tight line, and I forced them into a half-smile. "I'm fine, just a little tired. Noisy neighbors." I shrugged as if it was no big deal. It was almost the truth.

Mary's perfect smile was back in place in an instance. "Well then, shall we?" She gave Tara a curt nod and disappeared out of the kitchen.

I grabbed Tara by the arm sharply. "She said Mr. Weston? I thought it was Mr. West?"

"He's the West in West Lake and Associates, but his actual name is Weston, as in, Anthony Weston."

Blake's uncle was Anthony Weston, of West Lake and Associates? My stomach knotted tightly and then unraveled as it plummeted to the floor.

Tara's dark eyes narrowed at me. "Why all the questions?"

"Nothing, I, hmm, I, nothing. It doesn't matter."

She huffed. "Well, if you're finished getting your period, can we go do our jobs now?"

Our jobs, of course.

"Of course."

I followed Tara out of the swinging door and into the room. My eyes remained lowered, but it didn't stop me from peeking out from under my lashes to watch him. *Them.* Blake and Brittany were sitting slightly angled toward one another, his arm draped over the back of her chair. As I drew closer, I noticed they were talking to other people seated at their table, laughing and joking as if they were all old friends. Blake looked at ease with a playful expression on his face, the same one I'd witnessed so many times during the summer. The tailored, crisp white shirt molded to his broad shoulders. He looked good in a tux. Too good. His hair was shorter, styled to perfection, and even the scruff covering his jaw that I'd come to love over the summer was gone.

Who is this person?

No one even looked up as I approached the table. Not even a cursory glance. It was as if I was nothing. Insignificant… Invisible. I sure felt it.

I worked quickly; collecting the empty plates from each guest's left side, I risked only the occasional glance over at Blake and Brittany. They were in full conversation with the woman seated at Brittany's other side who I assumed was her mother. She had the same cold eyes as her daughter. Blake smiled at something she said, his lips hooking up on the side. It was such a simple gesture, but it caused the air to suck right from my lungs. It was the moment I realized that this wasn't all some dreadful mistake. A production crew wasn't about to leap out from hiding and announce that this was all part of some elaborate prank. No, the truth was staring me right in the face—Blake wasn't just with these people… he was one of them.

A wave of nausea slammed into me and I stumbled backward. The stack of plates balanced in my hand wobbled and a knife rolled off the edge and clattered to the floor. Ten faces glared at my incompetence, but I didn't see them; I only saw two blue eyes filled with shock and horror. We remained staring at one another for longer than we should have. Long enough to earn a confused look from Brittany as she tried to piece together how Blake could possibly know someone like me—the hired help. She laid a hand on his arm commanding his attention. I used the moment to collect the remaining plates and get the hell out of there.

My back pressed to the wall where I stood with the other servers watching Anthony Weston deliver his opening speech. His presence didn't live up to the rumors. He wasn't just formidable; he was terrifying. A tall, well-built man with a thick head of salt and pepper hair, he spoke with such poise and certainty that not a single sound could be heard. Guests raised a toast, clinking their glasses when required, but when Mr. Weston was talking, every single person in the room listened.

"Now that the formalities are out of the way, I have one last announcement to make before I hand you over to our emcee for the evening, Mike Carter. As some of you know, seven years ago, I discovered I had a nephew…" My heart slammed in my chest, and I inhaled trying to breathe. "The day Blake came to live with my wife, Miranda, and me, I gained the son I never had. Well, tonight I can announce that I am to also gain a daughter."

Mr. Weston raised his glass in the direction of table six, but I forced myself not to look. If I looked, the thread I was hanging by would surely snap.

"I can think of no better match for Blake than Brittany. The Arnold and Weston families have a history that goes back decades, and now, they also have a future." He said her name as if she was royalty, like everyone in the room would automatically know who she was. "Please raise a glass in toasting their engagement and wishing them a future filled with happiness and success. To Blake and Brittany."

The thread snapped.

I excused myself quietly and rushed into the kitchen unable to catch my breath. Heads whipped in my direction, but I ignored their confused glances as I made a beeline for the staff restrooms at the back of the building. My body crashed through the door, and I fell into the first stall slamming the door behind me. I crumpled down onto the seat and pinched my eyes shut trying to stop the tears from falling.

Fiancée.

He had a freaking fiancée.

Short, ragged breaths heaved in and out of my chest as my world crashed down around me. All summer, I'd slowly allowed Blake in. Smile by smile. Heated look by heated look. And although I felt the change in him, I thought it was time's doing. I was too blinded by his presence to realize the boy I'd once known was gone. The imposter sitting at table six looked like my Blake, smiled like him… but it wasn't him. He wasn't my lost, messy-haired kid with the crooked smile who showed me the stars and dreamed of a future where we made our own rules. The man out there in the designer tux drinking the expensive champagne from a crystal flute didn't have to worry about making his next rent check or working shitty jobs to make ends meet. He didn't know what it was like to be so haunted by the past that you didn't live, you only existed.

With each thought, each painful memory, my fragile heart shattered all over again.

I'd known Blake had someone—he had told me as much—but I was too lost in our memories. One look at him across the fire and my soul remembered even when I wanted to forget. I couldn't ignore the way our hearts called to one another. I'd spent the whole summer letting Blake back in, letting him mend the broken pieces of me.

Was it all a lie?

And if it was, where did we go from here?

The door to the restrooms opened, and Tara's voice called, "Penny, are you in here?"

I reached around, flushed the toilet, and then dried my eyes on some paper. "Yeah, I'm fine." Drawing a deep breath, I exited the stall catching my reflection in the mirrored wall opposite.

I looked like shit.

"Are you okay? You don't look so well." Concern flashed in Tara's eyes, but she quickly replaced it with annoyance.

"I think I have the stomach flu," I lied clutching my stomach and gagging for added effect.

"Shit," she cursed. "Mary will freak. Get out of here, and I'll cover for you. You had a family emergency, right?"

"Thank you."

"Go. Sneak out the back exit."

I nodded and hurried out of the restrooms. After retrieving my purse from the lockers, I left the clubhouse.

I didn't allow myself to cry again until I got back to the apartment.

"Oh, shit. How did I not know this?" Marissa's voice went all high pitched, and I moved the cell phone away from my ear. "Penny? Pen, are you there?"

"Yeah, I'm here." I sighed, exhausted from a night spent sobbing into my pillow. I cried until my eyes stung and there were no tears left to cry.

"Get your laptop," she ordered.

"Laptop? I don't have one," I replied meekly.

Marissa gasped down the line. "What the hell? Do you live in the dark ages? How do you watch Netflix or Google shit? How do you do that thing we all do called social media?"

I shrugged picking at one of the threads hanging from the couch. "I go to the library."

"We need to get you hooked up, pronto."

I rolled my eyes, a little annoyed at her presumptions. Didn't she realize I couldn't afford it? My reasons would only fall on deaf ears, though, so I remained silent.

"Okay. Well, then I'll Google, and you listen. Hang on. I'll put you on speaker."

The line went quiet except for the sound of the frantic tapping of keys. *Tap, tap, tap.*

"Ah-ha, I have something." Her voice startled me, and I leaned back on the couch feeling as if I might need the extra support. "Anthony Weston, founder of West Lake and Associates, blah, blah, blah, adopts nephew, Blake Weston, after discovering his estranged sister had died following a drugs overdose. Blake had been put in foster care following his father's arrest and subsequent incarceration for drug offenses. Anthony and his wife, Miranda, ask that reporters respect their privacy at this sensitive time.

"Oh, wait, there's something else. It's a photo of Blake with his aunt, uncle, and the Arnold family. That's her family, right? Piranha bitch… does she have long blond hair and eyes that could kill a girl dead with just one look?"

That's her.

"Yes." I sighed sadly trying hard not to conjure up the image of Blake pressing his lips to her cheek. Lips that had kissed me.

"Daughter of Trent Arnold, CEO of Arnold Holdings, is to attend Ohio State with a family friend and nephew of Anthony Weston, yada, yada, yada…"

My mental dam broke and images of Blake and Brittany flooded my mind. I imagined them attending class together, romantic picnics in Lincoln Tower Park, watching the Buckeyes on game day, and lazy mornings in his dorm room.

That should have been us.

The thought punched me in the chest, and I clenched my eyes tight forcing out my thoughts.

"Oh, I have more. They-"

"Stop."

"What?" Marissa said, and I could imagine the frown

etched across her forehead. "Come on, Penny, we need to know the facts. He left you the note, so he's obviously not happy with her. Who would be..." She launched into a dissection of their relationship, but I tuned out. Blake had said it was complicated; only now, I realized he didn't mean with Brittany. He meant with me.

I was the complication.

But that wasn't good enough for me. I didn't want to be someone's problem or hurdle... or temptation. I wanted to be someone's reason.

I wanted to be Blake's reason.

Foolishly, I thought we were getting a second chance, but now, all I saw was a million reasons why our story would never be rewritten.

chapter twenty

Blake

Age 16

I hated this fucking place.

And I hated Anthony Weston.

He had ruined everything.

Everything.

Ripped me from the only person I cared about. The one person who needed me.

My other half.

At first, when Derek and Marie had requested I join them in the living room—*their* room—I thought they were going to give me more shit. Any little excuse to hound me, and they were on me like flies on shit. But when the man in the expensive suit walked in, I knew something was up.

I didn't expect to find out he was my uncle on Mom's

side. Anthony Weston of West Lake and Associates, one of the biggest law firms in all of Columbus. He'd tracked us down—well, tracked Mom down only to discover she was six feet under thanks to my drug-dealing father who was now locked up in prison.

Derek and Marie sat with their smug grins as Anthony explained he had come to take me away. I would have been lying if I said escaping the Freeman's wasn't a tempting offer, but if Penny wasn't going, then neither was I. It had taken Anthony and Derek both to manhandle me out of the house and into the Town Car waiting at the side of the house. Now, I was prisoner in their damn near mansion on the outskirts of Upper Arlington.

"Blake. Please come down for dinner," Aunt Miranda called easing some of the storm in me. I'd tried to hate her—wanted to—but it was impossible when the woman looked at me with such understanding and patience.

I pushed off my bed and made my way downstairs. When I'd arrived at the house, a little over two weeks ago, they'd shown me to a bedroom furnished for your average sixteen-year-old. Neutral walls with blue painted stripes running across the wall that had a king-size bed pushed up against it covered with a dark blue comforter, and dark furniture complete with a flat-screen television and gaming system, a laptop, and docking station. We didn't even have a flat screen in the den at the Freeman's; we had one of those consoles that took up a whole corner of the room.

None of it mattered.

I wanted Penny and No Man's Land and stolen moments of freedom; I didn't want the Weston's money and gadgets. Or to be forty miles away from Lancaster.

I wanted to know Penny was okay.

Voices traveled through the vast hallway. "He'll adjust. Give him time." My aunt's voice was soft, a stark contrast to the commanding tone of my uncle's voice.

"Time? He should be thankful we saved him from that place. He will never want for anything again, and he can't even join us for dinner on time? It's unacceptable, Miranda," my uncle said with little emotion.

"Ant, please, give him time. You'll see."

I strolled into the kitchen as if I hadn't just heard them discussing me and said, "Did you contact the Freemans yet to see if Penny wrote me back? She should have gotten the letter by now, right?"

My aunt and uncle shared a look, and my heart constricted.

"Blake." My uncle was using his 'official business' tone as if I was one of his fucking cases. "I have already explained that it isn't that simple. We can't just call them up and-"

"Why? Why can't you just call them up and ask? You just turned up and took me away."

Uncle Anthony pushed away from the table, his chair scraping across the floor tiles, and stood abruptly. "Son, you need to listen and listen good. Forget the girl. Forget that house. I pulled a lot of strings to get you out of there. I'm sorry you had to leave your friend, but you need to let her go. It's for the best."

Friend?

Didn't he know Penny was more than just my friend?

That she was my everything?

Anger and frustration swirled together in my stomach, and I exploded. I grabbed the back of one of the chairs and picked it up and threw it at the wall. It didn't smash, but it did splinter. A shred of guilt shot through me when Aunt Miranda clasped her hand over her mouth and gasped. Uncle Anthony's eyes burned into me, but I didn't hang around long enough to feel his wrath.

I was out of there.

I didn't get very far.

Until two weeks ago, I had never even set foot in Upper Arlington. So I took a bag of chips from the overstocked cupboards and went to the perimeter of the grounds. The kitchen door walked out onto a beautiful decked area that led to a huge pool. Past the pool was a vast lawn area, which backed to Canterbury Woods. If I wasn't here under duress, I would have appreciated just how awesome it was. The yard seemed never ending, but I finally arrived at the fence. I dropped down to my knees and scooted onto my butt. It was still early, not even six. Darkness wouldn't fall for another hour or so. I didn't care, though. I just needed to feel close to her.

I lay there on the springy grass, staring up at the clouds with my fingers outstretched at my side, imagining Penny next to me. We'd talk about our day, and our dreams for the future. She'd lean over to kiss me and I would yank her down on top of me and take more.

Always more.

Never enough.

Pain sliced through my chest. We were going to give ourselves to one another. Once she turned seventeen, I was going to make Penny mine in every way possible. She was going to be my first.

My only.

It was as if Derek had known what we were planning to do and orchestrated the whole thing just to get back at me. The smug look on his face as Anthony announced I was leaving the Freeman home five weeks before Penny turned seventeen. I promised her the world and now she was all alone in that hell. And I had no fucking idea if she knew the real reason I had left. I had begged for a chance to explain things to Penny, to visit her, or at least, call her. But of course, Uncle Anthony wouldn't hear of it. So I did the only thing I could. I wrote her a letter.

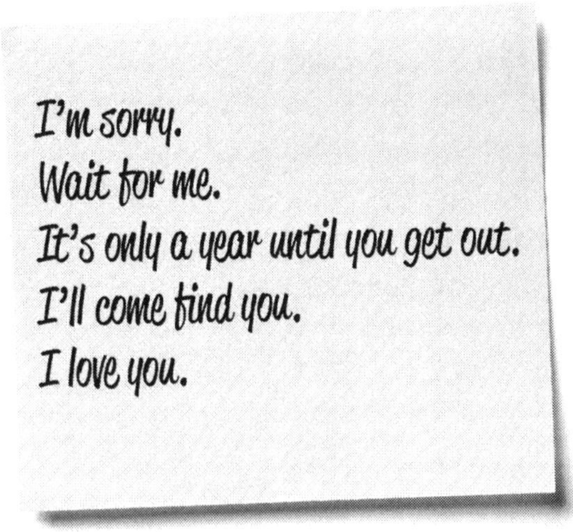
I'm sorry.
Wait for me.
It's only a year until you get out.
I'll come find you.
I love you.

One page of scrawl that promised her we would find our way back to each other. That one way or another, we would be together. Uncle Anthony promised me that he would make sure it arrived at the Freeman's; he was probably sending Max, his driver. I still couldn't get my head around the fact that growing up with Mom, we couldn't afford groceries, and he had someone to drive him. But as long as the letter got there, I didn't care who delivered it.

Anthony had to pull a lot of strings to get guardianship of me and wasn't prepared to have me jeopardize his sacrifices. *His sacrifices.* I scoffed into the air. I didn't know why he'd bothered—the man despised me. He had shown me nothing but contempt since taking me out of the group home. I'd only been here two weeks, and it was already as if I owed him the world. I didn't ask him to come and get me; I didn't want to be here.

Couldn't he see that?

I wanted to be with Penny. With Mason and Peter, even Ben. They were my friends, my family. Not the emotionally devoid robot back in the house. I didn't know him. He certainly didn't know anything about me, about what I'd survived. Where was he when Mom was strung out on her latest cocktail of drugs while Dad was out on the streets of Lancaster pushing that shit to kids looking to get a quick high?

Penny, tell me what to do?

What do I do?

A pained cry burst from my lungs. I closed my eyes and fought back the tears building. I couldn't cry. Men didn't cry, and I was a man now. Something told me that in my uncle's world, I would need to grow the hell up. He hadn't saved me from hell; he'd just replaced my prison.

"Disrespect mealtime again and you can eat in your room

like an animal." My uncle dropped his knife and fork onto his plate, rose from the table, and started for the door. He paused and turned back to me. "You register at Wellington in two weeks. I suggest you adjust your attitude before then."

With that bombshell, he left.

Wellington? The words were on the tip of my tongue, but I swallowed them down. Aunt Miranda sighed deeply. "He'll come around."

"Will he?" My plate of untouched food remained on the table. I sat down and picked at the salad.

"I can reheat the chicken?" Miranda offered.

"No, it's fine. I shouldn't have left." Why was I making it sound like an apology?

Miranda smiled and sat down opposite me. "You know, Blake, we really are happy to have you with us. When Ant found out that Imogen was, well, that she was gone, his heart was broken. He loved her more than anything, but then we discovered she had a son, you, and Ant was hell-bent on finding you. We could never have children, you see..." Her eyes glazed over with sadness. "Ant wanted to know his only nephew. News that you were in a foster home was the decider. He pulled every string he could to bring you home to us. Family. We're your family now, Blake. Please give him a chance." She reached across the table and laid her hand over mine. The feeling felt foreign, but a lump formed in my throat.

It had been so long since I'd had to look out for myself. And Aunt Miranda seemed nice. As if she actually gave a shit about me.

"Wellington?" I asked needing to fill the awkward silence. Aunt Miranda nodded and said, "Yes, it's the private school in Upper Arlington. Ant is good friends with the head. He pulled some strings."

I grit my teeth hard. *Of course, he did.*

Private school?

Things just got a hell of a lot worse.

Fourteen long days later, I found myself trapped in Miranda's Porsche as she drove me to Wellington. There was a school bus, but she wanted to see that I arrived safely. Although I figured it was probably just Anthony's way of making sure I didn't skip class. I stared out of the window tugging at the navy blue polo shirt Miranda had given me. It seemed all a little too convenient that they had a stash of uniforms waiting for me. It was the same with the fully decorated and equipped bedroom. I hadn't asked much about when or how they found out I was in Lancaster, but something told me it involved Uncle Anthony pulling a lot more than just strings.

"See the salmon colored building up ahead? That's Wellington. Alumni of eighty-eight. I have fond memories of this place," Miranda cooed as she turned off the main road and onto the private road. As we approached the main building, I noticed a playground off to one side.

"They have all grades here?"

Miranda rolled her Porsche to a halt and cut the engine. She turned to me. "Sorry, we're not doing a very good job of this so far, are we? Yes, it's a co-ed pre-school through grade twelve school. Small classes, excellent extracurricular program. I think you'll really like it here."

I nodded. What else could I do when the woman sitting opposite me was giving me such a hopeful look?

"You have an appointment with the head of the high school, Mr. Spellman. I'm sure he'll get you settled. I'll pick you up today and then maybe tomorrow you can try the bus or Max could drive you? I'm sure your uncle wouldn't mind."

Yeah, right. I nodded again and reached for the door handle. As I climbed out of the car and hitched my bag up my shoulders, I drew in a deep breath.

One year. You only have to survive one year of this shit.

For you.

For Penny.

"Thanks for the ride," I called back to Miranda as she watched me walk up to the glass doors. She waved, and I headed inside.

The silver Porsche disappeared out of sight. It shouldn't have bothered me; new situations were something you got used to growing up in foster care, but something about this place had me on edge.

I wasn't private school material.

In tenth grade, I spent more time goofing around and getting into fights than I did studying. It wasn't that I couldn't do the work, I just preferred not to. Penny was always yanking my chain about my study habits. I doubted a school like this would appreciate a kid like me bringing down their reputation.

Penny. A whole month away from her, and she still consumed my thoughts.

"Hello, can I help you?" An older lady with silver hair

and thick rimmed glasses smiled up at me from her desk behind the counter.

"I'm the new kid. Blake Weston."

She glanced me up and down, and her smile grew wider. "We're pleased to have you, Blake. Welcome to Wellington. I'm Mrs. Freids, but you can call me Dorothy."

Okay then. My lips drew into a tight line, curling up at one side. She seemed genuine, but I hardly looked the part. My polo shirt was already creased and I'd opted not to wear the shoes Miranda had left out for me. I preferred my worn in chucks.

"If you'll follow me, I'll take you down to Mr. Spellman's office. He's expecting you."

We walked in silence down a long hallway before she stopped outside a door. There were two seats to the left and I smiled inwardly. At Lancaster High, I was well acquainted with the principal's office.

Dorothy knocked, waited a couple of seconds, and then opened the door. "Good luck," she whispered before ushering me inside. The door clicked shut behind me. My eyes took in the room. It was light and airy with a huge glass window overlooking a playing field. It looked like the football team was running drills.

"Welcome to Wellington, Mr. Weston. Please, have a seat," said the man seated behind a huge desk positioned in front of the window. "I'm Dr. Spellman."

"Doctor?" The word just tumbled out, and I silently cursed. Taking a seat opposite him, I dropped my bag and sat rigid.

A slight smile broke over his face causing his eyes to wrinkle around the corners. "Doctor of Education."

I tipped my chin and waited. Spellman leaned forward to rest his elbows on the table and clasped his hands while he regarded me. "I'm good friends with your uncle. I feel confident your time here at Wellington will be smooth and enriching. I have taken a quick look at your files from Lancaster, and I think you have a lot of potential, son. We just need to…" His lips curved into a slight smile. "Focus your energies."

"I just want to graduate high school… sir."

"Of course, Blake. I understand this must be a difficult transition for you, so how about we give it some time. Let you settle and find your feet here at Wellington."

"Okay." What else was there to say? It wasn't as if I had much choice in the matter. Until I turned eighteen, my life belonged to Anthony and Miranda. He had made that perfectly clear.

"I've arranged for a student to help you settle. Brittany."

I turned around, following Spellman's line of sight. A girl in a Wellington uniform sat in the corner of the room. She smiled at me, and I gave her a slight nod. I didn't need—or want—a babysitter. Especially, not queen bee over there.

"Hi, I'm Brittany Arnold. Our families are good friends."

I bristled. I might have shared the same name as Anthony and Miranda, but they were not my family. The only family I had was back in Lancaster.

"Blake," I replied curtly.

She smiled again and smoothed her long blond hair over her shoulder. She was one of *those* girls; the mean girls who thought they were above everyone else. Just like the girls at Lancaster High who made Penny's life hell. It oozed from her fake smile.

"I can show you to second period?"

"Blake, I trust you'll be okay in Miss Arnold's hands?"

Penny's face flashed in my mind, and I wanted to close my eyes and lose myself in her chocolate eyes. But I couldn't. Spellman was burning holes into my head, and Brittany was looking at me as if she wanted to do more than just show me to second period.

Fuck.

chapter twenty-one

I stayed off work all week. Every time Mary called, I lied and said I was still attending to the 'family emergency.' I hated to lie, and guilt weighed heavy on my mind, but the alternative was worse. Part of me wanted to quit. I'd even written out my resignation letter, but something was holding me back. My heart was ready to walk away, to shut itself off and live a life of meaningless solitude again, but this time, my head refused to accept it had to be that way.

When Friday rolled around again, I knew it was crunch time. I wasn't being fair to Mary, and I needed to know if I was going to be looking for work again.

And I needed air.

I'd avoided leaving the apartment for fear of someone from Touch of Class noticing me. Like now, as I hurried along the sidewalk en route back to The Oriental Garden from the store. I'd finally run out of lavender scented candles and air fresheners and feared the smell of fried egg rolls was going to suffocate me.

In the short time from leaving my apartment to exiting the store, dusk had settled over Clintonville. I pulled my jacket tighter as I turned off the high street into the alley separating The Oriental Garden and Bernie's Bar. It was only just after six, but it was a Friday night and college students didn't need an excuse to start their weekend early. Usually, the crowds of students spilled out onto the street smoking and drinking paid me little attention, but it didn't stop me from holding my breath every time.

A couple of guys wolf whistled at me as I moved past them, but it deflected off me as my pace quickened. Focused only on reaching the stairwell to my apartment, I rounded the last corner and walked straight into somebody.

"Shit," a startled voice said.

"Marissa?" I asked, stepping back and blinking to make sure my eyes weren't deceiving me.

"The one and only," she smirked rubbing a hand where our heads had bumped. Without thinking, I launched myself at her wrapping my arms around her slender figure. She laughed and hugged me back. I didn't flinch or step out of her grasp—I embraced the feeling. Until now, I hadn't realized just how much I missed her. Marissa had played as much of a role in my summer—my healing—as Blake had.

Almost.

"I've missed you."

"I know." Marissa stepped back holding me at arm's length. "Douchebag guys look good on you. You need to tell me your secret. Now, are you going to make me stand out here all night or are you going to invite me up?"

Oh, shit. Marissa was here, standing outside of my apartment. The one that had damp rot, smelled like fried foods, and had no internet.

"Hmm, it's not exactly homey." I dropped my eyes; I regretted leaving it until the last possible minute to fetch more air fresheners.

"Please, I couldn't give a shit. We spent the whole summer sleeping on cots and being eaten alive by bugs."

She had a point.

"Okay, well, follow me."

Marissa didn't say a word as I led her into the apartment. I hit the lights and dumped the bags on the counter. When I turned around, Marissa was standing with her arms folded across her chest with her nose pointed into the air. "What in holy hell's name is that smell?"

I winced eyeing the bag containing the lavender air fresheners. *If only you'd arrived an hour later.* "Fried egg rolls with a hint of lavender," I said as if it was a normal everyday scent.

Marissa lurched, fake gagging, and then burst into laughter. "Lavender egg rolls? That's fucking disgusting."

"Tell me about it," I replied through my own laughter. "Coffee?"

"I might need something stronger than coffee to help me forget the stench."

"Expresso?"

"Geez." Marissa rolled her eyes playfully. "You're like party central up here."

I made us both coffee and joined Marissa on the threadbare couch sitting quietly while she glanced around the apartment. "I love what you've done with the place."

"It's not much, but it's all I have."

"You're a bit of a mystery, Penny Wilson, but I love you

for it." Her endearment rendered me speechless. We had forged a close friendship over the summer, but I wasn't sure it would extend much outside of Camp Chance. Marissa was full of surprises.

"It's so good to see you, and don't take this the wrong way, but what the hell are you doing here, Marissa? You never mentioned coming to visit." Marissa had an apartment in Mansfield just south of Akron. She had just started work as a fitness instructor at a private health club.

"Call this a friend intervention," she stated before taking a mouthful of coffee.

"Intervention?"

"Penny, don't you think I know what this last week has been about? You're in some kind of post-Blake funk, and I know you're thinking about quitting your job. Which, by the way, is a ridiculous idea." Marissa's eyes roamed over the room again, and I could see her mind ticking over.

My fingers gripped my mug tighter, and I stared down at the steaming dark liquid. "I haven't decided what to do."

"Penny, you can't quit. Don't give her the satisfaction."

"Her?" My head whipped up to meet Marissa's face, and she smiled sadly. "Okay, them. Don't give *them* the satisfaction."

"It's not about giving them the satisfaction, Marissa. It's about not putting myself through that again." I placed my mug on the table. "When I saw him sit down beside her, I thought there must be some kind of mistake. Even though I'd seen Blake kiss her, I didn't want to believe it. Couldn't believe it. But then I heard his uncle announce their engagement, and I almost puked right there in the middle of the gala dinner."

Tears rolled down my cheeks and dropped off my chin onto my sweater. Marissa cursed under her breath and set down her mug, reaching out for my hand. "Penny, I can't imag-"

"Don't. I spent the last seven years of my life closed off, Marissa. Do you know what it's like to live each day feeling numb? Void? Blake was a part of that. Not all of it, sure, but some. Seeing him again was like a dream. All my worst nightmares and fairy tales rolled into one. And I tried to deal with that, in my own way, but then he started proclaiming he never forgot? That he still feels things for me? What am I supposed to do with that?" My chest hurt—I couldn't tell if it was from the rush of words or the memories, but I needed air. Inhaling deeply, I let the stale air fill my lungs and give me the energy I needed to continue.

"I tried so hard to keep my past in the past, but he refused to stay there. Blake wormed his way back into my heart, and I let him. He told me he had someone, Marissa, and I still let him in. What the hell is wrong with me?"

Marissa released my hand only to wrap me in her arms. I sank into her comfort overcome by emotion. When was the last time I'd let someone hold me like this?

Blake.

Blake was the last person.

It always came back to Blake.

"Nothing is wrong with you. You did what anyone in your shoes would have done. You were confused and blindsided." She hesitated. I felt it in her. "You should call him," Marissa all but whispered.

I tore myself out of her arms and stared at her as if she'd just grown a second head. "Wh-what?"

"Blake. You should call Blake."

"Did you just hear anything I just said? I can't call him. He's engaged, Marissa, engaged," I said as if repeating it would make it any less painful. "There was a time when I thought we were the same, but we're not. We're from different worlds. Blake lives in a world I'll never fit in. He's freaking high society or something." I was starting to sound hysterical.

"Penny, just hear me out, please."

I shook my head frantically as my hold on reality started to slip.

I couldn't lose myself to him.

To her.

Because if I lost myself again, who would bring me back this time? I was all out of second chances. With a strange sense of resolution, I said, "No, Marissa, it's done. I refuse to live in the past. I can't. No more, I- I just can't."

Marissa stayed the whole night. We ate noodles and dim sum from The Oriental Garden and watched reruns of *Friends* on cable. She didn't mention Blake again. And I didn't bring him up. But I did heed one piece of Marissa's advice. I texted Mary to let her know that as of Monday I would be able to pick up shifts again, requesting local gigs when possible. I just hoped she would be okay with that. If she asked why, I was prepared to stick with Tara's cover of a family emergency. I needed the job, but I didn't need to run into Blake or Brittany anytime soon.

Before we had fallen asleep, I'd retrieved Blake's note

and set it alight with one of the lavender scented candles burning in the room. It was time to cleanse him out of my life for good. As the paper charred and burned into oblivion, a strange sense of acceptance washed over me. Maybe it was all the fortune cookies or pop or even the fumes from the takeout seeping up from the kitchen below, but I'd been doing well—too well—to let the revelations of the last week push me back into my mental prison.

When I woke, Marissa had already left, but not before sticking a note to my refrigerator. It simply said *a lifetime of possibilities.* As my eyes stared at her scribble, I smiled to myself.

I'd had one summer.

Now, I had my life to live.

It sounded simple enough, but until the summer, living was something I'd only had glimpses of over the last twelve years. I'd stopped living the day a truck ran my dad's car off the road and into a ravine. The day my parents died, I died.

Only I didn't.

I walked away from the accident with little more than a few scrapes and bruises. To the medical professionals and social workers, there was barely anything physically wrong with an eleven-year-old girl who watched her parents take their last breaths. But what they couldn't see was the emotional damage—the damage on the inside. My heart was broken.

Marissa had said something to me last night; she'd asked me to tell her about them, to tell her about Stephen and Alice Wilson, life givers to me. All these years later, and after countless therapists, I still couldn't talk to them about my parents without crying. But when my tears were all dried out, Marissa had taken my hand in hers and whispered, 'don't you think they'd want you to live, Penny?'

She was right; of course, they would want me to live. They would want me to date and get married and start a family. They would want me to take risks and fall and pick myself back up again. To fall in love and experience heartbreak, making vows never to love again, only to do it all over again. My parents would wish the world for me and more. But it had taken losing Blake again to realize only I could change my destiny. I didn't need to let my past define me; I needed to let it shape me and mold me and push me.

But I needed to do this my way. Baby steps. The apartment seemed like a good place to start. Okay, so money was in short demand and moving out wasn't an option, but it didn't mean I couldn't at least try to make the most of the place. After showering and changing into leggings and a baggy sweater, I texted Marissa to say thank you for stopping by and then grabbed my purse.

Operation egg rolls was about to commence.

chapter twenty-two

The weeks passed by and I replaced lavender with cinnamon and pumpkin. Thanksgiving was right around the corner, and it was the first year I had bothered to embrace the tradition. An oak wreath hung on the door, not that anyone ever came to visit except Marissa on the odd occasion, and I had a pumpkin display in the window. Marissa invited me to spend the holidays with her and her family, but I declined. Mary needed extra staff over the weekend, and I was saving up to move out of the apartment. It was going to take a long time… a really long time, to save up until I could afford anything nice, but I wanted more.

I'd been working for Mary for almost three months. Since the black tie gala dinner at the country club, I only worked events in the Clintonville and downtown Columbus areas. I didn't run into Blake or Brittany again. But I did find a new friend in Tara. She worked full time for Mary, and with me picking up all the shifts I could, our paths crossed on a regular basis.

"Penny, wait up," Tara said as people filtered out of the staff room. It had been a long shift serving an early Thanksgiving feast to sixty veterans, and I just wanted to get back to the apartment, take a shower, and sleep. "Mary asked me to ask you if you could cover for Milly tomorrow night. Cody's sick, and she can't get a sitter."

"It's my only day off all holiday weekend," I groaned, a painful burn shooting up through my feet.

"Grandview Heights. There's a Thanksgiving banquet fundraiser at The Grand."

"A hotel?"

Tara nodded.

"Black tie?" I asked zipping up my parka. The weather had taken a cold turn recently and having to walk everywhere or catch the bus required layers.

"No…" Tara shook her head as she jammed her hands in her knitted mitts. "It's a local organization raising money for some charity, I think. It's pretty low key. Nothing you can't handle."

I rolled my eyes. Tara knew I wouldn't say no. Nothing was a deal breaker unless I heard the words Upper Arlington, and Mary never asked me to work out there anymore.

"Okay, I'll do it. Have Mary text me the details. I need to get back and sleep."

Tara gave me one of her half-smiles and waved me off. With each step, I winced. My feet were on fire and I felt sure when I removed my shoes there would be gaping holes. The ice underfoot mocked me as I stepped out onto the sidewalk, and I almost tore off my shoes and walked the short distance home barefoot.

It didn't take long to reach The Oriental Garden, and for once, I was relieved to get back to the apartment. Everything was quieter at this time of year. Students returned home for the holiday weekend and local businesses, especially the bars, remained empty. Bernie's still saw a few regulars pass through its doors, but there wasn't the usual horde of students overflowing onto the street.

The first thing I did when I entered the apartment was crank up the heat. I stripped off and grabbed a towel from the pile of clean washing folded on the end of the bed. Twenty minutes spent under the steamy jet of water and I still didn't feel clean. Working for Mary was a good gig and it paid well, but the hours were usually long. And after hours spent serving people food and drinks, I usually came home smelling worse than lavender egg rolls.

But it was worth it.

Mary's could be my ticket out of the apartment.

Out of Clintonville.

The Grand was situated on Fifth Avenue, which ran all the way from the Scioto River right over the Olentangy River and out to Shepard. It looked more like a modern apartment building than a hotel, but certain I had the right address, I made my way inside.

The receptionist pointed me in the right direction, and soon, I arrived outside the Herrick Suite. When I entered the room, Tara was busy giving orders to two girls I didn't recognize. When she noticed me, she lifted a hand and gave me a slight wave. I waved back and gave the room my attention. If I'd learned anything in my time working for Touch of Class, it was to know your room, the layout, and the service areas. Mary's team rarely worked the same venue, and when we did, it was usually in a different suite or with a different setup.

"So service is for fifty. Five tables of ten. You and Jamie take tables one through three, the new girl and I will take tables four and five. Set courses, one vegetarian on table three." Tara handed me her clipboard, which outlined a detailed table plan. "Guests will be seated for seven. That gives us forty minutes to finish prepping the tables. The hotel did most of it, but some of the cutlery needs repolishing. Jamie," Tara yelled over my shoulder. "Can you grab a cloth and start on the cutlery?"

"Sounds good," I said. "Do we know what it is exactly yet?"

"Alumni of Ohio State or something. It's an annual thing. I just go where I'm told. You know that." She winked and snatched her clipboard back out of my hands. "Now, don't you have cutlery to polish?"

My laughter chased Tara away as she went to oversee the new girl. I assumed Mary had given her instructions to keep her eyes on her. "Yes, boss," I shouted across the room earning an eye roll from Tara and a strange look from the new girl.

Forty-five minutes later, we watched from our area toward the back of the room as people took their seats around tables decorated with orange roses and cinnamon stick displays. Once everyone was seated, we headed into the kitchen to collect the first course, which was spiced pumpkin soup. Tara was last in as she was doubling as server and maître d'.

"Piranha. Table two. Sorry, I didn't know."

Tara's apology was swallowed in the hollow pit carving its way in my stomach. Brittany was here?

Here?

She wasn't supposed to be here.

I loaded two bowls into my right hand and picked up another with my left.

"You good?" Tara had somehow cut in front of Jamie to stand behind me as we got ready to serve the course.

I nodded.

"Of course, you are." I heard the sarcasm in her voice but paid her no attention. My gaze was focused on the blonde at table two

Long blond hair curled at the ends, black bodycon dress hugging her slim figure, the huge fucking rock on her ring finger. I welcomed the anger swelling in me. For too long, I'd let my emotions cripple me, but looking across the room at Brittany, all I felt was red-hot rage. In a strange way, it was refreshing. Comforting.

I glided to table one, a fake smile plastered on my face. Brittany didn't notice me right away; she was too busy gossiping, no doubt, to the girl sitting on her left. I couldn't help but overhear as I served soup to three of the people seated at her table.

"... the venue is booked. Of course, Daddy and Ant insisted we have it at the country club. Exclusively..."

I threw up a little in my mouth but managed to swallow the bile down before hurrying back to the kitchen. It was as if those four little words unraveled all of my progress over the last few weeks.

The. Venue. Is. Booked.

Blake wasn't just engaged to the piranha; he was going to marry her.

Give her his name.

They were going to have a whole life together.

Fuck.

My breathing became shallow. As soon as I was out of sight, I leaned back against the wall and focused on catching my breath. She hadn't even spoken directly to me, and yet, she had managed to throw me into an emotional meltdown.

"Service," an angry chef yelled, ringing the bell one too many times.

I pushed off the wall and mentally checked myself before collecting three more bowls of soup and heading back into the suite. This time, when I approached table one, Brittany's eyes collided with mine and froze to the spot. It was only for a second, but it happened. A slow, knowing smirk spread across her perfectly made face. It snapped me back into action, and I placed the bowls in front of the next three guests.

If anyone noticed our exchange, they didn't let on, and as I walked away from the table for a second time, the only eyes that followed me were hers.

"Everything okay?" Tara eyed me cautiously as I entered the kitchen again. I nodded, pursing my lips. "Are you sure? I was pretty sure I just caught a moment between you and the piranha." Her eyebrow cocked, and I ducked out of her way unwilling to get into specifics while I was working.

"Okay, okay, I'll save it for later." Tara's chuckle disappeared out of the kitchen.

I loaded the last two bowls for table one into my hands and set off. Brittany was waiting for me to appear. Her narrowed gaze tracked me all the way to the table. I wished I were more like Marissa; she would have done something unsuspecting to throw Brittany for a loop. All I could do was concentrate on not dropping the bowls.

I saved Brittany for last and, without speaking, I lowered the bowl in front of her. As I imagined dropping the whole thing in her lap, her shrieking and jumping up covered in pumpkin and butternut squash liquid, I smiled to myself. She deserved it. For tripping me. For being a total bitch to me the first time she met me.

For stealing Blake.

After quickly checking that everyone was happy with the soup, I returned to the service area. I didn't play these kinds of games. I thought I had made my peace about Blake having someone. But why did it have to be her? Of all people. She wasn't even a good person. Maybe if he was with someone who was kind and warm and gentle, it would have been easier to come to terms with. I could have tried to, at least, been happy for him.

"I'm just going to the restrooms," I said to Tara, who was busy checking over her clipboard again. "Sure," she replied not even lifting her head away from Mary's checklist.

The Grand was nice, but it didn't have the facilities as some of the bigger venues we serviced. There were no staff restrooms in the vicinity, and I didn't have the time to go in search of somewhere else to pee. I hurried into one of the stalls and shuffled my skirt up my legs. When I was finished, I flushed and exited the stall and walked straight into Brittany. She scowled and backed me up against the stall door, which had flung shut behind me. "I know who you are, Penny Wilson."

"Wha- what? What are you talking about?"

It was a stupid reply; I knew exactly what she was talking about, but it was all I had. Panic had strangled all my intellectual thought processes.

"Don't act like you don't know what the hell I'm talking about." Brittany stepped into me again forcing my back up against the solid door. It swung open and I stumbled backward, scrambling to stay upright.

"Brittany, come on, I have a j-"

Her eyes were alive with pure hatred. I imagined the same emotion reflected back at her, and although she had taken me by surprise, I was starting to feel the anger boil underneath the surface.

"Don't you dare speak my name. You. Are. No one. If you come near Blake again, I will make sure you never find work again. If you know anything about my family and me, about Blake's uncle, you'll know I'm not lying."

Blake's uncle? What did he have to do with this?

"Blake is mine. Not some trailer trash girl of his past. Stay away from him or you'll regret it." Brittany swung around and left the restrooms. I sunk to the floor and let the door close. What in hell's name had just happened? Brittany knew who I was? But she knew more than that; she knew about our past… our connection.

The main door to the restrooms banged, and Tara yelled, "Second course is up, Penny. Come on."

"Coming, I'm coming," I yelled back, trying to hide the quiver in my voice.

Tara was wrong; Brittany wasn't just a piranha. She was

a shark, and I was swimming in open waters just trying to stay afloat. And I had a sinking feeling there was much more to Brittany's threat than I realized.

For the rest of the evening, Brittany ignored me. She didn't once look in my direction, but it didn't appease my nerves any. I was still shaking when I finally reached The Oriental Garden. Everything had closed up for the night. Tomorrow was Thanksgiving. Even Mr. Chen and his family were closing the takeout for a couple of days, but it wasn't being alone on Thanksgiving that was bothering me. It was Brittany's warning. Her words lingered with me the whole ride back from Grandview Heights. Growing up, Daddy was a huge football fan, and he always used to say that the best form of defense was attack. Brittany had attacked me, which got me thinking.

What was she trying to defend?

As I rounded the corner to the stairwell, I had my answer. My whole world slowed down until there was nothing except for Blake sitting on the bottom step with his head in his hands, the first snow of winter falling around him.

First, Brittany.

Now, Blake.

It was going to be a long night.

chapter twenty-three

Blake looked up, and our eyes locked. The emotion staring back at me left me breathless. Needing to ground myself, I wrapped my arms around myself and said, "What are you doing here?"

He rose from the step and took a step toward me. I sucked in a sharp breath. Blake was already affecting me. A single look, and I was already crumbling.

"Everything is so fucked up." His voice sounded so defeated.

The snow was falling harder now, the flakes covering everything with their white innocence. Funny really, that we were surrounded by something so beautiful when our history was the opposite. It was tragic and ugly and filled with what-ifs and could-have-beens. It was tainted. No, our story didn't deserve snow; it deserved a storm. The kind of storm that left a trail of devastation in its wake.

I closed my eyes and counted to three. When I opened them again, Blake was watching me. "Why did you do that?"

"I wanted to know if this was real. If you're really standing here outside of my apartment because tonight I served soup to your fiancée. Your fucking fiancée, Blake. So ask me again why I am sure this must be a dream? That this can't possibly be happening."

His face paled, and his hands came up to reach out to me. I stepped back. If he touched me, the last of my defenses would crumble. I had to stay strong.

"I'm sorry."

"Sorry?" I repeated unable to hide the bitterness in my quivering voice. "Sorry for what exactly? The summer? For letting me think you still felt something for me, that after all this time there was still something real between us?" I threw my hands up in frustration. "Or are you sorry for forgetting to mention you had a fiancée? That you're getting married—married, for fuck's sake. You're getting married, and you let me believe that you still loved me. That everything we shared, everything I felt all those years ago wasn't just something my mind made up to cope with all the bullshit life rained down on me. That it was real."

Somehow, I ended up standing right in front of Blake. I couldn't even remember moving, but before I could think about it, my hands lunged at his chest. "IT WASN'T REAL," I shrieked pushing hard against his solid frame. "NONE OF IT WAS REAL. IT WAS ALL A LIE. YOU LIED. I HATE YOU, I HATE YOU." My fists pounded against his chest while ugly sobs tore from inside of me.

Standing there, in the back alley of The Oriental Garden and Bernie's Bar with the snow falling all around us, I fell apart. My anger and frustration and hurt over everything that had happened poured out of me, and I continued to hit Blake. I cried for my parents leaving me on this earth alone. For Blake abandoning me when I needed him most. For Derek ruining my chances of ever having a normal healthy relationship. I cried for everything that had been and things that would never have the chance to be.

And Blake let me.

He didn't try to stop me, or comfort me, or fight me off. He just stood there, taking each pound of my fist against his sweater. And when I was emotionally exhausted and had nothing left to give, I collapsed against him. He wrapped his arms around me, lifted me off the ground, and carried me up the stairs to my apartment. Blake found my key, opened the door, and carried me inside. I clung to him like he was my tether to reality, and as he lowered me to the floor to find the light switch, I whimpered. The loss of his touch physically hurt me, and although my hysterical cries had quieted to gentle sobs, I knew I was only one step away from breaking down again.

The situation hung between us, thick and heavy. Blake regarded me, wariness dancing in his eyes. He was probably two seconds from splitting. I didn't speak. I couldn't. But I didn't look away either. Blake's eyes drew me in, holding me there. If only I could translate what they were saying.

Blake made the first move. He stepped toward me. Not enough that I moved back, but enough that if I reached out, I could touch him. I didn't. My hands remained firmly around my waist. If I moved them, I felt sure I would fall apart at the seams.

"It's always been you, Pen." Blake closed the distance between us, brushing my snow-covered hair out of my eyes. "My lucky Penny. I loved you when we were just two kids lost and alone…"

I squeezed my eyes tight. This was the part where he would finally be honest and own up to his mistake. His lies. This was the part where he would admit he loved Brittany. That whatever had existed between us was in the past. I held my breath, waiting.

Silence filled the room, and then an unsteady voice said, "... and I love you now."

My eyes flew open and connected with Blake.

He loved me?

Me.

"But… but you're marrying *her*." I didn't understand.

"There's so much I have to explain, but right now, I really need to do this." He pressed his lips to mine and everything fell away. All of the pain, the hurt, the betrayal disappeared in the feel of Blake's lips moving against my own.

What was I doing?

"Stop, stop," I murmured into his mouth, a war between my head and heart raging inside of me.

Blake sighed against my lips before pulling back just enough to look at me. "I can't stop. Please, don't make me stop. This last month has almost killed me. Do you know what it's like to live a lie, pretending to be someone you're not to everyone around you?" The pain in his eyes paralyzed me, and it was only when he dropped his forehead to mine that I managed to choke out, "Wha-"

Blake stole my words again. Strong hands skimmed underneath my butt and pulled me into him pressing us together until it was hard to tell where I ended and Blake began. This kiss was different from the one in the woods all those weeks ago. Even though that had felt desperate at the time, this was something else entirely. I could literally feel Blake's emotion with every stroke of his tongue, every graze of his lips against mine. I was broken—certain I had nothing left to give—and yet, Blake was taking everything from me. At that moment, I was his air as much as he was mine. As much as I wanted to fight it, to tell myself that I hated him, the man standing in front of me was my everything. Pain. Anger. Hurt and frustration. Fear. Hate. Hope and love. Blake Weston was everything I'd ever felt and wanted to feel again.

I'd been lost for so long, but at that single moment, I was found.

The realization startled me like waking from a dream. I wound my hands around Blake's neck and pulled him closer. I needed him to be closer, if that was possible. To know that he was really here. He smiled against my lips and scooped me up off the floor, cradling my body to his. We moved through the small room with me clinging on for life until the light faded into darkness. My back hit something soft as Blake covered my body with his own. He kissed me gently and then brushed the skin along the edge of my jaw with feather light kisses. A shiver started in my spine and ran through my whole body.

I'd imagined this. The feel of Blake's lips on my skin. How it would make me feel. Nothing compared. My skin burned for him. Feather light kisses became gentle nips and when Blake's teeth gently grazed the skin along my neck, I arched into him as my breaths coming in short bursts.

"Penny, I love you so damn much." His warm breath lingered on my skin and then he was looking down at me in awe. "Do you realize how many nights I have spent dreaming of this moment?"

Suddenly feeling very exposed, I dropped my eyes and squeezed them shut.

"Hey, hey." Blake tried to coax me to look at him. "Penny, please."

What was I doing?

Things had unraveled so quickly that I'd had little time to process what was happening between us. I was too caught up in Blake. But now, I was very aware that he was here, in my apartment, lying on top on me. Expecting what? Something I didn't know if I was ready to give.

"Penny, look at me. What is it?"

Slowly, I opened my eyes. The wariness in Blake's eyes was back and embarrassment started to unfold in my stomach. *What are you doing?*

"I…" The words lodged in my throat, and I shrugged Blake off me slightly. I couldn't breathe with him weighing down on me like that. "There's, hmm, there's something you should know."

Fear flashed in his eyes and my stomach knotted, but I needed to do this. This was a part of me. Inhaling deeply, I said, "I've never been with anyone, you know, in that way."

"I, I don't understand." Blake rolled off me and sat on the edge of the bed. I shuffled up and sat up against the headboard. "What do you mean, *that* way?"

"I'm a virgin, Blake."

"You mean, you've never…" He didn't say the words, so I nodded my head.

"But how. How is that possible?"

It probably wasn't meant as a joke, but a small laugh

bubbled up and tumbled out of my mouth. "If I have to explain that part to you, you're probably doing it all wrong."

"Fuck, Penny, I… I don't know what to say. Fuck." Blake leaped up from the bed and started pacing the length of my small bedroom. I thought I would feel a deep sense of embarrassment, but part of me was relieved. Relieved that I'd shared this with him. But then Blake stopped with a look of alarm on his face. "Does this have anything to do with what he did?"

All of the air was sucked from the room.

"Yes… and no," I answered honestly. "What Derek did left scars. The kind you don't just get over, but it wasn't just that. I've just never found anyone who I felt truly comfortable with letting touch me."

Blake's brows furrowed as he whispered, "But I've touched you. We've kissed." He dragged one hand over his face clearly struggling to put all the pieces together.

I smiled weakly. I couldn't explain it either—why I came alive when Blake touched me, but when others touched me, I wanted to retreat into myself. Neither of us spoke. Blake came to stand next to me and dropped to his knees. He grabbed my ankles gently and pulled me around until my legs were hanging over the edge and he was resting between them. Everything was silent except for the beating of our hearts. One of Blake's hands reached out and tucked a stray hair behind my ear and I dropped my eyes and blushed. It was such an intimate gesture. Something was changing between us. It was scary and intense, and yet, despite all of my better judgment, it felt right.

This was our chance.

I felt it with every fiber of my soul.

Blake opened his mouth to say something, but this time, I leaned forward and pressed my lips to his. If one of us spoke now, this moment would pass.

And we might not get another.

"Pen- Penny, what are you doing?" he mumbled into my mouth as I parted my lips urging him to kiss me. I pulled back slightly to reply, "I'm making a choice."

chapter twenty-four

Blake

Age 18

The square envelope taunted me.

Today, I turned eighteen. It was the day I would have aged out of foster care, but here I was, hiding in my room while crowds of people partied in the rooms below in my honor. I could hear their laughter and the drunken conversations. Uncle Anthony and Aunt Miranda had gone all out for me. A DJ was set up in the garden room, food and kegs filled the kitchen, and my whole class at Wellington was present. But it could all go to hell.

Until my uncle wished me a happy birthday this morning and handed me two cards, I was ready to pack my shit and go find her. I was eighteen, and legally, they couldn't stop me. Even if it meant turning up on *their* doorstep and demanding an address. I just wanted to know Penny was okay. Her feelings might have changed toward me, but mine hadn't. For a year, they had only grown stronger.

The envelope changed everything—my uncle was right all along.

The first time I'd asked about riding out to Lancaster to see Penny, Uncle Anthony had reminded me that I couldn't just turn up at the Freeman's house. There were rules and protocols about that kind of thing. So I'd asked if I could call. He said no. Email. Another no. So I did the only thing I knew how. I waited until the house was quiet and my uncle had finally retreated to bed. I made it as far as the thirty-three before a police car pulled me over. Turned out Uncle Anthony really did know everyone in the city, including the local police officers. They had recognized the black Prius my uncle insisted I drive once I passed driver's ed. It wasn't until the third time I tried to sneak out that Uncle Anthony really lost his shit. Officer Dalty walked me to the front door, the third time in less than three months, and waited until my uncle answered. He'd thanked the officer, grabbed me by the scruff of my neck, and hauled me inside.

"Sit," my uncle commanded, the vein pulsating in his neck.

I dropped into one of the leather chairs and glared at him. It was the first time he'd ever gotten physical with me, but he didn't scare me. After all, I'd survived Derek Freeman and lived to tell the tale. What worse could my own uncle do?

"Do I need to ask you where you were going, or were you trying to drive out to Lancaster again to see that Wilson

girl?"

Penny, her name's Penny.

I remained silent. We both knew where I was headed.

"Blake, have I not already explained that you can't just turn up on their doorstep?"

"Why not? I just want to see her, to make sure she's okay. It's been months, and I haven't heard back from her."

Uncle Anthony walked over to the cabinet pushed against the wall and poured himself a glass of whiskey. "Have you considered that she might not want to write you back? That maybe she has moved on with life?"

No.

No.

Pain ripped through me. I hadn't forgotten about her. Not a single day went by when I didn't think about Penny. She wouldn't just forget about me.

Would she?

"You're wrong. Are you sure you gave them the letter?"

He nodded. "Max hand delivered it himself."

"Maybe if we talk to the social worker. You must have their number, right? The ones who helped you find me?"

Something passed over Anthony's emotionless face. It was quick, there and then gone, but I saw it.

"What? What aren't you telling me?" I stood up too restless to sit. Everything pissed me off lately. It was here—this place—the money, the luxury—it was all too much.

My uncle regarded me for a second and then swirled his whiskey around in the glass. It sloshed up the sides, and he brought it to his lips and knocked it down in one. He placed the glass on the table dividing us and said, "I had to pull a lot of strings to get you here, Blake. Strings that usually take a long time to move. It would be bad for a lot of people if we draw attention to your situation."

Situation? *Is that what he thought of me; I was a fucking situation?*

"You bought me, didn't you?"

I don't know when it all started to click into place, but Uncle Anthony's admission seconds ago was the missing piece of the puzzle. He hadn't just used his position as one of the top lawyers in Columbus to get me out of the group home; he'd paid them off.

"You make it sound like I committed a heinous crime," he scoffed turning his back on me to stare out the window. "I saved you, Blake."

"At what price? That I never stepped foot in Lancaster again?"

"You're overreacting, son."

"I AM NOT YOUR SON," I yelled balling my hands into fists.

Anthony snapped. He marched up to me and stared me down, fury rolling off him. "Your father was a drug abusing son of a bitch who ruined my sister. Imogen was a good girl headed for great things before he came along and stole her from us. He poisoned her with empty promises and look how they ended up. Look how you *ended up. Without me, you have nothing Blake, nothing. What can you possibly offer Miss Wilson? Dreams and young love don't pay the bills. They don't secure your future."*

My mouth opened, and I stood there unable to speak. He thought he was saving me from a similar fate? It was crazy. Penny wasn't a drug dealer. She'd never even smoked, not even the time Mason had dared everyone.

"I can get a job," I ground out. "I can work. I don't expect life to be easy, but you don't know what it was like for us in there. What it's still like for Penny. She needs me."

My uncle's hard eyes softened, and he shook his head regretfully. "I will not see you end up like your mother. I won't do it. Even if you hate me for the rest of your life, I will not let you give up your chance at life for her. You're just children."

An idea crossed my mind and I said, "She could come here when she's eighteen. We can take her in, right? There's more than enough room and we cou-"

"No."

Just like that. He wasn't even prepared to hear me out.

"Why not?"

"Blake, please do not be unreasonable. We can't just take in some girl…"

"Some girl?" I closed my eyes in an attempt to calm the anger pulsing through me. When I opened them again, I said quietly. "I love her, Uncle Anthony. She only has me."

"Blake, you're seventeen. What do you know of love? Of relationships? Love is fickle, so-" he coughed covering up his mistake. "Blake. How do you think she's going to react when she realizes you're from money? When she sees that you'll never have to worry about anything ever again."

It wouldn't matter, would it? I wasn't from money; I just happened to have a rich family. Penny knew me. The real me. Not the me I was forced to pretend to be here.

But the more my uncle's words played in my mind, the more I questioned it. We'd already spent so long apart. What if she really had moved on? Met someone? What if she had plans when she turned eighteen? And then I turned up offering her what? A shitty apartment and dead-end jobs? Penny's grades were good; she could go to college, be anything she wanted to be. Without you holding her back. *Or, if Anthony did agree, I could offer the world. Would she come freely? Or would she look at me as if she no longer recognized me?*

A firm hand landed on my shoulder and squeezed gently. "Blake, you know this is the right thing to do. You both have your whole lives ahead of you. Young love comes and goes, family doesn't. I can see to it that Miss Wilson is given more than enough when she ages out. She'll have everything she needs to start a life for herself."

Tears pooled in my eyes. Was this the right thing to do? Every cell of my body was screaming no, but all I wanted was for her to be okay. I would give up everything in a second for her to be okay.

I don't know what hurt more—that Penny had moved on or that Uncle Anthony had been right. A knock on my door startled me, and I groaned. "What?"

The door clicked open and blond hair appeared in the crack. "Hey, it's just me."

"Hey."

"Can I come in?" Brittany said peering around the door.

I scrubbed a hand down my temples and squeezed. This had my uncle written all over it. He seemed to think us getting together would be a good way for me to move on. There was one huge fucking flaw in his plan: Brittany wasn't Penny. Not even close.

"I'm not really in the mood for company, Brit."

"Oh, don't be like that, birthday boy. You can't celebrate all alone."

"Fine, whatever," I relented. Sometimes, it was just easier to give her what she wanted. After enrolling at Wellington, I'd quickly learned that Brittany Arnold was used to getting what she wanted. She had guys practically falling over themselves to date her and girls kissing her butt wherever she went. But she also had a softer side, one she didn't let many people see. We became friends. I was upfront about not being interested, and she seemed cool with that.

"So, why are you up here instead of downstairs at your party? Which, by the way, rocks. Your Uncle Anthony outdid himself."

I rolled my eyes. These people were always so impressed by money. Who had the biggest pool, the fastest car, the most popular party. It was exhausting and fake and it wasn't who I was. I couldn't give a shit.

"Yeah, it's pretty great," I replied flatly.

Brittany sat on the edge of the bed next to me and nudged my shoulder. "Don't sound so excited. What's eating you?"

My eyes flickered to the envelope balanced against the lamp on my desk. "Nothing."

"You're a tough nut to crack, Blake Weston."

I didn't reply. Sharing and caring wasn't really my thing, especially not with the way our class gossiped. Silence filled the room. Thick and heavy and as awkward as fuck.

"Shit," I said feeling too bummed out to deal with Brittany. "Maybe you should just head back down to the party."

A soft hand glided across my knee and rested there. "Sometimes sharing helps. Try me. I can be a good listener. I promise," Brittany said, and I swore I heard a nervous quiver in her voice.

Was the queen bee of Wellington nervous? Around a guy?

Me?

Not possible.

I turned slightly and half-smiled at her. "Thanks for the offer, but trust me, you don't want to hear about my fucked-up life."

"Blake…" Brittany paused, and her eyes dropped to my lips. Next thing I knew, she was leaning into me and covering my mouth with her own.

Guilt fired through me.

And then I remembered Penny's card.

> Happy 18th Birthday Blake.
> We finally aged out.
> I hope you're happy. I am. I've waited for this day for so long, and it's finally here.
> I want to live.
> Go live, Blake.
> Be everything you can and more.
> I'll never forget you,
> Penny
> xx

Warm lips moved against mine again and some of the guilt peeled away, filling me with a numbness I welcomed. All of the pain and the hurt drowned out in a clumsy half-wasted kiss with a girl I barely liked. I wrapped an arm around Brittany's waist and dragged her closer as she pushed her tongue into my mouth.

I felt nothing.

But nothing was better than feeling everything.

chapter twenty-five

I felt like I was free falling.

Blake dragged his mouth over my neck again, and I panted as I gripped onto him, needing him to ground me.

"Is this okay? Tell me if you need me to stop," his own breathy voice asked.

I nodded, too full of emotion to reply.

Slowly, painfully, Blake pulled out of me and slid back in. I arched into him. It wasn't bad pain, that part had passed quickly; now, it was the most delicious pain I'd ever experienced, and as he moved inside of me, I felt the shattered pieces of my soul start to heal.

"Penny, I love you so fucking much. I never stopped." Warm lips lingered on my skin, searing each word into my heart.

He loves me.

Blake. Loves. Me.

My eyes fluttered shut overwhelmed by everything.

Blake was everywhere. His weight bearing down on me, strong hands entwined with my own above my head, our slick skin fused together. I was lost in him.

"Penny, Penny, come back to me," his voice coaxed me from the sensations running through my body, and I opened my eyes to find Blake gazing down at me. "I need you with me. Stay with me."

His lips came down on mine, and his tongue traced the seam of my mouth as he nudged it open. Fighting back the tears building, I freed my hands and slid them down to Blake's broad shoulders. I pulled him closer, circling his tongue with my own. He moved inside me again, deeper this time, and I gasped. Blake smiled through his kiss and released one of his hands to hook it under my thigh and pull up my leg around his waist. My pants came harder and faster. I was chasing my own breath, but I wanted more. Needed more. I wasn't sure I would survive without it.

"Blake, I… I, ahh God…" I murmured into his mouth, and Blake pulled back ever so slightly to whisper, "Just let go. I have you." He broke our kiss to tuck his arm around my neck and pull me into the crook of his neck. His teeth grazed my shoulder; his movements grew more frantic but never too hard or too fast. Just right.

Perfect.

Trembling wracked through me as heat uncoiled low in my stomach. I clung onto Blake with the fear that if I let go, I would fall into oblivion. As the feelings intensified, everything became a blur of limbs, kisses, breaths, and moans. I writhed underneath Blake needing it to stop and wanting it never to end all at the same time.

It was too much.

Not enough.

And when I thought I couldn't take anything else from him, Blake untangled me from his chest and laid me back against the pillows. His tongue trailed down my damp skin between my breasts, licking and sucking until his mouth closed around one of my nipples and my world exploded.

As my body shuddered with pleasure, Blake found his own release, collapsing on top of me and pressing a gentle kiss to my lips. "Thank you." It was no more than a whisper against my skin, but I heard it. Although, through my ragged breaths and the rush of euphoria flowing through me, I couldn't comprehend what Blake possibly had to thank me for.

Didn't he realize he had just given me everything?

We lay there in silence, our uneven breaths the only sound around us. After a couple of minutes, Blake pressed another kiss to my lips and rolled off me. In the sliver of moonlight illuminating the room, I could just make out the outline of his taut muscles as he walked into the small bathroom adjoining my room and disposed of the condom. He didn't say a word as he came back to the bed or as he climbed in beside me, rolled me slightly, and pulled me to him so my back rested against his chest.

As our breathing evened out so did the mood. The weight of what had just happened started to crush me where I lay. I had given myself to Blake—to a man who was promised to another. What in the hell was I thinking?

I wasn't.

That's what it all came down to. That, for once in my life, I didn't think, I just did. Tired of letting my past, my fears, define me, I hadn't been thinking when I leaned into

Blake and kissed him or when he'd slowly undressed me before kissing every inch of my bare skin.

I hadn't been thinking at all.

I was too blinded by him.

By us.

By those three little words.

I love you.

Now, everything was more confused than ever. Blake said he loved me, *showed* me he meant it, but what happened now?

He was engaged.

Engaged!

Just thinking the word made my stomach plummet and my head spin.

"Stop," Blake said brushing lazy circles along the soft curves of my waist.

"Stop what?" I replied, and Blake pressed another kiss to my shoulder. It was as if he couldn't help himself, and the thought made me smile.

"Overthinking things. Just let us have this moment. We deserve that, don't we?"

He felt it too, the consequences of our actions. We weren't children now; we couldn't just lay in No Man's Land and pretend as if everything was fine. We were adults, and we had responsibilities. *He has a fiancée.*

"Blake…" I started; the bubble had burst. I needed to know. "Wha-"

"No, Penny, not now. Not yet. I need this. We need this."

"But-"

Blake rolled me in his arms until we were lying side by side and our eyes connected. "I love you, Penny. I love you so much I can't see straight. For now, that's enough, isn't it? I know things are fucked up, but right now, I'm lying here beside you as yours. I have waited seven and a half years for this moment. Please, don't ruin it."

I closed my eyes and inhaled deeply. Blake pulled me to him tighter tucking my head under his chin. I would give him this, but we had to face up to our actions sooner or later.

I awoke startled. The comforter was pulled up around me, but something was wrong. My hand reached out for him only to meet empty space. Blake was no longer in the bed. I sat up and rubbed my eyes in an attempt to adjust to the darkness cloaking the room.

"We should talk," a strained voice said from the corner of my small room. I narrowed my eyes and made out Blake's profile sitting on the chair next to the dresser.

"Wha-what time is it? Did we fall asleep?"

"It's after two."

"Shit." I rolled over and hit the lamp on the bedside table. "Are you okay?" It was a stupid question; from the look on Blake's face, he was anything but okay.

Blake, now fully clothed, rose from the chair and came to sit on the edge of the bed. His hand reached out for me, and I interlaced my fingers with his. Why did I feel sick all of a sudden?

"Do you regret it?"

"Wha- what?" I said panic rising in my throat. "How could you even ask me that?"

"Fuck, I don't know, Penny. I felt you freaking out before we fell asleep, and it was your first time, and I'm…"

"Engaged." I finished his sentence. "I'm confused and my emotions are all over the place, but Blake, please know that tonight was everything to me. I could never regret it. Ever."

Relief washed over his face and he leaned over to brush my jaw with his knuckle. "I meant it. Every word. I love you, Penny. I have always loved you."

Blake uncurled his fist, and I pressed my cheek into his open palm needing to be close. I wasn't ready to say the words. Not after everything. Not with everything still standing in our way of a chance to be together. But hopefully, he knew.

"I have to go," he said, regret shining in his eyes. "It's Thanksgiving, and I can't just disappear, but I'll find a way to get away tonight. I'll come here?"

I nodded unable to talk through the huge lump lodged in my throat.

"This isn't me running out on you again, okay? You have to believe me, Penny. But things are complicated, and I can't just walk out of my life. Give me today." Blake pulled me to him and covered my lips with his. His tongue swept hungrily into my mouth and swirled with mine. It was different from the kisses before. This was desperate and full of frustration, and while it didn't feel like goodbye, it did ignite a ball of nervous energy in my stomach. When he pulled away, I couldn't stop the rush of tears from my eyes. Blake's face paled, and he wiped the stream away with the pad of his thumb. "Please don't cry. I promise I'll come back later. I won't lose you again."

I had to believe him.

What alternative did I have?

I spent Thanksgiving holed up in my apartment eating stale crackers and watching the Macy's Thanksgiving Day Parade. I couldn't stomach anything else. After Blake had left in the middle of the night, I had woken hours later to a blanket of bright white snow. I couldn't even make out Blake's tracks down the stairwell. Marissa had called before she sat down with her family to eat. I didn't tell her about Blake. For now, it remained our secret. Only, it was so much more than just a secret to me. I wanted it to remain that way for as long as possible because once it was out in the open, and people knew, it would taint what was the best night of my life.

Blake was always supposed to be my first. I'd wanted to lose myself in him long before we turned seventeen, the age Blake insisted we wait until. He said we weren't ready, that I wasn't ready. Not after what Derek did. I guess he knew best because looking back, I wasn't ready, and although it hurt so much more to lose Blake when I hadn't got to experience everything with him, it would have only made it ten times worse if I had.

I didn't doubt that what I experienced at the hands of Derek resulted in my inability to let people in—to let them touch me. But, now, after my night with Blake, I felt more certain than ever that the way I closed down and feared touch was also a result of being abandoned by the one person I trusted enough to give myself to. Of course, a shrink might have argued that my anxieties were a direct effect of my trauma—losing my parents, abuse by my replacement caregivers—but I felt it. Blake was intrinsic to everything I had lived with for the last six years. One single event didn't change me; it was a series of intertwined incidents, and one way or another, Blake was a part of them all.

He was the other half of my soul.

It's why I couldn't stay away. Why he couldn't stay away.

Why, after all this time, the connection between us still burned brightly.

But despite knowing this in my heart of hearts, as the time dragged on, I lost count of how many times I glanced at the clock. With each passing hour, the doubt I fought so hard to keep locked away inched its way closer to the surface. *He promised.* It was all I had. Until then, all I could do was wait.

I cleaned, showered, cleaned some more, applied some makeup, fluffed up the cushions on my embarrassingly threadbare couch, and checked all of the air fresheners over and over. I kept myself busy until dusk fell over the apartment. Still too nervous to eat and too restless to do nothing, I made myself comfortable on the couch and tried to watch reruns of *Friends.*

When Blake finally knocked on the door, it was past nine. Nervous anticipation coursed through me as I crossed the room to let him in. I reached for the door handle, and my hands trembled.

Blake and I couldn't change our past.

But could we finally rewrite our future?

chapter twenty-six

"Hi." Blake's eyes lit up as I opened the door and stood face to face with him, but I saw the dark circles underneath his eyes and wondered what had happened in the few hours we'd been apart.

"Hi." My heart fluttered as my body remembered last night.

"Can I come in?" His lips curved into a smile, and I blushed. "Of course." I stepped to the side so he could enter.

I'd waited all day to see him, but now all I could think of was what he would think of my place since he didn't see much of it last night. I closed the door behind us and turned to Blake. He was looking around the small open space. One side was my living area; the couch, a small table, and another housing the ancient television. The smaller side was the kitchen, if you could call it that. Pale units ran around the wall and a matching island split the area from the living room. At least The Oriental Garden was closed, which meant the usual smell of egg rolls wasn't lingering.

"It's not much, I know," I said quietly.

I didn't know the extent of Blake's living arrangements, but Anthony Weston was one of the richest men in all of Columbus. I doubted Blake lived in a shitty apartment like this.

When his eyes settled back on me, he looked ready to say something but closed his mouth again. His lips drew into a thin line. He looked torn. "How long have you lived here?"

"Hmm, a couple of years. Maybe longer."

"And before here?" His eyes started roaming over my modest furnishings again.

"I had a room in University District."

His eyebrow arched. "A room?"

"Yeah, in a shared house. It was… hmm, crowded."

That was putting it mildly. It was disgusting. I responded to an ad on Craigslist. The house belonged to two guys who attended Ohio State. It was trashed most of the time from their all-night parties and days spent on the couch eating cold pizza. I had lasted five months before I moved onto the next dive.

"I don't understand," Blake whispered to himself more than to me.

What did he mean he didn't understand? Was it that hard to comprehend that I couldn't afford to rent somewhere nice?

I wrapped my arms around my waist and felt shame crawl its way up my throat. My life hadn't been a bed of roses, but I made it work. We weren't all lucky enough to have a rich relative swoop in and save us.

Guilt hit me like a wave.

I was happy Blake hadn't endured the same life I had. One of us got away; one of us made something of our life, and I would never take that away from him. If anyone deserved it, Blake did. But I was only human and denying the sliver of envy coursing through me was impossible.

Needing to break the heavy mood, I said, "Can I get you a drink? I don't have much."

"No, I'm good. I didn't think it would be this awkward."

I didn't know if his honesty reassured me or made me feel worse, but then Blake was wrapping me in his arms and everything melted away. All my insecurities and worries of what lay ahead drifted into oblivion. In Blake's arms, I felt safe, warm… I felt loved.

Hands cold from the freezing temperatures outside swept into my hair, and Blake whispered in my ear, "I missed you." His warm breath tickled my ear, and I ducked my head away from him.

"Not so fast." Blake's fingers caught my chin, and he tilted my face up to his. He stared at me as if he was seeing me for the first time. And when his lips brushed against mine gently, it was as if he was kissing me for the first time.

I wound my hands around his neck and cemented us together, deepening the kiss. How could anything we were doing be wrong when it felt so right? Our tongues danced together, and heat pooled low in my stomach. Feelings so unfamiliar to me suddenly felt so innate, so essential to me; it was hard to believe I'd lived without them for so long. I craved to be with Blake again, and my body was already ready to succumb, but we'd left too much unsaid. Too much to discuss.

"Blake, wait." I tried to catch my breath, pulling away

from him.

"Yeah." He half-smiled sadly. He knew too. We were allowing our emotions, our need for one another, to distract us from what was important right now.

I shrieked as Blake scooped me up in his arms and carried me into the bedroom. He laughed but kept me cradled to him until he lowered me onto the bed and said, "Give me five minutes." His lips pressed to my forehead, and he disappeared out of the room. I lay there confused as I heard him leave the apartment.

A couple of minutes passed and the door to the apartment opened and closed again. "Everything okay in there?" I called out wondering what all the banging and rustling was.

"Yeah, stay put."

I couldn't help the smile forming on my lips. Blake had the ability to take an awkward, heavy situation and turn it on its head with his charm and playfulness. The laughter in his voice had me wondering what he was up to this time.

Moments later, he appeared in the doorway holding one of my dinner trays. It was loaded with chips, cookies, pop, and a pumpkin pie. "Happy Thanksgiving, Penny." Mischief sparkled in his blue eyes, but I didn't miss the way he gulped. He was choked.

So was I.

He was replicating our thing. When we'd lived at the Freeman group home, Thanksgiving wasn't any different to any other day. Sure, Marie and Derek hung a wreath on the door and arranged pumpkins on the porch, but it was all for show. Inside, there was no holiday spirit. The first year I was there, I'd been so distraught about my parents that Blake had tried to cheer me up by taking me out to No Man's Land. He had stolen whatever he could get his hands on to make us a Thanksgiving feast.

"You remember," I said overwhelmed at the sentiment.

"I never forgot a single moment." He moved to the bed and placed the tray down before pulling his snow-covered hoodie over his solid frame. His t-shirt stuck to it and rode up over his abs. "See something you like?" Blake smirked before rounding the bed and shuffling next to me.

"Jerk," I replied ducking my head to hide the blush staining my cheeks.

Blake pulled the tray between us and handed me a paper plate. "You came prepared."

"I figured a trip down memory lane couldn't hurt, you know, given the circumstances."

We ate in comfortable silence. I helped myself to a piece of pie and a can of pop. The snow was still falling outside, the shadow of the flakes reflecting on the wall.

"What happened to you, Penny, after you left the home?" Blake didn't look at me, but I didn't need to see his eyes to sense the change in him.

I set my can on the tray and shifted down slightly so I was lying back against the pillows staring up at the ceiling. "I left Lancaster. The social worker said she could help me find somewhere to stay and consider my options, but I couldn't be in that town for another second. I had some money saved. It wasn't much, but it was enough to get me to downtown Columbus. I'd already researched my options, and they were bleak. Finding a job was my priority. There was no way I could afford college, and after what happened with Derek, I wasn't in the right frame of mind to apply for scholarships…"

Blake flinched beside me. He was still sitting up against the headboard. I reached out and found his hand. Pushing the tray out of the way, Blake laced our fingers and shuffled down the bed to lie by my side.

"I picked University District as I figured there would always be work and cheap accommodations. The guidance counselor at Lancaster High had given me the name of someone at the University library, but I didn't know if I was ready for something like that. So I asked around for kitchen work. I-"

"Fuck, Penny, where did you stay?"

"I stayed in a hostel for a few nights, found a job, and then found a room."

Blake's hand clamped around mine. Something was wrong. I risked turning my head slightly to glance over at him. Eyes set on the ceiling, Blake's jaw ticked, and I could feel the anger rolling off him.

"Blake?"

"I can't imagine what that was like. It shouldn't have been like that. Things could have been different, Penny…" He sighed deeply. "If only you hadn't sent that card."

"Card? What card?"

Blake ripped his hand out of mine. He cursed under his breath and leaped up from the bed.

"Blake? What is going on?"

"I knew it. I fucking knew it. He lied, that bastard lied. I didn't want to believe it, but none of it made sense."

I pushed up on my elbows and watched Blake pace the length of the small room.

"Who lied? What are you talking about?"

"My uncle."

His uncle? What did his uncle have to do with any of this?

"Blake." My voice pleaded, and he stopped running a hand through his hair. He dropped to the edge of the bed and hung his head forward like a man defeated. I shifted up on my knees and slipped my arms around his waist pressing my cheek into his back. "Talk to me."

Please don't shut me out now.

"That first year I tried to come and see you. Three times."

He did?

"My uncle told me not to go. On the third time, he got physical. He didn't beat me or anything, but he lost it. My mom's disappearance and death hit him hard. He said he didn't want me to end up like her, like my father. None of it mattered to me, though. I just wanted to see you. The day I turned eighteen, I had planned to drive out to Lancaster. I knew the chances of you still being there were slim, but I had to try. Not a day went by that year when I didn't think about you, Penny." Blake turned his head slightly brushing his nose across the top of my head.

"Anyway, the morning of my birthday, he gave me two cards. One was from him and my aunt, Miranda, and the other was from you."

Me?

My heart stalled.

"We finally aged out. I hope you're happy. I am. I've waited for this day for so long, and it's finally here. I want to live. Go live, Blake. Be everything you can and more. I'll never forget you, Penny." He recited the words as if they were imprinted in his mind.

I inhaled sharply. I hadn't sent a card. Just as I had never received Blake's letter.

"Your uncle sent it." It wasn't a question; we both knew the truth. Blake's uncle had been so desperate to keep his nephew in Upper Arlington that he sabotaged any last hope for us. He had probably never delivered the letter to the Freeman's either.

"I knew he was desperate, but how could he do that?" Blake's voice cracked, and my heart ached for him.

"What happened, Blake?"

"The card was so, so final. It sounded a lot like goodbye, like you had moved on and wanted me to do the same. So that's what I tried to do. That was the day I stopped living."

A tear slipped from the corner of my eye. All this time, I thought Blake had abandoned me, but he never had. He had thought of me all these years, and he'd kept our memory alive. It was tragic, really. And yet, our time apart had changed things. Blake might have kept our memory alive, but he had also moved on.

"And now you're engaged."

The seconds the words left my mouth, Blake's whole body tensed.

"I don't love her," was all he said.

"Does that matter? You still made a commitment to her when you proposed." I was the one who winced this time.

A bitter laugh came from Blake. "Proposed? I didn't propose. My uncle arranged the whole thing. Things are more fucked up than you think."

It was my turn to pace. I climbed off the bed and walked back and forth trying to make sense of what Blake was telling me. He didn't propose? What in the hell was he getting married to Brittany for then?

"Penny, come sit down."

I shook my head. "No, no, I need to pace. It's too much all at once."

Blake eyed me warily, but I ignored him. I could concentrate on the pacing. *Five steps forward, turn, five steps forward, turn, and repeat.*

"My aunt and uncle couldn't have children," Blake started as I continued to wear a hole in the carpet. "Aunt Miranda told me that when my mom left, it crushed him. He was older by eight years—the typical overbearing, protective brother, especially since their parents were old. Mom was set for Brown. The world was hers until she met my father. It was love at first sight. Everyone was worried because Jason was unstable. No one knew about the drugs until later, but he was heading on a one-way track to prison and didn't care if he took Mom along for the ride. Uncle Anthony tried to make her see sense, but when you're eighteen and in love, you can't see straight."

I stopped in my tracks, and my eyes found Blake. He smiled sadly and then dropped his eyes jolting me back into action.

"One day, she was just gone. No note, no paper trail, nothing. Everyone knew she'd left with Jason, but they wanted to disappear and all searches came up empty. Uncle Anthony never gave up, though. Fast forward seventeen years and after numerous PIs, he finally got the call he'd been waiting for. Except it wasn't. Mom was dead, and I was in foster care."

As Blake said the words, I realized just how much

of our story I didn't know. During the summer, at Camp Chance, we had both been too paralyzed, too scared to talk openly about things. Hearing it now was hard enough.

"Uncle Anthony is used to getting what he wants, Penny, and he wants me to carry on his legacy. He wants me to work my way up in his law firm. Britt-" He hesitated as if the words were difficult to say and I froze. "Brittany's family and my uncle's family are old friends, and in my uncle's world, you marry your kind."

Pain sliced through my chest, and I gasped. I hadn't meant to, but it had happened all the same.

And I'm not your kind.

Blake pushed off the bed and walked over to me. His hand cupped my jaw and tilted my face to his. "I don't love her. I will never love her, and I will find a way to fix this. I meant what I said, Penny. I'm not losing you again."

chapter twenty-seven

Morning light filtered through the blinds. The light was so bright; I figured it was the reflection of the snow that had fallen through the night. My eyes squinted at the clock on the nightstand. It was only just past eight. Blake stirred next to me, and my heart swelled just knowing he was here. With me. In my shitty apartment overlooking a back alley of a bar and a Chinese takeout.

After talking into the late hours, we'd finally fallen asleep. At some point during the night, Blake had rid himself of his jeans and t-shirt and was now sleeping next to me in just his boxer shorts. My eyes traced over his body. The dips and planes of his smooth muscles. The way his lips quivered as he breathed. My mouth dried, and my legs clenched together as I adjusted to the feelings he evoked in me.

I sat up and reached out to touch him. I didn't want to wake him; I just wanted to feel his skin. His warmth. My fingers grazed his chest. Blake didn't open his eyes as his hand came up to grab my wrist. He yanked gently pulling me over his chest. "Best morning ever," he smirked, his eyes still shut.

Nose to nose, our lips were so close they were almost touching. "Good morning," I whispered, and Blake's eyes opened slowly. Drinking me in.

"I could get used to this."

I ducked my head, stretching my legs out underneath me, and nestled into his neck. I was still unused to the way he just said whatever the hell was on his mind. Blake's fingers hooked underneath my t-shirt and connected with my skin.

"Give me your eyes, Penny."

I lifted my head to look at him, but Blake had other plans. Capturing my lips, he ran his tongue along the seam of my mouth, sucking my bottom lip into his mouth. I moaned softly, melting into a puddle against him. I needed more. *Always more.* I let him deepen the kiss, swirling his tongue with mine all while his fingers continued to stroke my bare skin and leave a blaze of sparks in their wake.

"Do you know how much I love you?" Blake said without taking his lips off me. How had the moment gone from light-hearted to heavy and suffocating in a matter of seconds?

"Let me show you." Blake wrapped his arms around me, and then rolled us until I was underneath him, and he was peering down at me. "Let me love you, Penny."

I swallowed hard unable to think.

Blake leaned in, and I closed my eyes as I anticipated his kiss; only his mouth didn't find my lips. Warm air brushed my neck as his lips pressed against my skin. He licked and nibbled and sucked along my collarbone. The cold air of the apartment mixed with the warmth of Blake's breath had my body shivering in the best kind of way.

Deft hands grabbed the hem of my t-shirt and slid it up and over my body. Blake caught one of my pebbled nipples between his teeth, and I gasped. "Ah, Blake. More, please."

Always more.

Something about this time was different. Blake took his time with my body, caressing my curves, the rise and fall of my chest, stroking the soft muscles of my stomach. He kissed every inch of me until I was panting. I was so lost in the feelings running through me that I hadn't realized Blake was kneeling between my parted legs. With his hands hooked underneath my knees, he dipped his head and kissed my inner thigh. My whole body went limp, pressed into the mattress. No one had ever been there. So close. Cal, my last boyfriend, had tried, but in the end, I freaked out and couldn't go through with it. But now Blake was there, his tongue running along the curve of thigh up to my pelvis. With feather light touches, he alternated between licking and sucking, and each time he captured the burning skin in his mouth, I bucked off the bed. I felt him smile against me. But nothing compared to the way I felt when his fingers slipped between my center chased by his tongue. My whole body shuddered with pleasure as Blake slowly pushed one finger inside me followed by a second while his tongue glided over the sensitive bundle of nerves.

"Blake." His name was a prayer on my lips.

I buried my hands into hair holding on for life as he continued his sweet torture of my body. Skilled fingers worked me, in and out, and his mouth pleasured me to the point of seeing nothing but bright white behind my eyes. I cried out; over and over, I panted Blake's name. He crawled up my body and kissed me, my taste still on his lips.

"Penny." He pushed inside of me stealing my response, filling me so completely I felt sure I would fall apart all over again. I wrapped my weak arms around his shoulders and held on for life.

After Blake had left the apartment on Friday at lunchtime, I didn't see him again all weekend. I had back-to-back shifts, Friday evening through Sunday, serving dinner to stuffy business types at post-Thanksgiving functions in downtown Columbus. The whole time, I thought of nothing but my morning spent letting Blake love me. Nothing could dampen my high or the euphoric feelings flowing through me. Not even the reality of our situation. Maybe six months ago, I would have been waiting for the bubble to burst, for everything to crumble down around me, or I wouldn't have risked putting myself in this kind of situation in the first place. But this time, I wanted to believe things could be different. That, finally, I was getting my shot to live out from under the shadows of my past. Blake didn't want to marry Brittany, he didn't love her, and I believed him.

I *had* to believe him.

Of course, I wasn't foolish enough to think that the road ahead was going to be easy. Blake still had to find a way to tell his uncle without losing the only family he had left. He loved them—Uncle Anthony and Aunt Miranda—

and it showed in his voice every time he talked about them. Although his relationship with his uncle was strained, I didn't want to be the one who came between them.

You know you will be. Anthony Weston will never accept you. I silenced the little voice in my head. Blake said he would handle it, and I had to give him the time and space to do that. As long as I didn't cross paths with Brittany anytime soon, I could be strong for him.

For us.

I watched the city rush by in a blur of lights as I rode the bus back to my neighborhood. Three long shifts and I was ready for a break. My feet burned, there was grime embedded in my skin and hair, and I missed Blake. Forty-eight hours apart had felt like a lifetime. I now understood what people meant when they said they couldn't stand to be without their partner. My heart was lost without him; a feeling I'd switched off for the last seven years.

Blake had awakened me, and I didn't ever want it to end.

My cell vibrated in my purse setting off butterflies in my stomach.

I can't get away tonight. Sorry. I love you. Blake x

Disappointment flooded me. Blake had said he didn't know if he would be able to make it to see me tonight, but deep down, I had hoped he would find a way. I pocketed my cell, made my way off the bus, and started in the direction of The Oriental Garden. My pocket buzzed and excitement bubbled up. Maybe Blake had found a way to come.

"Hello," I said not even checking the screen.

"What the hell is going on, Penny?"

"Marissa?" I asked taken aback at her stern words.

"Yes, it's me. Tell me it isn't true?"

"True? Is what true? You need to spell it out for me, Marissa, because right now, I have no idea what you are talking about." I sighed picking up the pace. The snow had stopped, but temperatures were still well below freezing.

"You and Blake."

Me and Blake? My mind immediately went into overdrive wondering how she could possibly know.

"Why am I getting cryptic messages from Blake asking me to watch over you over the next couple of weeks? Watch over you? Penny, why the hell do I have to watch over you? What the fuck has he done?"

"Whoa, slow down, Marissa. It's not what you think-"

"It's not?" Her voice wasn't calming down any. "So what is it then? Did that fucker hurt you again? Because I have no problem driving down there."

"Marissa, calm down. Blake didn't do anything to hurt me."

The line went silent for a second, and then she said, "He didn't? So why-"

"We slept together."

"WHAT IN HOLY HELL'S NAME DO YOU MEAN YOU SLEPT WITH HIM?"

I held the phone away from my ear out of fear it might do permanent damage. Even slipping the phone into my pocket did little to reduce the sound of Marissa's shrills coming through the line.

"PENNY? PENNY WILSON, ANSWER ME RIGHT NOW."

"Hello." I rounded the alleyway and dug into my purse to retrieve my keys.

"Did you put the phone down?"

"Maybe. You were really loud." Treading carefully up the icy stairs, I balanced the phone between the crook of my neck and my ear. I quickly unlocked the door and hurried inside to get out of the cold.

"You can't just drop something like that on me and expect me not to lose my shit. Christ, Penny, what were you thinking? You do remember he's engaged, right? Betrothed. Promised to another. Shit, Penny."

Guilt knocked at my conscience, but I refused to let her in. I would not feel guilty about what happened between Blake and me. It was real and pure, and even though Blake's engagement overshadowed it, it was all I'd ever wanted. I couldn't regret that—I wouldn't.

"He loves me," I said without hesitation.

"Now, she realizes that," Marissa moaned. "Did I or did I not tell you that? What changed?"

"I love him too."

"Has anyone ever told you that your telephone manners suck? Well, durrrr, of course, you love him. You're like each other's lobsters or something." Her *Friends* reference lifted some of the heavy, and I laughed softly. "He doesn't love her, Marissa. It's all a front. His uncle wants him to marry her. Family politics…" I inhaled deeply to give myself a second to collect my thoughts, but Marissa beat me to it.

"So how is it being the other woman?"

"Marissa!"

"What? I need to know this kind of thing. I'm your best

friend. Was it good? The sex, I mean. Was it toe-curling, sweaty, heart-exploding good? Oh, tell me it was."

"I'm really uncomfortable right now."

She tutted. "Of course, you are. But back to the sex. It was good, right? I'm right, aren't I? Blake looks like he'd be a sure thing in the sack."

Everything.

It was everything.

The words were on the tip of my tongue, but I found myself saying, "Nice, it was… really nice."

"Nice? Penny, we really need to work on your sharing skills. I need details, girl, not nice. Nice is bunnies and fluffy clouds. I want to know if your world exploded."

I settled down on my couch and smiled. My life was finally falling into place. I had a job I enjoyed working at with people I liked. I had a good friend in Marissa. She pushed me to open up and trust her, and I loved her for it. My anxiety didn't define my life anymore. It no longer controlled me; I controlled it. And then there was Blake. The one person who knew me better than anyone else did, maybe even myself. It all felt too good to be true.

"This girl doesn't kiss and tell," I said with a hint of amusement in my voice.

Marissa snorted. "Wait until I see you. I'll get it out of you. You'd better watch out, Penny Wilson. But seriously, things are okay?"

"They are."

"So what, Blake's just going to tell his uncle and piranha bitch that he's out? I hate to be the voice of doom here, but that's never going to happen. You know that, right? That's obviously why Blake texted me because he knows shit is about to hit the fan."

My eyes fluttered shut.

I should have listened to the little voice in my head.

It was always right.

If things seemed too good to be true… they usually were.

chapter twenty-eight

Blake

Age 22

"Congratulations, honey. We're so proud of you." Aunt Miranda beamed as she hugged me tight and kissed my cheek.

"Welcome to the real world, son."

I winced. I hated when he called me that, but Uncle Anthony and I had reached an understanding in our relationship somewhere over the last four years. Maybe it had to do with me not living under his roof or maybe it was the fact he paid my way through school and had given me more than I'd ever had—could ever dream of.

"Thank you." I hugged my aunt back and nodded at Anthony over her shoulder. I would thank him properly, man to man, but right now, all I wanted to do was get out of this ridiculous gown and celebrate.

"Brittany, sweetheart." Aunt Miranda released me and met Brittany with open arms. "You look beautiful. Congratulations." She pulled her into a hug, and Brittany's parents, Trent and Sandi, came around to congratulate me.

"Son, congratulations." Trent took my hand in his firm grip and shook it. "We couldn't be more proud of the two of you. And thank you for looking after our girl these last four years." He winked; the fucker actually winked.

Brittany sidled up to her father and smiled up at him. "Daddy," she crooned. "What have I told you? Blake and I are just friends."

"Baby, I would be proud to call a fine young man such as Blake my son. Now, don't you two have somewhere to be?"

Son? What the fuck?

I was still gaping at Trent when Brittany slipped her arm through mine and tugged me away, waving at her parents and my aunt and uncle.

"Did your dad actually just suggest we get married?"

"Don't be ridiculous, Blake. He was just kidding. You know they'd love us to get together." She leaned in close as we walked toward the rest of our friends. "Although, we could celebrate tonight, you know, if you wanted to."

"Brit," I warned. It had happened twice. Okay, maybe three times, but I was always wasted, and she was usually rebounding from her latest boyfriend.

"What? I'm horny, and when was the last time you got laid?"

"I get laid."

"Oh, okay then, who was she?"

"Some girl." I shrugged; I was starting to feel pissed that she was pushing this.

"Some girl," she mocked. "There was no girl, Blake. Such a waste," Brittany mumbled under her breath.

We reached our crowd, and I shook her off me. I didn't need any of the guys giving me shit over her as well. I had enough on my plate with Trent and Uncle Anthony.

"What's up, guys?" Devon, one of our friends, said, pulling me in for a guy hug.

"We're ready to party, man, and I need to get out of this dress."

Everyone burst into laughter, and we headed back to our shared house to change.

"Shit, man, Brit is wasted." Devon tipped his beer in the direction of where the girls were dancing. The plan had been civilized drinks and dinner at Brindley's Brasserie. Uncle Anthony had made reservations for the eight of us, but the drinks flowed and before long, we were being ushered through the VIP entrance of Cashmere's. It was full of students celebrating graduation, but we had our own private booth and waiter service.

"Yeah," I groaned. "Maybe she'll hook up with someone and I can sneak out without playing babysitter."

"Dude, she's had a boner for you since freshmen year."

I scrubbed a hand over my jaw as my eyes watched the girls roll and pop their hips to the beat. Brittany was beautiful, no denying that. She had filled into her looks over the last four years. Killer curves, perfect rack. But what she had in physicality, she lacked in personality. College had mellowed her somewhat, but deep down, Brittany was as artificial and fake as the rest of the rich girls in our section of the club.

"Never going to happen," I said taking a long pull of my beer.

"Your loss, man. Your loss."

I shook my head with a smirk. These guys were my friends, but I still didn't feel like one of them. Sure, I'd adapted to the money and the extravagance of life in Upper Arlington, but it wasn't me. Not deep down. Not when I'd been the kid with nothing, the kid cold and hungry waiting for his mom to sober up and feed him.

"When do you leave for camp?"

"Not until June tenth. I can't wait. Out there all the shit in here," I tapped my head, "just disappears, you know."

"I'm not sure I could do it, man. All those brats and not to mention the bugs. Ugh." Devon shuddered, and I laughed. "It's Hocking Hills, Dev. It isn't Outer Mongolia."

"Blake." Brittany and the girls sauntered over; dressed head to toe in designer dresses and matching accessories, they left a trail of drooling guys watching after them.

"Easy, Brit." I held her at arm's length as she tried to slide onto my lap.

"Come on, relax. Have fun. Celebrate with me." She pouted and leaned forward a little giving me a good eyeful of her tits.

"I'm always available, Brit. Just hop on over here." Devon grinned that shit-eating grin of his and patted his lap. Brittany frowned before rolling her eyes. "I wouldn't touch you if you were the last man alive, Devon."

"Ouch," he responded clutching his heart pretending to be wounded.

Brittany gave in and shimmied between us before reaching for her cocktail. Her hand slipped and the glass went crashing to the floor. "Shit."

"Nice one, Brit." I couldn't hide the irritation in my voice. Her fumble had drawn attention to us; the thing I hated most.

"Sorry, maybe I'm a little more drunk than I thought. Take me home?"

"I can make sure y-"

I reached around Brittany's slender frame and squeezed Devon's shoulder. "Never happening, Dev. Might as well give it up."

"Never." He grinned at me. *Have you seen her tits?* he mouthed behind her back.

Shaking my head, I stood and offered my hand to Brittany. "Come on, let's go."

"Why don't you want me?" Brittany blurted out in the back of the cab. I eyed the cabbie, but he didn't seem to be listening.

"Brit, you're drunk, and it's late. Let's not do this now."

She leaned her head on my shoulder and sighed. I thought she had fallen asleep. Apparently not.

"We'd be so good together, Blake, and it would please our parents. You know they want us to make it official. Join together two of the most influential families in Upper Arlington. It would be perfect. We'd be perfect…" Her voice trailed off, and her breathing evened out. Brittany was asleep.

It wasn't that I didn't want her; I just didn't feel anything for her. She was a friend, but my uncle had forced even that. Aunt Miranda seemed indifferent about whether we dated, but on more than one occasion in the last three years, Uncle Anthony had tried to set us up.

I was partly to blame. After that first kiss on the night of my eighteenth birthday, I think I gave Brittany false hope that we would end up together. But the truth was I couldn't make myself feel something I didn't feel.

My heart belonged to another; it always would.

I paid the cabbie and lifted Brittany out of the taxicab. Our shared house was on the outskirts of University District. A modern two-story, four-bedroom house with a small pool and awesome roof terrace—just another way Uncle Anthony had sweetened the deal for me to attend Ohio State instead of applying to schools outside of Ohio. Attending college hadn't even been on the radar back when I lived in Lancaster, and for as much as I hated my life in Columbus sometimes, I couldn't deny that my aunt and uncle opened up doors for me and my future.

In some ways, it was as if I was two people: The Blake I showed to my uncle and aunt and all of their rich friends, and then there was the Blake I was in private. The Blake who still dreamed of nights under the stars in No Man's Land and a future with a girl who stole his heart when she was just twelve.

Maybe I should have pushed harder. Maybe I should have packed a bag, driven out to Lancaster, and demanded to see Penny. But in the end, I was weak. I let my uncle dictate the rules and I fell in line. Even when I received Penny's card, even after I kissed Brittany, I still wanted to go and find her. To track Penny down. Uncle Anthony had tracked me down for Christ's sake—I was pretty certain his resources could find anyone eventually. But somewhere along the line, I gave up. I accepted my fate and played the role expected of me. The only thing I had was Camp Chance—my sliver of normal among my life of fake.

My uncle had originally sent me to volunteer at the summer camp for foster kids in Hocking Hills as punishment for the final time I had tried to sneak out and see Penny. But my uncle underestimated my love of the outdoors and my patience with the teen boys I was there to guide. I saw so much of myself in those kids that after that first summer, I begged Troy, the owner-manager, to let me return the following summer. It had taken some persuading with my uncle, but Aunt Miranda stepped in and he came around. She felt it was good for me to have time away from the family business, and I think she was worried it would only push me further away if my uncle didn't agree. This year would mark my fifth season out at Camp Chance, and I couldn't wait. The sooner I was away from my uncle and Brittany and all of the shit that being a Weston brought with it, the better. My name didn't matter in a place like that.

All that mattered was who *I* was.

"Blake, I think I'm going to hurl." Brittany retched, and I scooped her up and rushed to the bathroom, Camp Chance suddenly feeling like a whole world away.

Brittany slid out of my arms and crumpled to the floor, pushing her head down the toilet. I stood outside waiting as she deposited her stomach contents into the bowl. When she stopped puking, I offered her a wet towel and some water.

"Thanks. I think I'm dying." She held an arm over her head.

"You're not. Come on, I'll tuck you in," I half-mocked. It wasn't the first time I'd played nursemaid to Brittany. She had a tendency to go overboard on Bellini's or Long Island Iced Teas or whatever the hell she felt like drinking. I wouldn't say she had a problem, but she enjoyed a drink. Part of me wondered if it was her way to cope with the pressures bestowed on her by her family. I shut down, and Brittany got wasted.

Brittany didn't argue as I scooped her up and carried her upstairs to her room. I laid her on the bed and pulled off her shoes. She groaned and rolled onto her side drawing up her legs. "Hit the light on your way out. Don't let me sleep past nine. I have to meet Daddy for breakfast."

"Sure thing," I said glancing back at her lifeless form on the bed.

"And Blake?" Her voice stopped me in my tracks as I reached the door. I turned back and said, "Yes?"

"I know you'll never love me, but maybe I could make you happy. One day." Certain I heard her choke down tears, I didn't reply. Nothing I could say would make her feel any better right now. I knew first-hand what it was like to love someone only to have her not feel the same way.

I lived it every day.

chapter twenty-nine

The next two weeks passed in a haze of stolen text messages, late night visits, and hours spent loving each other—erasing the seven years of separation between us. Blake didn't talk much about how things were between himself and his uncle—or Brittany—and I tried not to ask. I could see our secret was taking its toll on him. Each time he crawled into bed beside me, the circles underneath his eyes were darker and the tension in his shoulders tighter. But every time he slid inside me, things were okay. Just for a moment. But we couldn't continue like this. It would eventually break him… and part of me worried I would lose him forever.

"We need to talk about what's happening, Blake," I said. It was a normal visit, like all the other nights Blake slipped away to be with me. He tensed and pushed up on his elbows. The comforter fell away from his skin, and I rolled to my side tucking the material around me. "Blake," I said again gently.

He rolled onto his side and raked a hand over his face. The strain in his features was obvious and a deep aching stirred inside me. "Tomorrow." He sighed. "I'm going to tell her tomorrow."

"Okay."

"It's not as easy as I thought it would be. We haven't been together for weeks, months. Before the summer. She knows there's someone else. I can see it in her eyes."

I dropped my eyes and sighed ignoring the nausea swishing in my stomach at the thought of them ever being intimate. "She knows it's me."

"What?" Blake asked. "What do you mean she knows it's you?"

"That night you came to me, Thanksgiving, Brittany was at the banquet I worked. She cornered me and warned me to stay away from you."

"Fuck."

Silence hung heavy between us. I hated that, in an instance, the distance between us seemed more than ever.

"Why didn't you say anything?" Blake questioned me with his eyes.

"I don't know. I came back and you were here, and then we happened and everything was finally right between us. I'm sorry." My voice caught in my throat.

Blake rolled to his side and shuffled until he was at my eye level. His hand brushed away the hair falling over my shoulders. "Don't. Don't apologize. I brought you into this. It's my fault. I need to tell her. Tomorrow, I'll tell Brittany and then deal with Uncle Anthony. Okay?" He kissed me hard. Sealing his promise to my lips.

I nodded against his mouth.

The storm was coming for us; I just hoped we could survive.

I didn't hear from Blake all day. He'd left my apartment before sunrise, pressing his lips against mine, whispering he would talk to Brittany today.

Today.

Mary called me to work at two; it was supposed to be my day off, but since it was only for a few hours—and I didn't want to hang around the apartment worrying about Blake—I said yes. Tara was heading up the shift, which was a business dinner at a hotel in downtown Columbus. By the time we finished, I was desperate to check my cell phone for word from Blake, but when I dug it out of my purse and checked the screen, there was nothing. No missed calls. No text messages.

Nothing.

"Everything okay, Penny?" Tara asked as we left the Columbus Premier.

I nodded, clutching my phone in my hand.

Why hadn't he called?

"I'm meeting some friends for a drink if you want to tag along? You look like you could use some company."

"Really, I'm fine. I think I'll just head back to my apartment, but thank you. Maybe another time?"

Tara smiled weakly and said, "Anytime. Catch you later." She gave me a small wave before crossing the street and disappearing down the sidewalk. Another time, I would have pushed myself to accept her invitation and join Tara and her friends, but all I could think about was getting back to the apartment in the hopes that Blake would show up.

I tried to push away any irrational thoughts during the whole ride back. I watched people on the sidewalk, guessing their stories. Who they were, where'd they been, where they were going. I lost myself in the busy streets. When the bus slowed for a red light, I watched an elderly man and woman. His hand rested on her lower back, guiding her toward a coffee shop on North High Street. He held the door open for her and when she slipped past him, he leaned forward and kissed her, love emanating from them.

When I got off the bus, the elderly couple was still fresh in my mind. They must have been at least seventy, and their story gave me hope. I wanted that. Before the summer, I never opened myself up to the possibility of finding someone, of letting someone love me. But now that Blake was back in my life, everything had changed.

I rounded the corner and walked down the alleyway. I passed a black Town Car parked in the middle of the alley, which was strange. Cars rarely used the narrow passage for parking, but perhaps Bernie had visitors. Smiling to myself, I turned the last corner. Deep down, I knew that everything would be okay. Blake would be honest with Brittany and his uncle, and once it was out in the open, we could move forward.

Together.

All that plummeted as my eyes fell on the man standing at the bottom of the stairwell with his back to me.

I'd walked straight into the lion's den.

Anthony Weston heard my footsteps and turned narrowing his eyes right on me. "Miss Wilson. I believe we need to talk."

Funny how those small moments changed everything. A look. A kiss. Six little words. Because the disappointment gleaming in the eyes of Blake's uncle told me everything I needed to know.

He wasn't here to welcome me into his family.

"Mr. Weston," I said warily. My arms snaked around my waist as I succumbed to old feelings of vulnerability. "I wasn't expecting to see you here."

At my apartment.

The imposing man's lips drew into a tight line. He regarded me for a second and then said, "Can I come in? I have something I wish to discuss with you."

I wanted to say no, to pull a Marissa and tell him to fuck off or something to that effect, but Anthony Weston didn't seem like the kind of man you refused. Instead, I nodded and motioned for him to follow me. We walked in silence. Each step harder than the last, the burden of Blake's and my secret weighed down on me. And then the thought crossed my mind—*he knows.* I pushed the dread out and focused on the here and now. I had to face this man eventually. He was Blake's uncle, after all.

I opened the door and led Mr. Weston inside. Thankfully, I had cleaned the place before I left and the scent of lavender overpowered the smell of grease from the kitchen below. After closing the door behind him, Mr. Weston took in the small room. I could see the disapproval in his eyes, the judgment. But instead of embarrassment, I felt something else entirely. Who was he to judge me and my life? He didn't know the first thing about what I'd endured. Blake had told me that losing his sister—Blake's mom—had destroyed him, but I didn't see the expression of a man haunted by the ghosts of his past. I saw a man hardened and cold. His eyes shone with contempt.

"What can I do for you, Mr. Weston?"

I hadn't noticed the briefcase in his hand, but he lifted the aluminum case and laid it on the kitchen counter. "I'm sure you're aware, Miss Wilson, that I am a man of business. I am a partner in one of the most successful law firms in Columbus, if not Ohio, and I have my name attached to business ventures across the whole state."

I stared at the man before me unsure where he was headed with this. "I know who you are, Mr. Weston."

"Well, I am here today on business."

Business? Alarm bells started ringing at the back of my conscience. He moved his fingers over the locks and unclasped them. The lid opened fluidly and as he turned the case slowly toward me, he said, "I have a proposition for you."

My eyes fell over the neat rows of one-hundred dollar bills and my hand moved to my throat. I'm sure there was something I was supposed to say, but all I managed to choke out was, "Proposition?"

"It has come to my attention that you are somehow involved with my nephew. As I'm sure you are aware, Blake is engaged to Brittany Arnold. The wedding date is set and preparations are underway, and *both* of the families involved couldn't be happier."

A whimper escaped my lips, and I clasped my hand

over my mouth as the pieces slotted into place. Anthony Weston was here to make sure I wasn't a problem.

"As you can see," he nodded at the case, "I am willing to compensate you. This should be enough for you to relocate and start over." He spoke as if this was just a regular business deal. There was no emotion or feeling to his voice, and it was hard to imagine that my warm, charismatic Blake was related to this man.

"Mr. Weston." I managed to find my voice. "I'm not sure what you think you're doing, but I don't want your money." A tear slipped from my eye, and I dropped my head. I was trying so hard to stay strong, but Blake's uncle was here to end us. Before we ever truly began.

"Miss Wilson, let's not get emotional. You should consider this offer carefully. What do you think can possibly come of this misguided affair you and my nephew are involved in? He thinks he loves you, but he doesn't. He loves the idea of loving you. What happened to him, to his mother, it scarred him. Foster care scarred him. Blake should have grown up in this life, with his aunt and me and our friends. He has the world at his disposable, and with a woman like Brittany by his side, he will go far."

"We love each other. Isn't that enough?" I forced myself to meet his eyes. Couldn't he see my love for Blake? Was keeping face really more important than his own nephew's happiness?

A harsh laugh, full of cynicism and bitterness, rumbled from deep within Mr. Weston's chest. "Miss Wilson, I know you're smarter than that. Love is a fool's game. I'm sorry for what you went through as a child, I truly am. But I will not stand by and watch you ruin my nephew's life… for unrealistic dreams of what? Love? A life living in somewhere like this?" He glanced around my apartment again. "This isn't a fairy tale, Miss Wilson. This is life, and it's hard and ruthless and Blake does not need a distraction like you."

Like me? "I- I…" I had nothing.

He wasn't here to negotiate with me. He was here to seal the deal: To pay me to walk out of Blake's life.

Forever.

"You can hate me, Mr. Weston, and you can try your hardest to come between Blake and me. And, who knows, maybe Blake will see sense and decide a life with a fat wallet and an empty heart is the one for him, but please don't try to pretend you know anything about me or what I suffered in that place. You know nothing about me. Now, please leave. And take your business proposition with you." I walked to the door and opened it, holding onto the handle for support.

Mr. Weston watched me. His face was poised in the same expressionless pose it had been the duration of our conversation, but his eyes looked different. I couldn't quite put my finger on it, but there was definitely something there. Maybe he wasn't expecting me to put up a fight. Whatever it was slipped away and his mask was back in place. He slammed the case shut and lifted it off the counter. "You're making a mistake, Miss Wilson. The offer stands for twenty-four hours. I suggest you reconsider."

With that, he strolled past me and disappeared down the stairs. I closed the door and slumped down on the floor. Tears streamed down my face as I unraveled.

chapter thirty

I couldn't sleep. After Anthony Weston had left me, I'd cried on the floor until my eyes stung and my heart hurt. Once the heating had kicked in, I swapped my server's uniform for my pajamas and climbed into bed pulling the comforter up around my chest.

Blake still hadn't called.

Of course, there were numerous possibilities as to why he hadn't contacted me yet, given that his uncle now knew about us. I'd once welcomed solitude, but lying there cold and alone, I hated it. I hated that with the silence came irrational thoughts about where Blake was, about what he was doing. I hated that I felt weak without him there to reassure me it was going to be okay. But most of all, I hated Anthony Weston for making me believe I wasn't good enough for Blake.

A loud rapping on the door startled me, and I clutched the comforter in a panic.

"Penny, it's me. Penny." The desperation in Blake's voice

had me scrambling out of bed and hurrying to the door. I unlocked the latch and opened it. Blake reached for me and our bodies crashed into one another. "I've been going out of my mind. She tricked me into attending a dinner, and I only just managed to escape. I am so sorry."

I choked back the tears threatening to fall again and nestled my face into his neck. Blake cradled the back of my head whispering soothing noises into my hair. Just the feel of his arms wrapped around me lessened my anguish, and when familiar hands tried to peel him away, I resisted. I didn't want to leave the sanctuary of his smell.

"Penny, Pen, look at me." Blake's hand slipped between us and forced us apart. His fingers tipped my chin. "There's my girl. I told her everything. She admitted to knowing all about you. But she-"

"I- I had a visitor earlier," I rushed out. If I didn't say it now, I might never get the words out.

Blake's forehead creased. "What? Who?"

"Your uncle came to see me."

"He did what?"

I shrugged out of Blake's grip and paced to the other side of the room. This was likely to go only one way—Blake ending up mad as hell.

"Penny," Blake said sternly. "What did my uncle want?"

Taking a deep breath, I rolled back my shoulders and calmly replied, "He wanted me to leave Columbus. He offered me money if I walked out of your life immediately."

Blake's mouth dropped open, but his eyes gave away his shock. "He wouldn't. He's done some crazy shit in the past, but he wouldn't do something like that. Are you sure it was my uncle?"

"Blake," I said softly stepping forward. "It was your uncle. He had a case full of money with him. He was very clear about what he wanted."

When you spent most of your time alone, dealing with your own pain, the pain of others isn't something you have to experience. But watching Blake's expression change from one of shock to heartbreak was one of the hardest things I'd ever witnessed. He literally broke in front of me. I wanted to go to him, to wrap my arms around him and take it all away, but I was the cause of it all. And there was a chance he wouldn't want me to.

Defeated, Blake said, "He wouldn't. He- he wouldn't."

Tears rolled down my face, but this time they weren't for me, they were for the man I loved. I took another step forward aware that if I pushed him too far he might break. "Blake, he did. I am so sorry."

Blake closed his eyes, balled his fists at his sides, and dropped his head back. My control snapped. I rushed over to him and wrapped myself around him. His touch had healed me; maybe I could do the same for him in his moment of need.

"I'm so sorry, I'm so sorry," I repeated over and over.

I don't know how long we stood like that, but eventually, Blake's fists relaxed, and his hands found their way around my back. "I need you, Penny."

He needs me.

As selfish as it was, I needed to hear that. I needed to know that this didn't change anything between us.

"I'm here, Blake."

Blake lifted me off the floor and carried me to the couch. He pulled off the throw blanket and adjusted us so that he was sitting on the far end and I was lying with my head in his lap. He covered me with the blanket and slipped one of his hands underneath my sweater. Warm fingers began to draw circles on my skin.

"I'm sorry," he whispered.

"We seem to be saying that a lot to one another lately," I replied.

He leaned down pressing his lips to my forehead and my eyes fluttered shut. "Do you ever look back and wish things had been different?"

"Of course, I do," I said.

"I spent seven years of my life regretting that I left you in that place. Seven years. I told myself it was okay because you were smart. Told myself that you'd earn a scholarship and go to college and live out your dreams. I told myself every day that you were better off without someone like me in your life. I could offer you everything and nothing. How could we build anything real on something so fake?"

"Blake, stop."

"No, you need to hear this, Penny."

"I thought you'd given up on us, so I chose this life. It was the easy way, the coward's way, I guess. Get everything handed to me on a silver fucking platter but at what cost? I love my aunt, and in a strange way, I love my uncle. They are family, they will always be family, but you are my soul mate. I knew it all those years ago, and I know it now. Whether we have all the money in the world or have to live out of boxes eating leftover pizza out of the dumpster, I choose you, Penny Wilson. My lucky Penny."

I reached up and curled my hands around Blake's neck, yanking him down to me. Our lips fused together, hungry and desperate, but it wasn't enough. I broke away; sitting up and shifting onto my knees, I crawled onto Blake's lap, straddling him. He hadn't yet removed his jacket, and I was still in my pink striped pajamas, but it didn't matter. At that moment, everything else ceased to exist.

Blake wanted to go straight to his uncle's, but I needed time to process everything. It was all happening so quickly. And besides, I had to work a lunch meeting in University District. Which was where I was headed now. I'd left Blake back at the apartment wrapped in my sheets. He wanted to lay low—to face his uncle together. So I gave him my key and told him to make himself at home. I would only be gone three hours at the most.

The job was straightforward enough. Felicia and I served light refreshments to a team of designers working out of the Craven Building. After returning the service tray to the kitchen, we parted ways. I needed to pee before I left to catch the bus back to Clintonville. It felt a little strange knowing my apartment wasn't empty—that Blake was there waiting for me. I smiled at the thought.

I exited the glass doors onto the sidewalk. The icy air licked my skin, and I snuggled into my faux fur lined parka. The blanket of snow that had fallen over the last couple of weeks had started to thaw, turning the sidewalk into a slushy mess. Not paying attention to anything but my cautious footsteps, I didn't see the blonde whirlwind headed in my direction until it was too late.

My eyes widened as Brittany stormed over to me. The

gray fur muff pinned her hair in place giving her an air of perfection, but her eyes told a different story. She looked unhinged. Furious.

"You," she hissed jabbing her finger at the air between us. "I told you to stay away from him."

A couple of people passed us glancing back at us, and I shrunk further into my jacket. Brittany reached me. She stood taller in her snow boots than I did. Glaring down at me, her eyes burned with hatred. "What could he possibly see in someone like you? Look at you. You're nothing. Nothing." Her voice cracked. "You're the help, for Christ's sake. What does he possibly see in you?"

"Brittany, I'm-"

"No," she cut me off. "Don't say it. Don't you dare say you're sorry. We were happy before you showed up. I could have made him happy. Blake belongs in *my* world, with me. Not with some poor little orphan girl."

I closed my eyes and inhaled letting her insult roll off me. Of course, some of it stuck. She had a point. Somewhere in her wild, desperate ramblings she was right. Blake had everything at his feet… and I had nothing.

Aware that we were drawing a small crowd, I shuffled backward away from the door to the building. Brittany was clearly not finished and continued stalking forward.

"Do you really think you can keep someone like Blake?" She paused arching her eyebrow. "Well, do you?"

"I…" My mouth fell open, but nothing came out.

Why was I rising to her? Blake had made his choice.

Me.

But I couldn't shake her words.

Do you really think you can keep someone like Blake?

"Look at you. Cat got your tongue?" Brittany stepped right up to me, and my back hit the wall. "He might think he loves you, the pathetic broken girl from his past, but he'll grow bored soon enough and who do you think he'll come running back to? I've been the one there for him the last six years. Me."

I tried to swallow, but my mouth had dried.

"Blake is a Weston. He has obligations. Responsibilities. He will never walk away from his uncle. From the family business. And I'll be there every step of the way. Think you can handle that?" Brittany slammed her hand on the wall beside my head, and I jumped startled at her anger. She leaned in closely and said, "You. Are. Nothing. I'll make you wish you'd never turned up at that dumb camp and laid eyes on Blake again."

She righted herself and backed away. I released the breath I'd been holding. Our eyes locked and Brittany's lip curled up into a smirk. The crazy bitch winked at me before turning and setting off down the sidewalk as if she hadn't just threatened me. My body sagged against the wall and I dropped my head back closing my eyes.

A tear slipped down my face.

And another.

Was this how life was going to be with Blake?

And if it was, was I strong enough to live in his world?

The alley was quiet when I arrived back at the apartment. I'd walked along the sidewalk, my arms wrapped around my waist, lost in my own thoughts. Blake was expecting me back at four. It was after five. But Brittany's venomous words had wormed their way into my veins, spreading through me like slow acting poison.

I didn't doubt that Blake loved me. It wasn't about that, but we *were* from different worlds now. For the last six years, Blake had lived without wanting for anything when I struggled to make ends meet every day. I kept telling myself it was only money. But was it? Blake belonged in that world—*her* world. It was his birthright.

"Penny? What happened?"

I looked up to find Blake standing in the doorway staring down at me with worry shining in his eyes. My feet carried me up the stairs as if they knew I needed to be close to him. He opened his arms, and I collapsed against him.

"What is it? What's wrong?" Blake murmured into my hair, and I clung to him.

"She-"

Blake tensed and then his hands moved up my arms and gripped me pushing me back. "What the fuck did she do?"

"She… she was waiting for me after work. She's unstable, Blake. The things she was saying." My voice cracked and the tears followed. Blake pulled me back to him and encased me in his arms.

"Shh, don't cry. Please, don't cry. Whatever she said, it isn't true. Brittany isn't used to things not going her way. You know me, Penny, *you*."

Anger burned through me. I was angry with Brittany for planting the seed of doubt that what Blake and I shared was real. But, most of all, I was angry with myself for believing her. Because, as I stood wrapped in Blake's arms, I felt his love. It extinguished all of my doubts and worries. It filled the cracks in my heart until I felt like I might burst.

Brittany had it wrong.

Blake and I might live in different worlds.

But we belonged together.

chapter thirty-one

"Is this really a good idea?" I asked Blake for the third time. He kept his eyes on the road and said, "It needs to be done. Once and for all."

I leaned back against the leather seats. After spending the night wrapped in each other's arms, Blake insisted we pay his uncle a visit. Brittany's latest threat was the final straw—Blake had made his decision. My stomach disagreed, and with every mile that passed, I felt sure I would hurl.

"How you holding up over there?" Blake's hand brushed my knee, and I half-smiled. "I'm okay."

"After this, one way or another, we'll be free, Penny. That's all we ever wanted."

He was right. Once upon a time in a yard in Lancaster, two teenagers hadn't wished for expensive gifts or trips to the coast. They had wished to be free.

The neighborhood began to change. Modest family houses morphed into larger properties with long drives filled with expensive cars and preened lawns. Blake navigated his Prius with ease, a reminder that this was his home now. But when he drove to the end of a nice street and turned into a gated property, my eyes almost bugged out of my head. The Weston house was by far the biggest in the vicinity. I glanced down at myself. Blake had insisted I just wear what I felt comfortable in, but I'd decided on my knee-length pencil skirt, tights, a soft blue blouse, and my thick woolen coat. My hair hung loosely around my shoulders, curled out at the ends, and a light layer of makeup covered my face. It was more effort than I ever went to, and yet, I still felt inadequate.

"Stop." Blake's voice perforated my mental assessment of my outfit choice. "You look beautiful."

The car rolled to a stop. Well-tended bushes flanked the driveway and opened out in a circular parking area that had a water fountain in the middle. Anthony's Town Car was parked next to a silver Porsche Coupe.

"My aunt's car," Blake said noticing my line of sight. "Come on, let's get this over with." Some of the brokenness in his voice had gone overnight. He sounded more sure, determined to make his uncle see sense.

Blake exited the car and came around to the passenger side to help me out. As I slid out of the seat, a female voice called, "Blake, honey, how lovely to see you. We weren't expecting you."

I stepped out of the car and pressed myself slightly behind Blake. What I really wanted was for the ground to open up and swallow me whole, but the universe had never been on my side. I doubted it was about to start now.

"And who is this?" The lady's voice didn't sound annoyed so much as inquisitive, and I wondered if she wasn't privy to knowing her husband's way of dealing with unwanted problems.

"This, Aunt Miranda, is Penny Wilson."

I smiled weakly. Miranda regarded me for a second, giving me a cursory once-over. I closed my eyes just for a second already feeling the scrutiny of these people. When I opened them again, Blake's aunt was smiling directly at me. "It's lovely to meet you, Penny."

Taken aback by her warmth, I simply replied, "Thank you. It's very nice to meet you too."

Blake didn't let go of my hand as we walked to the house where Miranda was standing. "Is he here?" Blake asked. His aunt nodded and turned for us to follow her inside.

If the outside was anything to be impressed about, the inside of the Weston's home was stunning. I walked beside Blake in awe of the regal feel of the place. Soft, rich furnishings occupied the space, ornately framed photos covered the hallway walls, and everything just complemented everything else. Even the Christmas decorations matched to perfection. It was beautiful.

We stopped outside a door. Miranda knocked gently and pressed her ear to the wood. "Ant, we have guests."

My heart started to pound, and I squeezed Blake's hand for reassurance.

"Come in," a voice said from the other side of the door.

Miranda opened the door and motioned for us to enter the room. She followed behind us and shut the door. Anthony Weston sat behind a large antique desk. He looked up and his eyes glowered, dropping to where Blake's hand entwined with mine and all the air was sucked from the room.

I wanted to run—to get the hell out of there. My inner anxieties screamed at me to turn around and walk away. I wasn't built for this kind of confrontation. Not when I was the issue. But Blake kept my hand planted firmly on his. He squeezed gently and said, "Uncle, we need to talk."

Anthony Weston rose from his chair and stalked toward us. "I didn't expect to see you here, Miss Wilson. I take it you told my nephew about our little conversation." He honed in on our joined hands again, and I tensed.

"Uncle, don't."

"What is she talking about, Ant? You visited Penny? When?"

"Miranda, please stay out of this. This is between the three of us."

"Oh no, you don't, Anthony Matthew Weston. If this concerns Blake, it concerns me. I will not stand by and watch you drive him away."

I suddenly felt as if I was missing a whole part of the story. Miranda was nothing like her husband; her eyes were warm and friendly, and she had welcomed me into her home with no questions asked. A stark contrast to her husband who looked ready to burst a blood vessel.

"Fine, fine. Maybe we should make ourselves comfortable." He motioned to the leather sectional and armchair set in one corner of the room.

Blake led me to the couch, and I sat beside him trying to press myself as close to him as possible.

"Ant, will you please explain what is going on?"

Blake's uncle sighed deeply as if he was carrying the weight of the world. "I paid Miss Wilson a visit recently, in hopes of putting an end to their little affair."

"Affair?" Miranda gasped. It had me questioning who she thought I was. The girl holding onto her nephew as if he was her air.

"It would seem that Blake and Penny have been having liaisons."

I cringed. He made it sound so seedy, as if we were meeting in beat-down motels to have illicit sex.

Blake slapped his hand down next to him. It collided with the weathered leather creating a squelching noise. "What Penny and I do is nobody's business including yours." He glared at his uncle. They were locked in some kind of standoff until Miranda cleared her throat and turned to the two of us.

"Blake, is it true? Are you seeing Penny?"

He nodded never taking his eyes off Anthony.

"And does Brittany know?"

"She does now." Blake broke his connection with his uncle and turned to face his aunt. "I love Penny. It's always been her. Ever since you took me away from Lancaster."

"I knew this would happen, Ant. You pushed him too hard, forced him to sever all ties. I've read about it. How in group homes children can form unbreakable bonds. We should have considered what it would do to him."

Anthony scoffed at his wife and said, "Don't start quoting that nonsense you read, dear. We did what was best for *our* nephew. We have given him everything. Everything and this is the repayment we get."

"Repayment?" Blake spat. "I didn't ask for you to come swooping in. I didn't ask for you to rip me away from the only family I'd known in a long time. But *I* didn't get a say.

I was just expected to fit into your life, consequences be damned."

Miranda held her heads in her hands, Anthony sat motionlessly, and I sat there stunned. Blake's issues with his uncle ran much deeper than I could have imagined.

"I did it to protect you, Blake. To give you a life like the one your mother never had. You have the world at your feet and still it isn't enough."

"Penny, would you like to come with me?" Miranda said catching me off guard, and although I didn't want to leave Blake, I felt like an intruder on a very private moment.

"Yes, please." I nodded turning to Blake. "I'll be right outside, okay?" After squeezing his hand, I rose and followed Miranda out of the room.

"Can I get you some coffee, Penny? Or wine? I have a bottle of Chardonnay somewhere around here."

I glanced back at the hallway hoping I did the right thing by leaving Blake to hash things out with his uncle. A soft hand came to rest on my arm, which I had wrapped around my waist. "They'll be fine, dear. They need this. It's been a long time coming."

"I'm fine, thank you," I said offering Miranda a slight smile.

"So, tell me, dear, what is it that you do?"

I joined her at the table. "I work for a catering agency. Galas, banquets, business lunches, that kind of thing."

"Long hours, I imagine?" Miranda regarded me. I'd caught her doing that a lot since we arrived. I imagined she was weighing me up, trying to work out what someone like me could possibly want with someone like Blake. But then, out of the blue, she said, "Is it silly of me to be jealous of you for knowing Blake when he was just a child?"

"I, hmm, I don't really know how to respond to that."

"Excuse me, losing my tongue like that. It's just… you have this bond with him. I saw it the second you stepped out of the car. I've wanted nothing more than to know him in that way, but when Blake first came to us, he was angry and bitter. If I'm being quite honest, he was quite the handful."

I smiled wistfully, imagining the sixteen-year-old Blake with his messy appearance and teenage boy attitude.

"What was he like when you first met him? He must have been what, twelve?"

I nodded. "He was adorable. He wore his chucks constantly untied and his hair was longer, messy, always hanging over his eyes. But he had this goofy smile that, no matter what, made you feel better."

When I met Miranda's eyes, I was shocked to see hers laced with tears. "I'm sorry," I said. "I didn't mean to upset you."

Miranda reached across the table took my hand in hers. She smiled. "These are tears of joy, dear. When we found out that Blake was in foster care, I was sick with worry. You hear horror stories, reports of bad outcomes for children who age out of the system. But now, I can see that he wasn't alone. He had you, Penny. You saved him."

And he saved me.

For the next thirty minutes, I humored Blake's aunt, answering questions and trying to fill in the blanks to paint a picture of teenage Blake for her. By the time the footsteps sounded in the hallway, Miranda had tears streaming from her eyes.

"Thank you," she said in a hushed voice. "And please know that I support Blake's choice one-hundred percent. I know he never loved Brittany. I had hoped, that with time, he would open himself up to the idea, but he never got over losing you, Penny, and for that, I can only apologize. Ant may be misguided at times, but he really does have Blake's best interests at heart. He just has a funny way of showing it."

I was beginning to realize there was more than meets the eye with the Weston's, and while I still didn't trust Anthony's actions or judgment, I had warmed to Blake's aunt in a way I never thought possible.

"Penny, are you okay?" Blake's gravelly voice reverberated through me and a sense of contentment washed over me. As long as we stuck together, we could survive anything.

I knew that now.

It had always been that way.

"Miss Wilson, I believe I owe you an apology." Anthony Weston came into the kitchen and sat in the chair next to his wife. "Blake and I have reached an understanding. Blake is an adult, and while I do not wholly agree with his decisions, they are his decisions to make. You have my blessing, and you do not have worry about Miss Arnold any longer. I'll see to it that she doesn't bother you again."

Miranda beamed as she took her husband's rigid hand in hers, and I glanced back at Blake as he leaned against the doorjamb. He nodded confirming truth to his uncle's word, and although I didn't understand or care for the man's tone, I knew it was as good as an apology and it was the best I was getting today.

"Thank you, Mr. Weston. I appreciate the sentiment, but please know that I love your nephew with or without your blessing."

Anthony Weston shocked us all—he laughed. It wasn't belly busting or even a proper hearty laugh, but it was a laugh nonetheless.

Blake moved behind me, and his hands came down on my shoulders. It was the first time I'd said the words, and I was saying them in front of his family. But it felt right. I wanted them to know that I was standing by him no matter what. I loved Blake long before he fell in his life with the Weston's, and I would still love him even if his uncle decided to cut him off.

"We should probably get going."

"So soon?" Miranda said.

"If we're welcome, we'll visit again soon."

We will?

"You and Penny are always welcome. You know that, Blake. Right, Ant?" Miranda jabbed her husband in the ribs, and he spluttered. "Yes, yes. Was that really necessary?"

Miranda launched into giving her husband a verbal beating. Blake leaned down and whispered into my hair, "Ready to get out of here?"

I nodded my cheek brushing his. Yes, leaving seemed like the perfect plan.

Miranda and Anthony were still engaged in a war of words when we left the Weston house and made our way back to Blake's Prius. As soon as we climbed in the car, Blake's hands were on me, pulling me closer as his tongue dived into my mouth and swirled with my own.

As Blake's lips moved against my own, I still had questions. There were still things that I needed to know, to understand, but this—the kiss—was everything. It was a dedication to our past, an acknowledgment of our present, and a promise to our future.

Our future.

When I was a teenager, I laid out in No Man's Land under the sky and fell in love with a messy-haired boy wearing ripped jeans and unlaced chucks.

Seven years later, things were different. *We* were different.

But one thing had survived our story—the thing that defined it.

Our love.

epilogue

Blake

Age 24

"How are you feeling?" I glanced over at Penny from my seat and smiled.

"Okay, I think. I mean, it's all happening fast, and I'm a little scared about going there again, especially in court. But it's time he was brought to justice." Penny turned her head and pressed it to the cool glass as my stomach knotted.

So much had happened in seven months. Penny and I had moved in together. A nice little apartment in Grandview Heights. Of course, Uncle Anthony wasn't pleased about it, but I wasn't going to let him dictate everything in my life, including where we lived. If he wanted to keep me in his life, he had to accept that I wanted to live by my own rules.

Part of me was pissed that it had taken revealing the true extent of what we suffered at the hands of Derek and Marie to make him understand why our relationship wasn't just the first love crush he took it for, but I couldn't knock everything he'd done since.

"Why?" I waited until my aunt's and Penny's voices were far enough away. I didn't want Penny to hear any of this conversation. This was between the man standing in front of me and me.

My Uncle resumed his spot by the window looking out over the yard. "You're engaged, Blake. The wedding is planned. Brittany lov-"

"Don't. Don't you dare use her feelings for me as an excuse for the stunt you pulled," I snapped and started pacing back and forth. "Love has no place in business arrangements, isn't that what you've been telling me for the last four years? Love is a fool's game?"

"Blak-" Anthony turned to face me, but I cut him dead. "No. I am done listening to you. I have sacrificed my soul to keep you happy. Played my role as dutiful nephew for too long. I told you I didn't want to marry Brittany. I told you I didn't love her. You promised me she knew it was a business arrangement. Was that all a lie too? Were you secretly hoping I would finally fall in love with her? She threatened Penny. Twice. Did you know that? Did you put her up to that?" I stared at the man who had searched for my mother most of my life. He had never stopped looking for his sister, and I didn't doubt that in a different time, love had guided Anthony Weston. Family. But losing Mom to a criminal like Jason

Bellmont had changed him.

It was ironic, really, that although Mom ran away to be with my dad, she had, in some ways, clung to her past. To her family. It was the reason I had my uncle's name, and not my fathers. I think it was her attempt at giving me a chance in life; hoping that, one day, Anthony might find us. Me.

Or, at least, that was what I told myself when I agreed to start dating Brittany.

Uncle Anthony moved toward me, his tailored suit hugged his frame. "What is it about the Wilson girl, Blake? You were just children."

He wanted to understand? Now? After everything?

I dropped my head and thrust a hand into my hair, dragging it over my scalp, frustration boiling under the surface. "You wouldn't understand what Penny and I have."

"Explain it to me. Miss Wil- Penny, she said some things when I visited her."

My head whipped up. "What things?"

"You never talked much about what it was like in the Freeman house."

"You never asked." I moved over to one of the chairs and my uncle took the seat opposite me. He inhaled deeply as if undecided about what to say next. The three words that rolled off his tongue were not the ones I ever expected to hear.

"I'm asking now."

The words were on the tip of my tongue. It wasn't my story to tell, but I was desperate for him to understand how deeply Penny's life was entwined with mine. Maybe if we'd spoke up sooner—when we were just kids—we wouldn't be here now. Maybe things would have been different.

Before I could stop myself, I rushed out, "Derek was a

sick bastard."

Something flashed in my uncle's eyes, and he loosened his tie. "Excuse me?"

"You heard me. That sick fuck had a thing for young girls. Penny, in particular."

The color drained from Anthony's face. A man who rarely lost his cool looked ready to hurl onto the floor. "Did he- did he..." The words almost choked him. I'd felt the same when Penny had revealed to me what Derek tried to do to her.

"Rape her?" I said. "No, but he tried. He abused her. Abused his position. They neglected us, hated us. You were right." I looked him straight in the eye. "You did save me. You saved me from hell, but you also left the only person I'd ever cared about in there."

"I-" he stuttered. "Blake, I didn't know. You didn't say anything."

"I tried, but you didn't hear me. Do you have any idea what it's like to be in foster care? A strange home with strange adults and strange kids? That was my life for four years before Penny arrived at the Freeman's. And then things were better. She was a ray of light in the darkness." I stopped overcome with emotion.

Uncle Anthony had a point. I hadn't opened up since he took me away from Lancaster. I rebelled at first, sure, but after the fake card from Penny, I stopped fighting. If she had set me free, what else did I have left to fight for? I became compliant. Weak. And I had to carry that with me for the rest of my life. But I wasn't about to make the same mistakes twice.

"I love Penny. I have always loved Penny, and I will not lose her again. Even if it means walking away. I left her once, but it will never happen again."

Anthony rose from his chair and moved back to the window as if the view held the answers to the universe. I knew that look etched on his face. He was considering my argument, weighing up all sides of the case preparing to give his verdict. Only this time, it made little difference to me. I finally knew where my home was—and she was sitting down the hallway in the kitchen with my aunt.

"This is your final decision?" his strained voice asked.

"There was never a decision to make. Not this time," I replied.

My uncle turned to me and smiled sadly. It changed his whole face, and for the first time, I felt sure I was seeing a glimpse of the man my aunt talked of so fondly. "You have my blessing. I will handle Brittany. We have lots to discuss, but that can wait, for now."

Just like that, it was back to business, and I knew my uncle was referring to my revelations about Derek Freeman.

"Thank you," I said rising, the burdens I'd carried for the last four years melting away. "In a strange way, I understand why you did it. You were trying to protect me. Protect your family. I get it, I do. But I'm not Mom and history is not repeating itself."

With that, I turned and left the room, laying rest to my past and moving into my future.

In less than five months, his legal team at West Lake and Associates had collected enough evidence and tracked down enough witness testimonials that they were confident Derek Freeman would be locked away behind bars for a very long time. Surprisingly, my uncle also managed to talk Penny into giving a statement. She had been adamant that she didn't want to dredge up the past—not since everything in her life was finally on the upswing—but Anthony Weston didn't work in shades of gray. To him, Derek Freeman had committed a crime—exploiting and abusing the young people in his care—and he needed to be brought to justice. They had eight cases of sexual misconduct with a minor against Freeman, including Amy, the girl who had lived with us. It was going to be harder to prosecute Marie with neglect, but the team was working their asses off to make it happen.

I reached over the stick shift and brushed Penny's hand with my fingers, coaxing her back to me. The looming pressure of the court date weighed heavy on her. I saw it in her eyes, the way she'd started wrapping her arms around her waist again as if she might fall apart. "Hey, Penny, come back to me."

She settled back into the leather seat and sighed. That one sound could bring me to my knees every damn time. I hated that the past still had such a hold on her—that even with things between us better and stronger than ever, she still had demons preventing her from moving forward.

"I'm okay, really."

"You don't need to put on a brave face for me. You can crumple and breakdown and I will always be here to catch you."

Always.

She had to know that I would walk to the ends of the earth for her.

Penny intertwined her fingers with mine. "I know."

The trees lining the road grew familiar, and before long, the dense green walls thinned out. Camp Chance's freshly painted sign welcomed us, and I couldn't help the grin tugging at my mouth. I loved this place. For so long, it was the only place I felt free. Since moving in with Penny, waking up next to her every morning had earned my top spot, but driving through the gates of camp still came in at a close second.

"You love it, don't you?" Penny asked, and I turned to her; it wasn't as if I didn't have the road into camp memorized. "Almost as much as I do you."

She blushed, pink spreading across her neck and into her cheeks. Almost a year together and I still had that effect on her. I never wanted it to end—I wanted a lifetime of these moments.

The Prius rolled to a stop, and I put it in park. Reaching over, I pulled Penny to me, my hands buried deep in her hair as my lips captured hers. She fisted her hands in my hoodie, holding on for life, letting me explore her mouth. By the time we came up for air, our chests heaved between us as our breaths came in short, shallow bursts.

"How are we going to uphold camp rules for ten weeks?" she asked blushing again.

I laughed. My vulnerable girl needed me as much as I needed her. "I have my ways. You forget I was once the master of sneaking out." I winked; I couldn't help it.

Penny's mouth formed an *o*, and she sucked in a breath. "Blake, I don't want to get into trouble. Tina was very clear about the rules last year."

Capturing her mouth again, I mumbled, "Rules are meant to be broken." Besides, there was no way on earth I was going ten weeks without feeling Penny underneath me.

"Are you sure they're okay with our..." She hesitated.

"Our situation?"

Releasing Penny, I frowned. "Situation? One day, Penny Wilson, you are going to be my wife. The mother of our children. Please don't ever call our relationship a situation again."

Her jaw dropped slightly, and I saw the flash of panic in her eyes. Feeling like a total shit, I pulled her back into me. "I'm joking. Well, about calling our relationship a situation. The rest of it, not so much."

"Blake," she hissed, batting me away with her hand. "That was mean."

I noticed movement in front of the car and glanced out of the corner of my eye. Troy, the big goof, was pretending to make out with himself. I swear that guy was forty going on twelve.

"Well, come on, we have company."

Penny turned her head slowly and the blush from earlier returned. "How long has he been standing there?"

"Oh, I'm pretty sure he saw everything."

"Perfect, just perfect..." Penny started muttering to herself, and I laughed, pressing one last kiss to her lips before climbing out of the car. I retrieved our bags out of the trunk, and Troy came around. "Looking good, brother, and you don't look so bad either."

"Troy," I warned. Penny was embarrassed enough without Troy hitting on her.

"What? You two almost caught fire." He clapped me on the back and grinned. "Get out here, Penny, I have some Troy love for you."

Shaking my head, I said, "Seriously, where do you come up with this shit?"

"Just sharing my love, my man. Sharing the love."

The passenger door opened, and Penny stepped out. I could tell she had withdrawn into herself. Getting away for the summer was supposed to take her mind off the impending trial, but now, I wasn't so sure it was a great idea.

"There she is." Troy started to move in her direction, but I shot a hand out in front of him. He raised an eyebrow at me, but I just shook my head. His overenthusiasm was usually infectious, but Penny, although mostly okay with touch now, still had a tendency to fall back into her old ways when her stress levels were high.

"My bad. Hey, Penny, it's really good to have you back."

Penny slammed the door shut and looked over at us. "Thanks, Troy. It's good to be back." She ignored Troy as she stared right at me. A small smile broke over her face, and my heart skipped a beat.

She was telling me we would be okay.

Always.

"Pssst, could you two be any cuter?" Marissa tipped the bottle of lukewarm beer in our direction and grinned like a fool.

Penny giggled from her position between my legs as I perched on one of the overturned trunks. In usual fashion, Troy led the circle in song while we toasted marshmallows and drank warm beer. Tina had already given the whole 'don't fool around with each other speech' earning Penny and me a stern glance. We knew the rules. After tomorrow, we had to keep our hands to ourselves—for the most part.

If Troy and Tina thought I was going to go ten weeks without kissing or making love to Penny, then they were more deluded than I realized. It was all about discretion, and I intended to be discreet. After all, it was what I did best.

"Are you okay?" I brushed Penny's ear with my lips and felt her body shudder. My dick twitched. Perhaps ten weeks was going to be harder than I first thought. She turned her head slightly and whispered, "I'm fine. Pay attention."

Her warm breath lingered against my face, and I closed my eyes lost in her. "I can't. You're distracting me."

She started to shuffle forward. "Maybe I should sit somewhere else?"

"Not happening." I looped my arms around her tighter, drawing her back to me.

Troy continued to sing but kept winking in our direction, the fucker. But for as goofy as he was, he had been a great friend over the last six years. He and Tina had given me a chance, no questions asked, and in an ironic kind of way, the owners of a camp for fostered kids had saved me. If it hadn't been for Camp Chance that first summer after I left the Freeman house, who knows where I would be now.

The music stopped and people broke off into their own huddles. New faces had replaced a couple of the regular counselors, and Tina sat with them to fill them in on the dos and don'ts, no doubt. Where Troy was carefree, she was uptight, but they worked. In fact, I'd never seen a couple stronger than the two of them.

Marissa stood and dusted herself to come sit with us. "I miss you guys."

"We told you, door's always open."

"Not too open, though," I added smirking at Marissa.

She scowled and flipped me off.

"Ignore him. He's just jealous at the thought of sharing me," Penny said amusement heavy in her voice.

I rested my chin on her shoulder. "Damn right, I'm not sharing."

"I don't know whether to cry or puke watching the two of you. I mean, we're all glad you sorted shit out, but we can't all be lucky enough to find our lobsters." Marissa leaned over to kiss Penny's cheek. "Show a little thought for the rest of us, yeah?"

We watched Marissa sashay away and join the regular staff. Everyone was busy talking, catching up and stuffing their faces with Troy's grilling efforts. Now was my chance. "Come on." I pulled Penny up with me and curled my hand around hers.

"Blake, we can't just leave. Everyone will notice." The caution in her voice was so fucking cute. It reminded me of every time we had escaped from the group home.

I didn't give her time to worry, pulling her along the path that snaked around the main cabin and out to cabin row. Penny dragged her feet behind me until I slowed, letting her catch up, and wrapped an arm around her waist hugging her to me. "I miss you."

"Blake, it's only been twenty-four hours." She knew exactly what I was referring to and rolled her eyes at me.

"I don't care. It's too long. I need you. Always."

Our eyes locked and my love for Penny reflected back at me in two dark pools. Was it still supposed to be this intense between us? After all of this time?

Eight years.

Snapping myself out of it, I walked us to the spot. The

one I'd brought Penny to last summer. Earlier, when she'd been catching up with Marissa and unpacking in their cabin, I'd come out to prepare things. I released my hold on Penny and took her hand so I could go in ahead of her, just to see the look in her eyes when she realized what was happening.

We broke through the small clearing, and I turned around not wanting to miss it. Penny's eyes widened and then filled with tears. "I, I- Blake, this is, this is everything."

Mission accomplished.

I'd laid the picnic blanket in the middle of the tree circle. Cartons of juice and cookies were scattered in one corner and a bunch of hand-tied flowers lay in the middle. Those were new, and with her hand in mine, I tugged a speechless Penny over to the blanket and pulled her down with me.

"Eight years ago, a lost, sad, and afraid girl showed up at the group home where I was staying. I was pissed because it was another girl. Until I saw her. Saw the pain in her eyes and the way she held herself together with just her arms. I wanted to make her smile. I was only twelve, and I didn't know why I felt that way, but I did. Over the years, I watched this girl grow into someone special. My friend. My partner in crime. My heart. She became everything. The light in my dark. My hope in despair. I lay out in No Man's Land with her looking up at the stars planning our future. One where we were free. Where we could make our own rules. And then, one day, I was ripped away from her." A lump stuck in my throat, and I gulped back the rush of tears behind my eyes. Penny's eyes were already glazed over, and I saw her inhale a sharp breath.

"Not a day went by when I didn't think about her. Even when I thought she'd moved on, I still dreamed of her. Of where she was and what she was doing…" The lump grew, and I swallowed hard trying to choke down the emotion running through me.

"Blake…" My name on her lips almost broke me, but I reached my hand for her and pressed a finger to her lips. "No, I need to say this. If I could go back and do everything differently, I would. I would pick you every time, Penny. I would be brave and strong and fight for you. But I can't turn back the clock, so all I ask is for you to let me be that person now. Let me hold you when you're sad and cry with you when you're hurt. If you let me, I promise I'll spend my life loving you."

I exhaled. Really, inhaling would have been better to let me catch my breath, but I felt like a huge weight had been lifted. After everything with my uncle, Brittany being a total bitch in the aftermath of finding out about Penny and me, and then the charges against Derek and Marie, the last seven months had been a whirlwind. I told Penny I loved her all the time, but I needed her to know that I never *stopped* loving her.

My hands buried themselves deep into her hair and I drew her to me, pressing my lips to hers. I needed her to know I hadn't just saved her, but she had also saved me.

My tongue traced the outline of her mouth, and she parted her lips. The kiss was hungry, needy… desperate. I needed her to know she was my lucky Penny.

She always would be.

lucky penny playlist

Young Love – Eli Lieb

From Eden – Hozier

Body Talk – Foxes

Wings – Birdy

Yours – Ella Henderson

Sweet Nothing – Gabrielle Aplin

XO – John Mayer

Second Chances – Imagine Dragons

Please Don't Say You Love Me – Gabrielle Aplin

Tears and Rain – James Blunt

Say Something – Boyce Avenue

Leave A Trace – CHVRCHES

Wasn't Expecting That – Jamie Lawson

Let It All Go – Rhodes / Birdy

Scars – James Bay

Alive - Sia

about the author

Contemporary romance and romantic suspense
... written with feeling

L.A is author of the Fate's Love Series and Chastity Falls Series. Home is a small town in the middle of England where she currently juggles being a full-time mum to two little people with writing. In her spare time (and when she's not camped out in front of the laptop) you'll most likely find L. A immersed in a book, escaping the chaos that is life.

Official Website: www.lacotton.com

You can connect with her on:
Facebook: www.facebook.com/authorlacotton
Twitter: www.twitter.com/authorlacotton

Or email her at:
contact@lacotton.com

acknowledgements

A whole heap of people helped me get this story just right, and without them, Penny and Blake's story would not be what it is here.

Firstly, my good friend and writing buddy Jenny Siegel. Jenny reads everything I write as I write it, and Lucky Penny was no exception. Thank you for always being there.

My beta readers: Claire, Kirsty, Lorena, Lucy, Sam, Shannon. My test readers: Ewelina, Courtney, and Maria, and my proof-readers: Caroline, Christie, and Nelly. As well as my unofficial proof-reader Ginelle (you spot those mistakes like no one else!) Thank YOU all for being so awesome and showing Penny and Blake so much love.

Jennifer Holter, my friend, my assistant, my go-to gal, you are awesome, and I'm lucky to have you in my corner. Please stick around!

My editor, Jenny Sims, thank you for making my words pretty, Daniela Conde Padron, thank you for such a beautiful cover, and Stacy from Champagne Formats for making Lucky Penny as pretty inside as it is out!

Give Me Books for handling the release events—it was great working with you. And to all of the blogs who continue to share, support, and review my work. Thank you. I appreciate each and every one of you!

And lastly, to my readers—the people who support my work and buy my books… you make it all worthwhile. I poured my heart into this story, I hope you enjoyed it as much as I did writing it.

56385972R00167

Made in the USA
Charleston, SC
21 May 2016